CELLULOID CRIMES

CELLULOID CRIMES

EDITED BY
DEBORAH WELL

LEVEL
SHORT

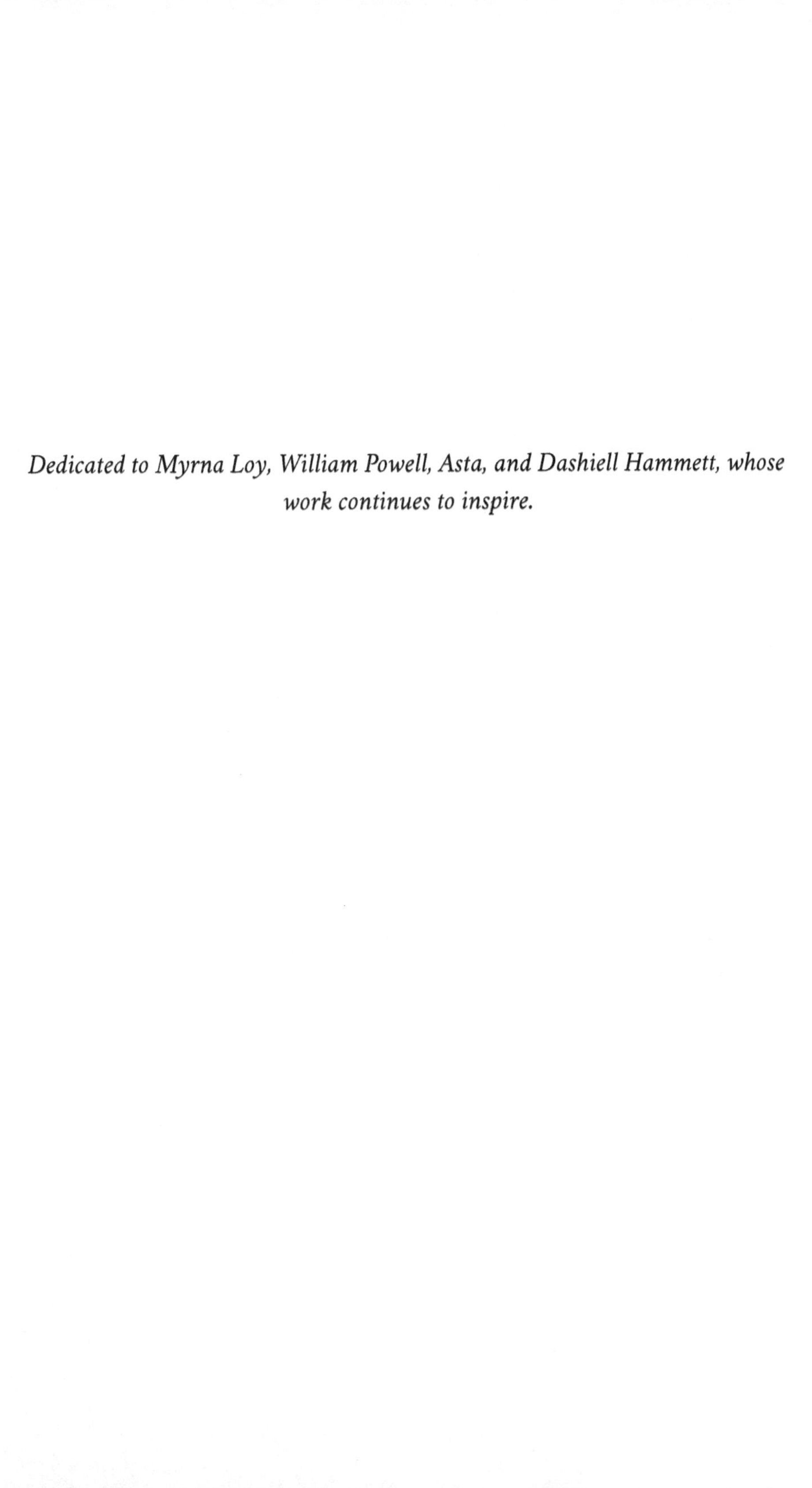

Dedicated to Myrna Loy, William Powell, Asta, and Dashiell Hammett, whose work continues to inspire.

Contents

The Fixer

By Gabriel Valjan

Y ou must not worship any other gods except…"

That line from Exodus makes me laugh every time because if Tinseltown has taught me one thing, it's this: whether you attend services at a temple or sit in a pew in a church, image is everything the studio says it is. Actors are told how to dress, whom to date, and how to behave. Deviate from the script, and the foolish beau or belle from Peoria will learn that Los Angeles is a desert city. The sand will bury you, and the Santa Ana winds will carry you away.

I ought to know because I am a fixer.

People may pray to Saint Jude, the saint of Impossible Causes, but studio heads call me to clean up messes. There are five moguls and five plantations in this town, and the moguls own everyone and everything on them. Actors are a property, a commodity that could be traded and sold. The Contract became the chains around hands and feet, and it includes a clause for moral turpitude. Make no mistake about it: both god and money are green as jade, and the Movie Capital of America is one jaded town.

Slavery never ended in this country, only the terms of servitude changed. For the ordinary Joe or Jane, bondage meant either work in a factory or on a farm, or in some crummy office in a metropolis somewhere. Mr. and Mrs. Smith were obligated to sweat for what amounted to a long sentence in the penitentiary for the mortgage, kids, and the car in the driveway. Nobody will admit it but that's why they look up at the screen on Saturday night. The price of admission includes the fantasy of freedom.

For the cost of tickets for two, hamburgers, and soda, John and Betty could enjoy celluloid dreams and escape their troubles. Actors and actresses have it no different, though the scale is different. They live in palatial houses, drive the most expensive cars, and they live for the adulation of fans and what the magazines say about them. With the stage lights come glamour and privilege, but when the lights are off, there's a darker side to the champagne life. There's envy, rivalries, secrets, and decadence in the Hills where more than eucalyptus and jasmine bloom at night under the moonlight.

Directors, studio executives, and producers understand that talented people are flawed, driven to excess and inclined to indiscretion. Money is religion. It fixes almost everything, and when it doesn't, my phone rings, and I'm called in.

I've shepherded booze hounds to safety and saved the virtue of young ladies whose virginity was as perennial and poisonous as the Lily of the Nile in southern California. I've babysat the addicted and counseled the lovelorn and conflicted. I've seen it all, from drug parties to orgies that were both color-blind and indiscriminate, and I've delivered payoffs.

My reputation is such that I can negotiate 'situations' I prefer not to handle. I dislike anything to do with child actors or their parents. The kids within the studio system are so screwed up that I'd rather chase butterflies with a pair of tweezers, and mom and pop are often parasites who give tapeworms a bad name.

The worst of the worst in my professional life was the time I handled the daughter of a bombshell starlet who allegedly killed her mother's boyfriend. If it weren't bad enough to make murder disappear, I had to separate darling daughter from mother dearest because mom was madder than Medea when her dearly departed had put the moves on her kid instead of her. The whole affair made Bugsy Siegel's demise seem quaint. Everyone thought that Bugs was a Syndicate hit, when in fact it was a jealous husband who didn't like the idea of Mr. Flash and Cash bedding his wife.

Life in La-La Land offers no intermission, folks, and the call last night provided proof there are second acts in American lives.

* * *

The butler led me to the bedroom where I found LB practicing his golf stroke. It was carpet, cup, and a movie mogul with the wrong choice of club in his hands. He'd been born in Russia when czars ruled the country, emigrated to Canada, and his first foray into the world of entertainment was managing a theatre called The Garlic Box in Haverhill, Mass.

LB was wearing silk, and he spelled his nightwear pajamas, and not the British way, pyjamas. His eyes and hands concentrated on putting the little white ball into the mouth of the cup.

"I've got two jobs for you. One is a message, the other one is involved."

"A message that needs to be delivered in person?" I said.

"In person, in a way that only you can."

"Is persuasion required?"

He nudged the ball and missed the cup. "Nuts. What was that you said?"

"At this hour of the night, you could upgrade the profanity. I asked if persuasion is necessary?"

"I doubt it. You're discreet, and Scotty is known for his discretion."

He retrieved and planted the ball a greater distance from its destination.

I said, "The message is for Scotty then."

"Nope, for a friend of his. You bring down the commandment from the mountain and let Scotty play Hermes with the pagans. It's best this way, since he knows how to work that crowd."

"That crowd?" I said. The look I received provided the subtitles. "Got it, and the second job?"

"A case of hormones."

"Now, hold on, LB," I said and stomped the metaphorical foot. "I thought I made it clear that I don't handle kids, especially teenagers."

"They're not teens," he said.

"They, as in plural?" I said. "You've got better people for the assignment, and plenty of aspirin or penicillin for that kind of problem."

He took his stroke and almost made it into the holder. "Put your horse in the stable, it's not what you think."

"Boys or girl?"

"Girl times two," LB answered and rearranged the ball and cup on the rug.

"Two," I said, voice inflected for dramatic effect. "Any boys in this scene?"

"Civilians and taken care of." His eyes met mine. "It's not what you think."

"You said that twice, LB. Can't Eddie handle this?"

"He's unavailable."

"Since when?"

"Since he decided he wanted to write a book."

"Is this a book with words or with pictures?"

His club worked the air next to his ball. "Eddie is writing what he thinks is the great American novel. I believe it's called *The End of Fury*. I know you're going to say it's an ironic title, given Eddie's personality."

It was ironic with a thumb in the I. Everybody called Eddie Eddie, although his first name was Edgar. Call him by his Christian name, and there's a good chance Mr. Mannix would put you in the hospital, and that's if he was being gentle. Eddie had earned his notoriety, but it wasn't for writing. I couldn't frame the picture inside my head. The closest I could see Eddie writing a novel was if he dropped a typewriter on someone's head.

Eddie and I never saw eye-to-eye, but we respected each other. He was there day and night for Gable when Lombard died. Most people don't know he was the one who found her body in the snow and brought her remains down from the mountain. I'm also one of the few people Eddie told about what she looked like after TWA Flight 3 crashed into Mount Potosi. It was a horrific ending to a beautiful lady. Carole of the Curves was a good egg.

I looked at the time on my wrist. "What's the juice with these two ladies?"

"Ladies?" He smiled again. "Those two would make an Irish priest blush. Let's just say the party started with each other, and then it included some male company. I've got the hotel and their play pals covered. Where you come in is that I heard someone else was there, and this individual either took photos or filmed the festivities. Your task is to find the negatives or reel. I don't need to know how."

"Name of the hotel?"

"The Georgian in Santa Monica."

He sank his shot. I asked if there was anything else I needed to know about the two unladylike ladies. LB sighed the sigh, and he didn't do it for effect. "Girl one is the goddess as in the case of the goddess and the gangster you once worked. I'm sure you remember it."

"Remember it like amnesia. And her girlfriend?"

"She is less of a problem. It's her bobbysoxer ex that makes this situation special."

"Special how?" I asked.

"He carries a torch for her, and he has dangerous friends who can be bad for business."

"Okay, what else should I know?"

"What God didn't give him for height, he gave him in a third leg, and only so much blood between it and his brain to work. While I can't prevent him from knowing about her escapade, I'd like to see to it that he not find the auteur first because we know what that means."

"Yeah, a one-way ride to the sandlot called Palm Springs."

* * *

Scotty owned the Richfield gas station on Hollywood Boulevard, at the corner of Van Ness Avenue. Scotty knew everyone there was to know, and everyone but the Vice Squad knew about Scotty. He wasn't a proper pimp, in the sense that he taxed his stable, but he had a network, and his company motto was 'Discretion with Integrity.'

A nice guy, a good guy, an honest guy was Scotty.

He pocketed a twenty from each liaison, and clients either used the trailer behind his station or the motel across the street. Customers came for the pump, stayed for the canoodle, and Scotty's reputation grew, even when the skunks at *Confidential* magazine offered him a thousand bucks for a scrap of gossip. He refused, and the debauched in Hollywood loved him for it. Scott fixed up queer, straight, and the curious of both sexes.

Scotty walked up to the car. "This is a first."

"It's not what you think, Scotty."

"If no conversion on the road to Damascus, what then?"

"Here with a message, friend-to-friend, cable to shore."

Scotty, for all his friendly demeanor, didn't broadcast tough because he didn't have to. He'd fought as a Marine in Guadalcanal and then at Iwo Jima. He lost a brother on that hellhole of an island in the Pacific. We had something in common. I went from Omaha Beach to the Battle of the Bulge.

Without naming LB, I conveyed the mogul's message:

"A friend wants you to tell your friend George that one of his guests at one of his cottages ought to scale back on the revels. The monthly budget to the rags has been spent. Let it be known that he should dial down the noise."

"Like Western Union, I'll deliver the telegram. Sure there's nothing else?"

"How are the nights for you?"

Scotty looked at me with those eyes, and he understood I wasn't talking about what men didn't discuss over beers when they were together. Combat left most of the men who'd seen it with other kinds of fragments, those awful memories that visit us at night.

"Some nights are better than others. You?"

"Like you said, some nights are better. Alive is always better than the alternative." I looked around, at his station, which was neat and clean, in plain sight, whereas sections of the Boulevard were already headed for Babylon. "Not for nothing, Scotty, but you know it's only a matter of time. Vice works a quota, and they don't play nice. A collar on a sheet is one thing, but guys like you could get hurt. My unsolicited advice is you start looking into another line of work or relocate the office."

He understood. Homosexuality had been declared a pathology that was legion, a national epidemic. Alan Turing had taken a bite of the poisonous apple to avoid jail time and public humiliation. Oscar Wilde rotted in gaol. In the US, our legal system hadn't read the New Testament, the part about compassion. Leviticus is what the judges knew by chapter and verse, and they ordered the wayward and especially repeat offenders to be incarcerated, lobotomized in asylums, castrated, or all of the above.

Scotty said he wanted to show me something. He pulled a black-and-white picture of a buck private in his dress uniform from his shirt pocket. "A friend?" I asked.

"Foxhole buddy. I'm alive because of him."

I studied the face that had seen the horrors of war. Compare any picture of Jimmy Stewart's face before he did *It's A Wonderful Life*, and you'd understand what I was looking at. His own mother didn't recognize her son, the actor and pilot of multiple bombing raids. I said to Scotty, "Does he, you know?"

"He couldn't care less. We survived what we did, so what's there to be scared of?"

"Society, Scotty." I pulled the gear out of park. "It scares the hell out of me every damn day. Deliver that telegram for me, please."

* * *

I drove to the hotel in Santa Monica in the morning.

The Georgian had first been a speakeasy by the ocean, then a hotel, the tallest building in town in the early Thirties. In a former life, it was where you came to lose your inhibitions during Prohibition. The place attracted the likes of Capone and Company. The gorgeous vista of sand and surf lured the A-list crowd of Arbuckle, Chaplin, and Gable and Lombard for their trysts.

I found the manager and asked for a word in private. He sold the hospitality brochure verbatim until I cited the date in question, and I described the ladies without naming names.

He said no truer or more patriotic words from an American. "What's in it for me?"

I leveled a stare that stiffened his spine and left his smile on the ground. He blathered several paragraphs for platitudes about how the hotel guarded the privacy of its guests.

"Appreciate the foreplay, so you neither saw nor heard a thing?"

"There might be someone." The guy snapped his fingers, and a bellhop in a powder blue outfit sauntered over. The choice of color for a uniform seemed more appropriate to a newborn in the Maternity Ward, and the square hat on his lid wouldn't do him any favors with the homeliest girl in the Hollywood Canteen. The young man stepped up to me, a look of confusion on his face because there were no bags at my feet, but the same mug lit up when I held up a bill between two fingers.

The manager snapped the Benjamin out of my hand and screwed off to give us some privacy. It's not the first time I've seen this gauche move. Rank didn't guarantee manners. I looked at the kid, embarrassed, as if my fly were unzipped. I asked him the same question I'd put to his boss.

The more he described the guy, the more a certain creeper's face came into focus. There was no Vaseline on this lens. No blur. No uncertainty, either. The person he detailed was a familiar snake in the garden called *Confidential* magazine. We'd danced before.

"Hate to say this, but if a story or photos of any kind break, your boss will blame you for violating hotel policy."

"Mister, I need this job."

"I know you do. I appreciate the info, so here's what I'm gonna do. You have a missus?" He didn't respond, so I asked, "A friend? Don't answer that. It's none of my business." I pulled out one of my cards, reached for a pen inside my jacket, and scribbled a name and number. "My name is on the front. Call this guy on the back of the card after I leave. Tell him I sent you. He'll get you a VIP tour of the studio and your name into the system for starters. Then, you and your plus one will enjoy a weekend in the ritziest room at the Hotel Roosevelt on the company's dime. This friend of mine tends bar at the Lido Room at the Roosevelt. If the studio doesn't offer you a job, he'll get you one that doesn't require a ridiculous uniform like the one you're wearing. Either job will pay better than this gig, too."

He examined both sides of the card, read the names, and thanked me.

While I walked to my car, I thought of when Carole and Clark cavorted in the Roosevelt's penthouse. It cost the couple five dollars a night. She told me she would have paid more if Gable had given her a serious case of rugburns, instead of the Minuteman's sprint. Clark had no spark between the sheets, she told me.

I realized how much I missed her.

* * *

Sid Hackett was his name, but everyone called him either Hack or Hatchet because he was the male incarnation of Lizzie Borden. He destroyed reputations, one syllable and one innuendo at a time. He preferred pictures to text because it meant less time for him to exercise his limited vocabulary. The man had no decency, no scruples, and he worked every nasty number and trick from the days of yellow journalism.

He'd write who liked reefer, who dropped the popular tranquilizer Miltown into their martinis, and who was the pinko-subversive who had escaped Joe McCarthy. His forte was insinuating who enjoyed what in the bedroom, and the more outlandish their kink, the better he hyped the titillation factor because it sold stacks at the newsstand.

Sid, however, was predictable. I prowled Wilshire Boulevard to see if he was at the original Brown Derby. He celebrated whenever he scored a major coup. Sid wouldn't dare show his mug at the Derby on Hollywood and Vine, the preferred site for wrap parties. The man had made so many enemies that anyone who spotted him there would've spat in his food. Sid's celebratory meal of choice was a Cobb Salad, and then he'd visit the Zephyr Room, where he'd be seen at the bar throwing back Manhattans. If he tippled too much, he'd rent a room for the night at the Chapman Hotel and sleep the hangover off.

He'd seen me first, in the mirrors. He knew he'd been made, and he acted unrepentant as a cat caught in the act of stealing food off the dinner plate. He invited me to take a seat and called over a waiter. I ordered a Silver Bullet and watched the tuxedo walk away.

"Why can't you keep it simple and call it a martini like everyone else?"

"Because I can't decide whether you're a vampire or a werewolf, Sid, but I do know that a silver bullet can kill them both. Let's make this quick."

The waiter returned and placed my drink down. He disappeared.

Sid raised his glass. I didn't raise mine. "Suit yourself," he said. "I would've thought LB would've sent Eddie. Oh, I forgot, that bulldog from Jersey thinks he's Hemingway, though I'd put him next to Edgar Allan Poe on the shelf for the horror that he is."

I sipped and tasted strong gin. "We both know he'd erase you in a heartbeat."

Sid dished it back. "I have enough dirt on Eddie to bury him somewhere in the Pine Barrens, and you can tell LB I said so because I've said as much to Eddie's face. If you haven't noticed, I'm still breathing with both lungs."

Eddie's list of accomplishments in the dark arts was known but never corroborated. He hunted down every known copy of *Velvet Lips*, a blue film that featured a hot studio property. He tampered with all kinds of evidence, cleaned up crime scenes, and was physical with both men and women. He broke his first wife's back, and that was before she died in a dodgy car accident. His second wife had herself a boy toy, an upcoming actor named George Reeves, and Eddie wasn't thrilled about it.

"What will it take, Sid? Let me guess, you want a particular starlet to roll your bones for a night?"

We both imbibed. Sid cracked open a cigarette case and offered me a cig. I declined.

"Don't insult me. Say what you came here to say, and then shove off."

"I thought I did, but okay. Was there any film footage taken at the Georgian?"

"No, only photos. That's the honest truth."

I squinted with suspicion. "What gives, with you being so forthcoming?"

"Feeling generous, and I'm enjoying my Manhattan."

"About those photos, Sid."

"Don't have them. This may shock you, you big lug, but you've got it all wrong. I didn't snap those glossies, nor did my staff."

This surprised me. "You're lying," I said.

"I'll swear to it on a Bible if you want, but that means nothing. Between the two of us, you know we'd both burst into flames if either of us stepped into a church or touched holy water."

The waiter hovered, and I tilted my head as a signal to him to hit Sid with another Manhattan. I was at a loss, because I thought the photos and photographer were part of some usual score Sid was working on against Eddie and the studio. I could keep guessing from now until the trumpet for the Apocalypse sounded and still come up short. Wherever Eddie went in the afterlife, there were fans doing the Bronx Cheer on both sides of the escalator.

I looked at him. "You're telling me someone beat you to the photo session?"

"Someone beat me to it."

"And you couldn't persuade said someone to cough up the goods?"

"And deal with her ex? No thanks."

"You're scared of a singer more than you're scared of Eddie?"

Sid smirked. "Eddie has had how many heart attacks?"

"Don't know and don't care, but there's no discounting that some people are too mean to die."

Sid nodded. "Fair enough, but unless you've forgotten, all the studios have lost their court cases with the government, so you've got but one question to ask yourself here: Who should I fear most, LB, or the runt from Hoboken himself?"

It was my turn to grin. "Seems to me you answered your own question."

Sid had valid points. The moguls made movies, and owned the picture houses where they were shown. Uncle Sam had stepped in and declared Monopoly. Eddie had damaged his health since he partied from sunrise to sunset, which may explain why he was writing a novel. He'd seen signs of his mortality, along with the San Gabriel Mountains before the sun could burn off the smog.

"I need to talk to this photographer."

"Pen and paper, please."

* * *

West Adams was in USC's backyard, within distance of Automobile Row on Figueroa and the huge Felix the Cat outside of a Chevrolet dealership. The street was row after row of Craftsman and Tudor homes, with a dash of Victorian mansions. While I parked the car, my mind considered the motivations. I was thinking of the long game of blackmail, a handsome sum per picture, or that this might be some college kid looking to supplement his family allowance.

The University of Southern California had grown up a lot since its days as an orange grove. It was now a playground for the next generation of tycoons. Known as a hothouse for actors such as John Wayne, home to a meritless rumor about Clara Bow and the football team, SC was where the rich sent their sons to foster business connections and their daughters to obtain their MRS degree.

I rapped wood like a missionary with The Word.

A shorter version of Rock Hudson answered the door with, "May I help you?"

My first thought was that this guy would be popular with Scotty's crowd. I was hoping he didn't give me a reason to send him to the dentist for bridge work. I opened with business, "How about you give me the negatives to the photos from Santa Monica?"

"I don't know what you're talking about?" he said.

"Wrong answer, kiddo."

He went to shut the door, but my foot stopped it, and my hand came up to brace the frame. "Look, I have no quarrel with you. Hand over the negatives, and we call it even."

He pushed the door forward, and I pressed back. "This is me being nice," I told him. I tried to talk sense into him. "There's someone not in those pictures you need to consider, someone who is an impediment to your health."

"Who might that be?"

"A crooner who will keep the beat with his foot on your face until your heart stops."

"Is this you throwing the fear of God into me?"

"God isn't who you should be afraid of, kid."

"Then who?"

"My boss, for one. He is one of the Ms in MGM."

"Metro-Goldwyn-Mayer?"

"More like Morons Gets Mauled."

"You're not funny, Uncle Miltie," he said.

"Let me tell you what's hilarious. MGM has a lion named Slats for a mascot, and nobody would know it if you were to become kibble for the house cat."

I forged forward, into the foyer. I saw a camera on a table under a mirror. I reached for it.

We collided and struggled with the camera. All the while he pleaded, "Don't manhandle it," and I said, "All I want is those negatives."

We went round and round, me holding the contraption out of reach. I shoved him away from me, and he crashed into the table behind him. He winced as the wood caught him in a kidney. "The negatives aren't in it," he said between huffs."

"Then why put up such a fight?"

He pointed to the camera. "Because it's expensive is why."

I glanced down and made out the name Contax. "Fine, but I want the negatives."

"How much you willing to pay?"

"How about I leave you in one piece and you keep your teeth?"

"Whatever you do, don't break the camera."

I held his toy over my head. "Negatives and prints, or I break your toy."

"I need money."

"Who doesn't?" I surveyed the room. "You don't look like you're hurting any."

"My family cut me off. They want a doctor and a lawyer."

"So?" I said.

"So, I want to be a photographer, but they told me to do that on my own time, not on their dime. A hobby, they called it."

I sighed and shook my head. I'd seen it all. I'd watched parents turn minutes of dubious pleasure that resulted in a kid with talent into a lucrative return on investment. I'd watched stage hens and nasty roosters for moms and dads do all kinds of horrible things to their kids, but I'd never heard of a pair disowning a kid over the love of a camera. He pulled the drawer to the table open and pulled out a set of prints. He tossed them over to me.

"Negatives, with contact and storage sheets included."

I thumbed through the prints he had developed. He wasn't Max Autry or Cecil Beaton, but he had a good eye and a knack for composition. The subject matter was explicit, graphic as it got for sexual congress. One of the girls seemed to enjoy a position I'd call the BLT. She was the turkey between two strips of bacon.

"Satisfied?" he asked.

"I bet they were. Need a job?"

"Not interested in working for *Confidential*. He offered."

"Forget that heel. I have you sized up for a different pair of shoes."

"What did you have in mind?"

"Someone who could put your talent to good use and to his advantage. Come with me, kid."

The Little Death

By Robert Lopresti

Some of the reporters who have interviewed me over the decades seem more interested in my encounters with Hollywood greats and ingrates than in the crimes I have solved so brilliantly. Ronald Reagan's election to the presidency last year has made the obsession with old Hollywood even worse. That's annoying, but I suppose it's bad taste to complain about America's worship of celebrities while being interviewed for a magazine.

And it's hardly a new development.

I remember one summer morning in 1941, I was sitting in the breakroom of the Los Angeles office of the national detective agency which employed me. I was astonishing two secretaries with tales from my years as a circus performer.

"Shot out of a cannon!" Betty said, wide-eyed. "I can't imagine!"

I could imagine, which was good because I had run out of true stories weeks earlier. I didn't feel bad about making things up. Quick invention was an important skill for an operative, so by practicing I was giving the agency its money's worth.

Not that I was being allowed to earn it in more practical ways.

"Tell us about the strong man again," said Angel. She was a busty redhead from Nebraska who said she was only pushing papers until an agent discovered her and raised her to stardom.

Betty, on the other hand, grew up on an orange farm in the Central Valley and considered working for a detective agency sufficiently exotic.

"You and your strong men," she scolded. "There's more to men than muscles, ya know."

"I'll say," Angel replied with a dreamy smile.

Then the office boy called me to Nolan's office.

* * *

My boss didn't like me. The agency had hired me as a publicity stunt after I famously solved a murder. They figured L.A. was the best place to situate a crime-solving lady dwarf.

Nolan was stuck with me and, when forced to acknowledge my existence, tended to say so.

As I entered his lair, my hopes weren't high. I expected another reporter seeking a human interest story. But this visitor was no newspaperman.

I don't mean that a woman can't be a reporter—far from me to insult females in unusual jobs—but I never saw a journalist who looked that good.

She was a blonde, early twenties, with a figure that demanded a bathing suit. If Angel resembled her, her Hollywood dreams would have already come true.

"Matty." Nolan sounded both irritated that I had taken so long to arrive, and more so that I had shown up at all. "This is Miss Paige DuChamp."

"Charmed, I'm sure," the guest said with a surprisingly deep alto.

As often happened, she first looked over my head. When her eyes finally met mine, they widened. "Why, you're a midget!"

"A dwarf, actually. Pleased to meet you." We shook hands.

"A dwarf. Like in Snow White?"

"Not exactly." I tried a smile. "I'm not a miner, for one thing."

Miss DuChamp shook her head as if she were trying to clear it. "I know you played a Munchkin in The Wizard of Oz, but I didn't know you were short in real life."

"I'm sorry. How do you think…" I couldn't even phrase the question.

"I thought you were just playing a short person."

Nolan and I exchanged glances. Miss DuChamp was a rare subject in which we were in complete agreement.

I tried another smile. "As you can see, I'm the genuine article."

Nolan cleared his throat. "Miss DuChamp—"

"Call me Paige, please." She batted her eyes at me. "Both of you! I insist."

"Paige wants a guard for a party she is holding. She specifically asked for you." His tone indicated this was more proof of her poor mental acuity.

Paige nodded. "Vivian Shaw told me that if I ever needed security, to trust no one but Madame Matilda!"

That had been my circus name. I preferred to be known as Matilda Mason, but it hadn't caught on.

But now I understood why I had been summoned. The only assignment Nolan had given me so far was as part of a security detail for a costume party hosted by the great British actor Vivian Shaw. The boss had hoped to humiliate me by making me wear a Munchkin outfit, but I had saved Mr. Shaw from a deeper humiliation by catching some criminals. Now he had gallantly returned the favor.

"I'd be honored," I told her. "Will it be a gala like Mr. Shaw's?"

"Oh no," she said. "I don't have a mansion like Viv. I live in a little bungalow in Rayvenhurst. This will be a tiny private party."

"But you think you need a guard," Nolan said, more irritated than usual.

"It's complicated," Paige said. She took a breath. "I'm starring in a movie. My first big role! It's called The Little Death?" She looked at us, expectantly, but we hadn't heard of it.

"I play an artist's model. Well, that was easy, 'cause I did some modeling before I discovered my true calling. Acting," she added, in case we weren't sure.

I nodded.

"And the movie posters the studio made were terrible! Just embarrassing." She shook her head. "So I had this brilliant idea. Why not have one of my former clients create the poster?"

"That is brilliant." I hope I didn't sound surprised. "Great publicity."

"That's what Tommy said."

"Tommy?"

"Tommy Feinstein."

Nolan and I both sucked in a breath, again in agreement.

Tom Feinstein—I'd never heard anyone call him Tommy before—was the president of Hemispheer Studio, a Hollywood giant.

"Tommy's taking a real interest in the movie," Paige said. "He's involved in my whole career."

Nolan muttered something.

"He even agreed to sponsor the contest."

"Contest?" I asked.

She nodded, blond curls bouncing prettily.

"The three boys are making posters, and Tommy and I will give the best one a big prize."

"These are famous artists?" I said. "And they agreed to this?"

Paige looked solemn. "Well, they weren't happy at first, but it's big publicity for them. And they all get prizes. That's what I need you to guard."

"What are the prizes?"

"Wine." She shrugged. "I'm not a big drinker, but Tommy's got a famous collection. He keeps it in his cellar, for some reason. The first prize will be really old wine. Why would people want old stuff?"

"Wine improves with age," I said. "How old are the prizes?"

"Well, the first prize is from, I think, a hundred years ago. Chatto Lafitty?"

"Chateau Lafite?" Nolan said, awed. "I can see why your artist friends agreed to play along."

Next, he tried to convince Paige to hire more guards. He had several reasons: it would be more money, and he had no faith in me, but mostly he wanted to impress Feinstein. The studio could send us a lot of business.

But the client knew what she wanted. "Madame Matilda is good enough for me."

I couldn't argue with that.

* * *

"Was it really her?" Angel asked during lunch. "Paige DuChamp?"

"It was," I said. "You've seen her films?"

Betty snorted. "Hardly. There's only been a couple. She had two lines in a gangster B-movie and played a corpse in a western. I'll give her this; they say she was pretty convincing as a stiff."

"Don't be mean," Angel said. "She's gorgeous."

"That doesn't mean she can act," Betty said.

"Wait a minute," I said. "If she's so unknown, how did you hear of her?"

"Not because of her talent," Betty said. "Acting talent, I mean. She probably has other abilities."

"You're just nasty."

"Please explain," I said.

Betty sighed, but was clearly enjoying herself. "DuChamp got into the trades a few months ago because Feinstein announced she's starring in a movie. That was news to the director, who threw a fit in the Brown Derby. Then Mrs. Feinstein found out, and she threw a fit."

"Oh," I said. "So DuChamp and the studio head—"

"Are just good friends, they claim. But she moved into a cute little house in Rayvenhurst, and who do you think is paying for that?"

Angel sighed. "When I'm a star, I'll live there."

"The closest anyone in this room will get to stardom," Betty said, "was Matty in Munchkin Land."

* * *

Nolan was too cheap to spring for a taxi, so another op, Larry Carlstrom, gave me a ride in his Hudson Terraplane on the afternoon of the party.

"You're so lucky, Matty. They say the parties here are wild."

"I'll be on duty."

"How come I never get duty like that? I spent last week spying on an accountant to see if he cheated on his wife."

"Did he?"

"He wouldn't cheat on a crossword puzzle. Rayvenhurst." Larry sounded awed. "I'll bet there's enough whoopee going on there on a weekend to keep the divorce courts busy for a month."

Rayvenhurst is long gone now, replaced by a big bank. In the thirties and forties, it was one of the most stylish places to live in Hollywood. It was officially a hotel, but most of the bungalows were rented on a permanent basis—as permanent as anything was in this town.

"They say," Larry continued, "that on a summer evening you can see as many stars around the pool as at the Oscars banquet. And more writers than…"

He stopped, not knowing where to see writers.

"Than the Pulitzer Awards," I said.

"Yeah."

At the east end of Sunset Boulevard, he stopped beside a complex of Mission-esque buildings. "Here you go. How you getting home, Matty?"

"I'll call a taxi. Thanks for the ride."

"Happy to oblige." He shook his head. "Bring back some good gossip."

* * *

Following Paige's directions, I took a winding path from the main building. Bungalow 17 was a small cottage, far from the center of the action.

A maid let me in through the front door, straight into the living room.

Paige was wearing a dazzling red dress. She was arguing with an overweight older man I recognized as Tom Feinstein. When I arrived, they separated, and the studio boss looked down at me, in both senses.

"This is the best guard you could get?"

I ignored his manners. "Matilda Mason, sir. Pleased to meet you."

"About time. Where have you been?"

I was early, but before I could say so, Paige spoke. "Tommy, you didn't want her here when we were—"

Feinstein went red. "Never mind. Just do your job."

"Yes, sir. Are these—"

I stopped because what I saw on display could not have been wine bottles.

There were three easels, and on each was a package wrapped in paper. Paintings, by the shape of them.

Paige smiled. "These are my posters. I'm so excited to see them! It's like Christmas morning, isn't it?"

Feinstein sighed. "Not a big holiday at my house. Let me show you to the wine, Miss, uh—"

"Matilda," Paige said.

He led me down a hallway to the far end of the bungalow. The sunroom faced Rayvenhurst's famous pool, barely visible from this end of the complex.

Among the casual furniture stood a tea cart bearing three elegant wooden boxes with glass lids, each showing off impressively old bottles of wine.

Feinstein snorted. "Can you reach to push the cart, little girl?"

I would look and feel ridiculous shoving it around like a waitress, but I wasn't there to argue. "All part of the service, sir."

* * *

The first artist to arrive was Dom Rosetti, a man of about fifty whose large head was covered with unruly gray hair. He wore glasses so thick I was amazed he could find a canvas to paint on.

I heard him in the living room exchanging greetings with Paige and Feinstein. When he came to the sunroom, he barely glanced at me—which was unusual, since my size typically attracts notice. Rosetti's attention went straight to the bottles, and he licked his lips like a thirsty man.

A few minutes later, the next guest arrived. Rosetti could have passed for an accountant, but Web Jahns might have been mistaken for a Hollywood star. He was tall, muscular, with oily black hair.

Striding into the sunroom, he saw me, did a double-take, and grinned. "You! You're the dwarf who solved the circus murder!"

I nodded. The newsreels had made a big deal of me for a while.

"Francis," Paige said to the maid. "Get the drinks, please. We're just waiting for Sammy now."

The artists seemed surprised.

21

"What about everyone else?" Rosetti asked, peering around for an invisible crowd.

"I'm afraid it's just us, plus Sammy." She did not sound pleased. "Tommy decided a big crowd wasn't appropriate."

"Oh," Jahns said. "Your wife couldn't come, Tom?"

Feinstein glared at him, and I understood. His spouse resented his relationship with Paige, and this tiny event was a compromise. It was probably the smallest party ever held at Rayvenhurst, where police were frequent latecomers.

The exec looked down at the Navajo rug. "There wasn't time to arrange a big party, my dear. I promise the premiere will make up for it."

Rosetti cleared his throat. "Where's Sammy, anyway?"

"Probably trapped under a case of empties," Jahns said. Sneered, to be more accurate. "Or he wrapped his Caddy around a palm tree again."

"Don't be mean," Paige said. "Sammy's a great artist."

Rosetti snorted. "The man can hardly hold his brush straight these days."

"In more ways than one," Jahns said, with another smirk. He smirked a lot, when he wasn't sneering.

"Watch your mouth," Feinstein growled.

"I'm not sure wine is a good prize for a drunk," Rosetti said.

"Don't call him that," Paige said. "Sammy's sweet."

Feinstein snorted. "Well, you would know."

She pouted. "That was a long time ago, Tommy."

The studio boss looked embarrassed. "Humph. Right now, your nice guy is keeping everyone waiting. You know what happens to people who make me wait?"

We could guess. Rumors said anyone who annoyed Feinstein never worked in Hollywood again. Of course, that was a bigger threat to an actor than a painter.

Jahns looked longingly at the bottles on the tea cart. "How about some more drinks here?"

Paige nodded and called the maid, who brought whiskey, beer, and some lovely canapes.

I never drink on the job, but I was getting hungry. No one invited the help to eat.

"If he never shows up, it's fine with me," Rosetti said. "He's old-fashioned and overrated."

Jahns snorted. "You're just mad because he judged that exhibit last year and called your work—what? Inferior to a Barney Google cartoon."

Rosetti colored. "Shall we discuss why you hate the man?"

Paige jumped up. "Tell you what, boys. We can open your paintings at least."

"About time," Feinstein said.

She led them to the front of the house.

I stayed in the sunroom near the prizes, feeling useless. The maid started picking up empty glasses.

I helped myself to some appetizers.

"These are wonderful, Frances."

She dropped an ashtray onto a coffee table. "My name is Francoise! That woman—" She gestured toward the living room. "C'est une idiote."

"I'm sorry." I paused. "How do you feel about the others?"

She sniffed. "That Mr. Feinstein. He is so scared of his wife, he threatens to deport me if I tell anyone he visits." She pointed out the glass doors toward the distant pool. "As if half the dégénère don't know."

I didn't know French women could be so straightlaced.

"And that dog, Jahns. He pinches me, you understand?"

I nodded.

"The one with the glasses, he dumps his cigarettes on the table when there is an ashtray right there. Then I get yelled at." She paused for breath.

"What about Mr. Laurence?"

"I have not met him, but he is the worst."

"How can that be?"

"On the phone, when he heard my accent, he joked about France and—" She paused dramatically. "He insulted the General!"

"What general?"

"de Gaulle!"

I had heard about that man the previous year, slipping out of France, past the Nazis to Britain. He claimed to be the leader of the free French now.

Paige called me from the living room.

I went, pushing the tea cart with the precious wine, feeling like a waitress in some silent comedy.

The artists were arguing loudly about their paintings.

They weren't movie posters, really: just paintings with some spots left blank. I realized the empty spaces were left for the text the studio would put in.

How had they interpreted The Little Death, a movie about an artist's model?

Rosetti chose what you might call a symbolic approach: His whole painting was an artist's canvas with the painter's brush just visible, touching a picture of DuChamp, who stood with another canvas beside her, showing a different pose of her beside a smaller canvas…a hall of mirrors effect.

Jahns, on the other hand, had shown Paige embracing the actor who played one artist, while his romantic rival glared from the background.

The third easel held Sammy Laurance's contribution, still wrapped in brown paper.

"Those are both sweet!" Paige said. "Wonderful work, boys."

Feinstein snorted. "Let's hope Laurance has something better."

"Better?" Jahns growled. "Better than Dom's little art school exercise, sure, but not mine."

"Why you dirty—" Rosetti said.

"Neither one could be a movie poster," Feinstein growled. "Miss DuChamp is practically naked in yours. And nobody in the sticks will understand the other one."

Rosetti sniffed. "I don't work for peasants."

"Who do you think fills movie seats? Harvard professors?"

"Like any intellectual would want your crap," Jahns said to Rosetti.

"Boys!" Paige said. She looked at me, hoping I would think of a way to calm the argument.

Naturally, I did. "Miss DuChamp, I think Francoise is putting out more food."

She blinked at me. "Who's that?"

"Francoise? Your maid?"

"Oh, I thought her name was Frances." She forced a smile. "Come on, gentleman. Food and drink await."

I followed, carefully pushing my cart past the three easels.

Shrimp, crackers, and booze improved everyone's moods, although Feinstein announced he would give Laurance only ten more minutes. Then he returned to the living room to make more calls.

Paige decided to talk about the movie.

"It was so exciting to have those cameras pointed at me," she said. "Especially the love scenes."

"Love scenes," Jahns said thoughtfully. "You know, I was amazed the Hayes Office let you get away with that title."

"The Little Death?" Rosetti frowned. "What's wrong with it?"

Jahns grinned. "It means—"

He stopped and looked at Paige and Francoise, suddenly aware that women were present. He ignored me, which was no surprise. Many people don't think of dwarves as being male or female.

Jahns cleared his throat. "It refers to something I doubt any woman has ever experienced with you, Dom."

Rosetti gawked. Then he turned red. "That's big talk coming from a man whose wife left him for a drunk!"

Jahns punched him in the face.

At the circus, I saw many fist fights, but they mostly consisted of drunks windmilling their arms and shouting. There was seldom any real contact.

This was nothing like that. Jahns fired off the punch like he'd been waiting all day for the chance.

Rosetti's head snapped back, and his glasses flew off. He shrieked and stepped forward, flailing like the drunk battlers I mentioned earlier.

I quickly wheeled the prizes out of harm's way. Painters-turned-pugilists weren't going to knock over the bottles and ruin my career.

Once those were safe, I turned and saw Feinstein looking amused, while

Paige and the maid wrung their hands.

I yelled, "Murder!"

Everyone turned to look at me. Down at me, actually.

I pointed a finger like an angry schoolteacher. "Stop! You're embarrassing yourselves."

"He broke my glasses," Rosetti said.

"I think he broke my nose," Jahns said, sounding like Donald Duck. "Ow."

"Get washed up," I told him. "Paige, help Mr. Rosetti find his lenses. Francoise, get bandages, please."

Feinstein said, "Don't dare give me orders."

"I wouldn't assume."

"The word is presume."

Actually, I had meant I wouldn't assume he could be useful.

The next few minutes were hectic as Paige and Francoise rushed around gathering first aid and cleaning supplies, and the two combatants cleaned themselves up.

Then I smelled smoke.

I moved quickly toward the front of the house. There I saw one of the strangest sights I had ever witnessed—and keep in mind I worked in a circus, and acted in *The Wizard of Oz.*

The painting by Sammy Laurence, still wrapped in brown paper and sitting on its easel, was ablaze.

"Fire!" I yelled.

I grabbed the easel from behind. I managed to open the front door with one hand and dragged the easel outside without spilling its burning burden. I dumped the whole mess on the well-watered grass.

"What the hell are you doing?" Feinstein asked.

I saw a hose on the lawn and ran to find the tap. I put out the fire quickly, but the painting was certainly ruined.

All the party-goers stood near the doorway, staring at me.

"What happened?" Paige asked.

"Someone set fire to it," I said, although it seemed unnecessary.

"Sammy's painting?" She shook her head. "I never got to see it."

"Must have been hot stuff!" Jahns said.

Nobody laughed.

"How the hell did this happen?" Feinstein asked.

I walked back inside and pointed to two objects on the bay windowsill. "Lighter fluid and lighter were already here. Someone squirted the fluid on the paper wrapping. I smelled it on…the remains."

"Where the hell were you?" Feinstein snapped. "Some guard!"

I stayed calm. "I was hired to protect the prizes, sir. If you wanted the paintings guarded, you should have hired two operatives."

"This is terrible!" Paige said. "Sammy will be furious."

"If he ever shows up," Jahns said.

"Why did you do it?" Rossetti asked.

Jahns gawked. "Me? What the hell are you talking about?"

"Just because Laurance stole your wife—"

Once again, Jahns hauled back an arm for a punch.

I wedged between them. "Cut it out! We don't know who did it yet."

"Yet?" Paige said, wide-eyed.

I was thinking fast. Who had a motive? Both artists were competing with Laurance, of course. And he had apparently stolen Jahns' wife. And insulted Rosetti's art. He had even sneered at Francoise's beloved general.

Feinstein was clearly jealous because Paige had once been Sammy's lover. It seemed she was the only one without a motive, unless the affair had ended badly. But if it had, would she invite him to compete in the contest?

All this went through my head as the painters moved to neutral corners of the living room, so to speak.

Feinstein told the maid to fetch drinks. She rolled her eyes and complied.

There were motives aplenty. Method was easy: the lighter and fluid had been plain to see.

Opportunity? I concluded that the fight and subsequent clean-up had given everyone a chance to slip into the living room for a little light arson. Everyone except me, of course.

If I didn't solve this mystery, Nolan, my grumpy boss, would never let me live it down. I was considering my next move when Francoise gasped.

"Ce nest pas bon! Look!"

A tall, well-built man was ambling up the sidewalk. His bald head only made him look more striking, and he was mopping it with a red handkerchief. With his other hand, he waved a bottle of champagne.

"Am I late?"

We stared at him.

Sammy Laurance stared back. Then he noticed the burnt painting on the grass.

He grinned. "Having a bonfire?"

* * *

Paige got the job of telling Laurance what had happened. Francoise kept the drinks coming—although Laurance had clearly started celebrating before he arrived. Feinstein made more phone calls in the sunroom, trying to keep his characteristic roar down. The rival painters were subdued.

"My painting," Laurance said, over and over. "My beautiful painting."

He explained that he was late because he had had to use a taxi. His car was in the repair shop due to an accident, which might possibly have involved a bottle of bourbon.

Paige showed remarkable sympathy and patience.

I had expected outrage from Laurance, but he seemed merely stunned, like the victim of a natural disaster.

"My beautiful painting…"

His rivals looked awkward and embarrassed.

Only Feinstein, done with his phone calls, was ready for decisive action. "That's it. The contest is canceled."

"What?" Rosetti shrieked.

"You can't!" said Jahns.

"What about the movie?" Paige demanded.

"My art department will come up with something better than those two scrawls." He glared at Laurance. "I was hoping yours would be acceptable, but we'll never know, will we?"

"My painting…" He sounded ready to weep.

"And you," Feinstein growled at me. "Your boss will hear about this farce. Sending out a woman to do a man's job, and not even a real woman, just a midget."

I stood as tall as I could. "Make sure you tell him that the bottles I was hired to protect are perfectly intact. And that I saved the house from burning down."

"That's right!" Paige said, glaring. "Stop picking on Madame Matilda. Besides, she isn't a midget, she's a dwarf, like Snow White."

That silenced everyone for a moment. And speaking of silence, nothing worth repeating was said for the next hour. Finally, the artists decided it was time to leave.

Sammy Laurance was first. He gave Paige a hug—Feinstein scowled—and picked up his gray homburg from a table.

"This has been the worst day of my life," he announced. "I'm going home to get drunk."

"Won't take much," Jahns muttered.

"Paige, thanks for your kindness. As for the rest of you…" He tried to toss his hat jauntily onto his head, but it bounced off. With an angry mutter, he picked up the homburg and dusted it off. "Damn it."

I took a breath. "Excuse me. I don't think you want to leave yet."

"Pipe down, squirt," Feinstein said.

I gave him my most innocent look. "Don't you want to know who burned the painting?"

Everyone stared at me. Laurance, standing on the stoop, swayed to a halt.

"You know?" Rosetti croaked.

I nodded and pointed at the arsonist.

Feinstein snorted. "Ridiculous! You're making things up."

"I'm afraid not. Mr. Laurance burned his own painting."

"Little girl," the artist said. "What are you talking about?"

Paige dropped to her knees to face me. "Matty, that's nuts. We all saw Sammy arrive after the painting burned."

"Exactly. We saw him coming with a bottle in one hand, wiping his head with a handkerchief in the other."

"So?" Feinstein growled.

"So where was his hat?"

We all looked at the homburg Laurance was holding. Even he looked at it.

"Under his arm?" Rosetti asked.

"No," Paige said, standing. "He was waving his arms."

"So how did the hat get into the house?" I asked. "We just saw him pick it up off that table."

Feinstein turned red. "Has he been here, Paige? Have you been seeing—"

"No!" Laurance shouted, throwing his homburg to the grass, where it almost landed on the ashes. "Your dwarf is right, damn her. When I came up the walk, I heard you arguing at the other end of the house. I torched my painting and fled."

"But Sammy," Paige said. "Why did you do it?"

Now he colored, right up to his bald forehead. "This is embarrassing."

"Embarrassment is the least of your problems," Feinstein roared. "We should call the police!"

Paige grabbed Laurance's hands. "Sammy, explain."

He closed his eyes. "Well, the fact is... I'm a drunk."

"That's your big news?" Jahns asked.

Laurance was weeping. "I've had a problem for years, but it never affected my work. At least, I didn't think so. But when I saw your beautiful paintings –yours and Dom's — I realized mine was garbage."

"Oh, Sammy," Paige said and hugged him.

Feinstein growled. She backed off.

"I was ashamed," Laurance continued. "I couldn't bear the thought of you seeing my awful, awful work, so I destroyed it."

"Why didn't you burn them all?" I asked. "Then no one would know the target. So to speak."

He looked horrified. "Destroy those beautiful paintings? I couldn't!"

Rosetti actually blushed. "Aw, Sammy..."

"You're an idiot," Jahns said.

Laurance stood up straighter. "You're right, Web. I am an idiot, but a reformed one now."

He looked at me. "I'm sorry for calling you names, Miss. You made me see the truth, and I swear I am done with drink. From today on, only art will intoxicate me."

He was true to his word. And that is why the first painting of his so-called Sober Period, which hangs in Los Angeles' Contemporary Art Museum, is a portrait of me. The title "The Little Death" does not refer to my size nor, as some have suggested, my personality, but to the movie that changed his life.

As for the film, the Hays Office realized what Jahns had pointed out and forced the studio to change the title before release.

The Artist's Model was a failure, and Paige DuChamp never starred in another movie. She did become a great favorite of the G.I.'s during the war, performing at countless USO shows.

I saw her obituary in the paper recently, and it said she married an army captain and had three children. I drank a toast in her honor then because, unlike Sammy Laurance, I have never had trouble holding my liquor.

Night Passage

By Peter W. J. Hayes

To Doran Black, driving across the Golden Gate Bridge after nightfall was like gliding weightless through the sky, tethered only by the shiny, flat rounds of his headlight beams on the bridge deck. His Ford Super Deluxe growled, and a throaty wind rushed past his open windows. A memory of 1943 rose to him, of standing on the stern of his troop ship watching this same bridge fade into fog and distance.

That was before the fighting on Okinawa molded him, changed him, and spat him out like a slug punched from sheet metal.

Now, four years later, the bridge behind him again, Doran turned onto Alexander Avenue toward Sausalito. His headlights probed the darkness. He was glad the call to his insurance company came at dusk. It let him handle this case the way he wanted.

Alone. In the darkness.

The bay-facing storefronts of Sausalito loomed out of the shadows. Doran smelled smoke and followed it to a scatter of fire engines and police vehicles alongside a one-story brick building half the size of a football field. Crisscrossing spotlight beams from the fire trucks probed past a collapsed front wall into a roofless and scorched interior.

Doran parked and approached. A funk-smell of wet ash and charred wood—undercut by a chemical tang—was so strong Doran tasted it. A memory of bodies blackened stiff by flamethrowers gripped him, and his hands started to shake.

"Hey!" A bull-necked police officer appeared, gold buttons glinting in the darkness. "Walk away, bud. Nothin' to see here. Especially if you're a newshound."

Doran steadied his hands and extracted a business card from his coat pocket. "Insurance investigator." He nodded toward the building. "This is one of ours."

The officer peered at the card. "Pacific Mutual, huh?" He squinted. "Doran? What the hell name is that?"

"Mine." Doran gestured at the fire trucks. "Need to speak to the fire chief." He waited as the officer sized him up, then added, "Tonight."

The officer's face hardened. "Keep your pants on, wise guy."

Doran watched the officer present the business card to a heavyset man in a white helmet. The chief studied Doran's card and, finally, tiredly, walked over to him.

"You're here fast." The chief had four inches and fifty pounds on Doran and stood close enough so Doran knew it.

Doran noted sweat-streaked black smudges on the chief's face and liked him better for it. "I was in the office. This is pretty close, and I work best at night."

"Nighthawk, huh?" The chief considered him, a memory moving in his eyes. "You serve?"

Doran's stomach clenched. "Yeah. Army. Seventh Infantry."

The chief was motionless. "Okinawa."

"Okinawa." Doran knew the word sounded like a curse, but couldn't help himself.

"I had a boy from the Seventh with us for a while." The chief's lips tightened. "He liked working nights, too."

Doran noted the past tense. "I need to know if this was accidental or set."

"That's up to the fire marshal." The chief glanced at the hollowed-out building. "But I smelled chemicals when we rolled up, and the fire spread fast. Feels like a firebug, to me."

Doran slid his hands into his pockets. "Thanks. How about the freight inside?"

The chief shook his head. "Gone." He held up Doran's business card. "I'll tell the marshal you need the report."

Doran thanked him and wanted to turn away, but couldn't. He looked at the chief. "That boy from the Seventh. What happened to him?"

The chief's jaw tightened. "He decided the bridge and the bay were best for him." His voice was thick.

Doran wanted to shout in anger, but couldn't. He understood. The night offered peace and stillness; it was why he preferred it, but memories circled and hunted there. Those creatures, he knew, took the soldier—just as, more than once, they'd almost taken him.

* * *

Sitting in his car, Doran checked the insurance file on the property by flashlight. It belonged to a Chester Krouther, one of eleven buildings he insured for his shipping business.

Doran recrossed the Golden Gate Bridge, trying not to think of stepping over the railing and, just, letting go.

He felt more like himself as his Ford ground to the peak of Nob Hill's Washington Street, tires chattering on the streetcar tracks. He parked and walked the cool night to a three-story mansion with a recessed front door.

A stocky Asian man opened the door. A flare burst in Doran's brain, transporting him to Okinawa's Arakachi. In the glare, men scrabbled toward him, their eyes just as slitted as this man's. Instinctively, Doran lurched for the man's throat, but the man dodged and threw his weight against the door. Doran barely managed to block it with his brogue.

"What do you want?" The man's voice was sharp and unaccented.

"I'm here for Chester Krouther," Doran panted. "I work for Pacific Mutual. I've news on the warehouse fire."

Somewhere, a car engine groaned uphill. Doran's body was so tight he thought one of his bones might snap.

"Your name?"

"Doran Black." Doran retrieved a card and offered it through the gap between door and jamb.

The man plucked it from Doran's fingers. "Move your foot, and I'll tell him."

Numbly, Doran freed his foot, and the door clunked shut. Doran retreated to the sidewalk, turned, and bent at the waist. Straightened. He tried to breathe in the night's stillness. Absorb it. Before Okinawa, he'd thought he understood hatred. He hadn't. Not how it fish-hooked into your marrow, made you want to rip flesh with your fingers.

The shape of the man's eyes haunted him. His black hair.

Behind him, the door opened.

Doran turned. The Asian man evaluated him. "I'm Chin. Chin as in Chinese. Get it? Not Japanese."

Doran breathed through his mouth. "Yes."

"Mr. Krouther will see you. Follow me."

* * *

Chin led Doran through the dim entry and upstairs to a brightly lit sitting room that ran the depth of the house. The furniture and fittings were art deco, as heavy-set and overwrought as the tall man talking into a telephone by the door.

"Just get it done!" The man shouted. He slammed the receiver onto its cradle and pivoted to Doran. "Chester Krouther." He extended his hand. Doran took it, surprised at its softness.

A young woman glided from the recess of a bay window. Her platinum-dyed hair matched her silk dressing gown. She smiled at Chester, a mixture of enticement and haughtiness.

Chester waved at her. "This is Grace, my daughter-in-law."

"That's all I am to you now?" Her voice was little more than a whisper. "The daughter-in-law?"

Chester's face mottled. "Not now. Please."

"Grace, give it a rest."

Doran turned to this new voice and spotted a young man in a leather club chair with oversized armrests. He looked like a stringy, younger version of Chester Krouther.

"My son, David," Chester said.

The young man clambered to his feet, a drink almost sloshing out of his crystal rocks glass.

"What's the news?" David asked.

Chester stayed David with his hand. He turned to Chin and told him to bring tea. As Chin disappeared through the doorway, David strode to Chester's side.

Doran faced them. "I talked to the fire chief. He suspects arson. He recognized a chemical smell, and the fire spread too quickly."

"Ridiculous!" David swigged his drink. "Who would burn our warehouse? For what?"

The muscles on Chester's jaw flickered. "Anything left of the building or freight??"

Doran liked the way Chester was trying to size the problem. "No. The front wall collapsed, and the ceiling dropped. It's a total loss."

"I think you're missing the point, David." It took Doran a second to understand that Grace was speaking.

David slurped his glass dry and glared at Grace. "Are you stupid? Who did this has everything to do with it. Go back to your paintings. The men are talking."

Doran couldn't reconcile why David spoke so bluntly to Grace, especially in front of a stranger.

"David." The word was sharp. A middle-aged woman stood in the doorway, frowning in concentration, her eyes glassy. "Don't speak to Grace that way."

Doran knew that dazed stare. He'd seen it on wounded men with empty syrettes of morphine pinned to their uniforms. It looked out of place now.

"My wife," Chester intoned. "Anne Krouther."

Doran noticed that Chester ignored Anne as she crossed to a day couch.

Grace stepped closer to David and raised an unlit cigarette to her lips, waiting for him to light it. David mocked her with a smile and didn't move.

Chin appeared in the doorway, balancing a tray of tea cups and saucers.

Doran was swamped by this family, by its riddles and feuds. He wanted control of the conversation. And there was Chin, his narrow eyes baleful as he passed. Bile rose, and Doran pivoted his nearest foot outward. Chin's toes caught Doran's shoe midstride, and Chin sprawled to the parquet floor in a clatter of shattering crockery.

Chester gaped. David guffawed, then broke into raucous laughter. The haughty smile returned to Grace's lips. Doran glanced at the day couch. Anne Krouther seemed oblivious.

Chester sighed. "Chin, careful now."

Chin rose from the floor, ignoring Doran.

"Hell of a swan dive, Chin," called David.

Chin picked up the tray and used it to collect the shattered china.

Doran took his chance and turned to Chester. "David has a point. Is this going to hurt you financially?"

Chester looked pensive. "Well, sure. But business is good. I just gave our drivers a raise."

"How about your competitors? Anyone make demands of you lately? Threaten you?"

"No." Chester focused on Doran. "Why are you asking? Isn't your job just to decide arson or accident?"

Doran shrugged. "You know the ropes. If it's arson and you set the fire, we don't pay. But if someone else set it, maybe we do. My job is to figure out which."

Chester waved a fleshy hand. "Then get at it. Chin, please see Mr. Black out." Chester turned, checked a small black book, and started to dial the telephone.

Chin nodded to Doran to follow him. At the front door, he placed the tray of broken crockery on a side table and reached for the doorknob.

"Are you getting Mrs. Krouther her opium?" Doran asked, quickly.

Chin stopped mid-motion and turned to him. A distant room light illuminated one side of Chin's face, leaving the other in shadow. "I'm the house chink, so of course I got her opium? Boy, aren't you the top-notch investigator."

"Somebody gets it for her."

Chin shook his head. "I can take you two ways. Maybe you tripped me because you hate how I look. Maybe the war did that to you, maybe it's sheer pissiness. I don't care. Or, you tripped me because you wanted to stop the arguing and see everyone's reaction when I fell. So tell me, round eye, how does it play?"

Doran let out a small breath. He'd expected Chin to be angry, not guess at his motivation. "Maybe it's both."

Chin shook his head. "Confucius say, never trust an asshole who doesn't answer a question." His imitation Chinese accent was so thick Doran felt mocked.

Chin held open the front door, his face still divided between darkness and light. All Doran could do was walk outside. When the door shut, he stopped and turned to the house. He noticed, for the first time, a banner in a first-floor window. It showed a single gold star. He looked up. Grace stared down at him from the bay window, surrounded by light. Suddenly, the family's behaviors made more sense.

Grace was a widow, not David's wife.

Above him, Grace lit her cigarette with a silver lighter, breathed out smoke, and turned her gaze to the night sky.

* * *

Doran sat at his desk on the darkened fifth floor of the Russ Building, his desk lamp the only light in the room's phalanx of desks. He typed steadily, the key strikes like the tap-tap of someone driving a railroad spike. It was almost two-thirty in the morning. He finished and stripped the paper from the roller.

The report was preliminary and carefully worded. Doran didn't want his boss to deny Krouther's claim until more questions were answered.

The first was why the Sausalito warehouse was targeted. It was the smallest Krouther owned, the loss manageable. An odd choice. The second was the fire itself. Fires were set to destroy either failing or overly successful businesses. Failing businesses meant investigating the owner. Fires involving successful businesses implicated the competition.

But this fire didn't fit. Krouther had just given his workers a raise, and he'd received no warnings or demands from his competition.

He would check Krouther's statements, of course, but another possibility nagged at him. Suppose the Sausalito warehouse was burned as a test? To see if the method of starting the fire worked?

If true, the firebug had their answer, and more fires would come. Doran could even guess the location of the next one. If someone wanted to destroy Krouther's business, the obvious target was Krouther's largest warehouse.

* * *

Just after four o'clock the next afternoon, Doran steered his Super Deluxe along Route 101, past Candlestick Point, and turned into a dusty industrial park. He'd inspected the security on Krouther's warehouses earlier in the day, saving the largest one for last.

Unlike Sausalito, this warehouse was the length of two football fields and backed against a railway spur. Truck bays lined the side walls. Across the road stood a two-story building with a large neon sign on the roof, angled at drivers on the 101.

Doran parked near the front door, alongside several Haulthrifts and Fleetmasters. As he headed to the office door, he noted two Cadillacs, one a convertible with its top down, sparkling and out of place.

Interested, Doran walked around the convertible. A collapsed painter's easel lay on the back seat, as did a blank stretched canvas and a wooden box for carrying oil paints and brushes.

Doran entered a dingy reception area and went through another door into the warehouse. Naked bulbs hung from the ceiling, lighting hundreds of wooden crates stacked like islands across the interior. A forklift operator was emptying a boxcar on the railway spur, helped by several men with long wooden pry bars. A second forklift was loading a truck at one of the bays.

"Help you?"

Doran turned to a short man in shirtsleeves, his tie tucked between two buttons on his shirtfront, a fedora pushed back on his head. He carried a large clipboard with a stubby pencil under the clip.

"Yes. I'm with Pacific Mutual. Who's in charge here?"

The man shrugged. "Down here, it's me. Up there," he jerked his thumb at a wooden staircase that led to several glass-fronted, second-floor offices above the front door, "It's whichever Krouther shows up. Today that's David."

"David, it is." Doran thanked the man and climbed the steps. Hearing David's voice, he stepped quickly through the nearest door.

The conversation stopped.

David was sprawled on a couch in a small seating area to the right of a large desk. Perched beside him was Grace, a rakishly tilted red beret hiding much of her platinum hair.

"Oh," Grace said. She rose and stepped away from the couch. Slid her hands into her pants pockets.

"Don't you know how to knock?" David didn't bother to hide his anger.

"Didn't know it was a requirement." Grace, Doran noted, was framed against a row of windows that looked onto the neon sign across the street. He couldn't read the expression on her face.

"What do you want? We're busy." David dropped any pretense of politeness.

"Just wanted to know if I can look around. Do you mind? It's part of my investigation."

"Sure." David waved his hand. "Go."

Doran retreated through the door. He smiled. Perhaps David and Grace were arguing the night before, but other games were afoot today.

* * *

Doran walked the perimeter of the warehouse, trying to think like a firebug. Once it was dark, he would check again, still certain this was the next target.

He returned to his car and a mostly empty lot. The convertible was gone.

He moved his car behind a neighboring business and walked along the railroad spur, hiding in the now-empty boxcar.

At seven o'clock, Chester Krouther walked along the spur, testing the locks on the loading bay doors. Doran guessed Chester wasn't taking any chances, either.

At ten o'clock, Doran dropped out of the boxcar into blissful dark. He crossed to the back door and picked the lock.

The warehouse interior was pitch black. As Doran chastised himself for forgetting a flashlight, light bathed the warehouse for several seconds and disappeared. It took Doran several cycles of light and dark to understand the source was the large neon sign on the opposite roof, shining through the windows and glass front walls of the offices.

Doran started a loop of the warehouse perimeter, halting in darkness and walking in the light.

Before he'd gone ten yards, a chemical smell flared in his nose. He followed it, and near the far wall, spotted a low, flickering orange light.

Another revolution of the neon sign carried him around a stack of wooden crates to a swath of crumpled towels soaked in chemicals. The stench was dizzying. The towels covered a wide area of the floor and led in lines to the back and side walls. In the very center of the sodden towels stood a lighted candle, the flame barely a quarter-inch above the nearest towel fold.

Doran backed away, unsure how to extinguish the candle. Walking on the towels might squeeze out the chemical, risking fire. Pushing towels out of the way might knock the candle over.

Doran heard a shuffling noise and spun toward the sound. The warehouse plunged into darkness.

Doran squatted and duck-walked forward. The neon sign cycled into light, and Doran glimpsed the slitted eyes of an Asian man not five feet away. Hatred coursed inside him, and he leaped forward.

The men crashed together as darkness fell. Doran scrabbled at the man's chest searching for his neck. He clutched soft skin. Fingers spider-walking across his face, and a thumb dug into his eye. Doran screamed and wrenched away from the man. The warehouse lit up long enough for Doran to locate his target, and in the next bout of darkness, he leaped forward and drove his fist into the man's gut.

The man's defense was identical. Doran's breath left him in a ghastly bray as the other man whooped.

Doran dropped to his hands and knees, unable to breathe. Light surged, and Doran saw the other man in the same position, gagging, black hair falling across his face.

In the next bout of darkness, Doran managed a trickle of breath, and in the light looked intently at the man.

"Chin?" He croaked.

"Black?" Whoops bracketed the word.

Doran concentrated. "You…set fire?"

Chin gagged. "What…fire?"

"Need…" Doran dry heaved and dragged a breath into his lungs. "Stop it."

Two less-violent whoops from Chin. "Show me."

Together, they swayed to their feet. Doran fought nausea and took another shallow breath. Half bent over, he led Chin to the flickering candle.

Still hunched, Chin said, "Clever."

"Flame can't…touch towels."

Chin frowned. "Wait. Here."

In the next pulse of light, Chin hobbled away. Several sequences of light and dark later, Doran heard a scraping sound. Chin appeared in the candlelight, dragging a six-foot wooden pry bar.

"We can lower this on the candle. Put it out."

Doran understood. "Like a candle snuffer. Okay, but hold it on the candle. If you lift too soon… the candle might fall."

"Small problem."

Doran looked at Chin, for the first time not bothered by Chin's narrow eyes.

"I can't lift the pry bar. My stomach. Where'd you learn to punch like that?"

Doran touched his own tender stomach. "Same place you did. Let me try." He took the pry bar from Chin and lifted. His stomach muscles screamed in protest.

Chin started to laugh, but swallowed it down with a grimace. "Damn. Even laughing hurts. Look at us." He swiped black hair out of his eyes. "Okay. Together?"

A wave of bile rose in Doran, but he tamped it down. He turned the pry bar around so the thick end was nearest them. Together, they lifted the bar, watching the end near the candle waver. Doran's stomach muscles were red hot, obliterating his disgust at standing so close to Chin.

"Soon as the light comes on, we lower it," Chin said, through clenched teeth.

"Then wait two rotations to lift."

Chin breathed heavily through his nose. "If I can."

They waited through the darkness. When the warehouse illuminated, together they lowered the pry bar onto the candle. The warehouse plunged into darkness. They waited, their breathing strangled. In the next few seconds of light, Doran saw candle smoke curling around the end of the pry bar. Interminable darkness, and then light.

"Okay," they both said, together.

"Swing to the left," Doran groaned as they lifted.

In the moment before the light disappeared, Doran glimpsed the candle stuck to the end of the pry bar as they swung it clear of the soaked towels.

* * *

The pry bar discarded, Doran and Chin stared at each other through two cycles of the neon light, breathing heavily.

"Now what?" Chin asked.

"I need the cops. And to document all this. The last person I saw was Chester Krouther. Not sure why he'd burn his own business, but that's what it looks like."

"I don't think so."

The old anger stirred in Doran. "Why not? And why are you here, anyway?"

Chin smiled. "Anne Krouther. She asked me to follow Chester."

Doran blinked in surprise. "Why would she do that?"

"She thinks Chester and Grace are sleeping together."

Doran stared at Chin, at the way the pulses of light illuminated only half his face. Something shifted in Doran's mind. "Wait, you followed Krouther here. I saw him check the rear bay doors."

"Right."

"So why didn't you follow him when he left?"

"Because he didn't leave."

Doran blinked and looked around. "You were looking for him and ran into me?"

"Bingo."

"Enough of this," Doran said. "Let's get the damn lights turned on."

* * *

Doran and Chin found Chester Krouther tied up behind some crates just ten feet from the mass of sodden towels. The bump on his head was the size of a golf ball.

When Doran loosened his gag, Krouther sputtered and shouted, "What happened? Who hit me?"

"Just tell us about it," Doran said to him,

Krouther needed several seconds to calm himself. "I came to check the warehouse. If this one burns, so does my business. I checked the back unloading bays and started on the truck bays. Someone hit me on the head. When I came to, I'm tied up, it's dark, and the whole place stinks of paint thinner."

Something moved inside Doran. "Paint thinner."

Chin gave him a knowing glance.

Excited, Doran said, "I think we need to get you home, Mr. Krouther. I'd like a talk with your family. And I'm going to ask a local detective I know to meet us there."

* * *

In the second-floor living room of the Krouthers' house, Chester Krouther stood by the telephone, holding a towel filled with ice cubes against the bump on his head. Anne Krouther lay on the daybed, looking alert. Grace stood near the bay window, wearing the same white silk robe. Doran thought she looked serene. David sat in one of the club chairs, sipping whiskey.

Jack Gunther, a SFPD detective who investigated arson cases, had just arrived and taken a seat in the club chair across from David, his fedora resting on his bent left knee. Doran had explained his theory to Gunther when he called, and Gunther's beady eyes were bright with interest.

Chin stepped into the room and nodded to Doran.

"Okay." Doran glanced from one family member to another. "As you know, someone tried to burn down Mr. Krouther's warehouse tonight. Detective Gunther has men investigating the scene now."

Gunther nodded to Mr. Krouther.

"Chin and I," Doran hesitated, wondering if Chin was a surname. "Um, we found the setup to start the fire. We neutralized it and found Mr. Krouther tied up nearby."

Doran took a breath. "The method of starting the fire was ingenious, and because of a time delay, let the firebug establish an alibi." Doran silently counted to three and turned to Grace. "You must have felt great when the Sausalito warehouse burned, Grace. You were at home, a perfect alibi, and you knew you could destroy your father-in-law's business whenever you wanted."

"What?" Chester Krouther managed to spit out.

David opened and closed his mouth.

Grace didn't move, or even blink. Her platinum hair looked frozen.

"Anything to say for yourself?" Detective Gunther asked Grace.

Grace glided away from the bay window. "You don't know what you're talking about."

"I think I do." Doran gestured at David. "You visited David at the warehouse today. Is that correct, David?"

David nodded.

"And where did Grace say she was going when she left?"

David frowned. "To paint."

"Exactly," Grace said quickly. "I had my paints and an easel in my car."

"Yes." Doran nodded to Chin, who stepped into the hall. "You even had a blank canvas with you. I saw it."

Chin returned holding a canvas, its front toward him.

Doran gestured to Chin. "That's the canvas from your car. Chin and I grabbed it on the way here."

Chin turned the canvas around. It was unpainted.

"You weren't there to paint, Grace, you were there to burn down the warehouse," Doran said quickly. "And I bet if we check the trunk of your Cadillac, we'll find traces from the towels you used. Like we found candles in your studio matching the ones used to ignite the fire." He looked at Gunther. "Any luck with fingerprints in the warehouse?"

Gunther grinned. "Yep. We pulled lots from some empty tins of paint thinner. I think we'll need a full set of your fingerprints, Mrs. Krouther."

Grace's lips thinned, her eyes hard. She whirled at Chester. "Fine. Yes. I wanted you dead. It was only fair." Her cheeks flushed. "You murdered my Alfred! Your own son. You killed him. Alfred was safe here, in the Quartermaster Corps, but you talked that Senator into transferring him to the Pacific. To a combat unit. And what happened?"

"He asked for that transfer," Chester said thickly.

"No, " Grace shouted. "You wanted a war hero in the family. That's all it was. You didn't need to transfer him. You murdered him, and you deserve the same."

Detective Gunther struggled out of the club chair. Handcuffs appeared in his right hand, and as Grace panted at Chester, Gunther folded Grace's arms behind her back and clicked the handcuffs in place.

* * *

An hour later, with Grace transported to jail, Chin saw Doran to the front door. This time, he followed Doran onto the sidewalk.

They stared at one another in the darkness.

"Not what I was expecting from an insurance investigator," Chin said, finally.

Doran felt the night's stillness on his cheeks. "Tell me something. Why do you work as a servant? You know how to fight. You figured out Grace when I did."

Chin studied the gold star in the house window. "Penance," he said, finally.

"What the hell does that mean?"

Chin was silent, organizing his thoughts. "When the war started, I joined the Navy. They made me a steward in an officer's mess. I'm a third-generation American. My grandfather came here two years before the Exclusion Act. I'm as American as you, but no way they would give me a weapon."

Chin let out a deep breath. "But it's funny how things work out. One of the officers in the mess was a Commander Miles. I got along with him. One day, he asked me if I spoke Chinese. I said sure, and next thing I know, I'm in Chungking, China."

Doran stared, unsure where the story was going.

"Turned out," Chin continued, "Miles was ordered to set up a spy network in China with the help of the Kuomintang. Fight the Japanese there. Miles had one of their generals, Dai Li, put me in counter-intelligence. We looked for Japanese sympathizers."

Chin's voice was suddenly thick with emotion, his hands shaking. Doran knew what came next.

"We executed them as fast as we found them," Chin said hoarsely. "Men, women, children. It didn't matter."

"And the war ended," Doran said gently.

"Well, ours did. I was sent home, but it was like I lived in my shadow, not myself."

"And so, penance," Doran breathed.

Chin looked up. "Meeting you woke me up. That raw emotion you have. I realized I hadn't let myself feel anything since I got back." His voice sounded stronger. "It's why I help Anne Krouther. She stopped feeling anything the moment Alfred died."

Emotions crawled under Doran's skin. "You did the opposite for me. I hadn't realized until I met you, but I wasn't really back. My body was, but not me. I still hated people the way I did over there. Acted like I was still there. I know now I don't have to."

Chin huffed a laugh. "Look at us."

Doran held out his hand, and they shook.

"Let's get a beer," Doran said, surprising himself.

Chin was quiet for several seconds. "I don't know. Last I heard, round eyes can't hold their liquor."

Doran stared at him. "Oh. So you're one of those kinds of guys."

"What kind is that?"

Doran smiled. "The good kind."

The Whispering Arch

By P.A. De Voe

Exhausted after the long trip from San Francisco, but also excited to be in St. Louis, Frances stepped up to one leg of the grand arch marking the Union Station's main entrance. Such opulence! Everything about this place spelled vitality, strength, and most importantly, security.

Turning around, she took time to appreciate the train station's Grand Hall. Marble slabs encircled the lower section of the room. The walls above were covered with intricate patterns created out of glazed tiles and gold, three-dimensional, elaborate designs. Frances stared, absorbing the room's magnificence.

Lastly, she looked up at the enormous Tiffany stained-glass window of three women—the Allegorical Window—dominating the arch. They gazed serenely down onto the Grand Hall. Amidst the station's frantic hustle and bustle, its beauty offered her a sense of stability and peace.

Frances set her worn, brown, leather suitcase, with its identifying red scarf tied to the handle, next to the arch's wall and searched the crowded room for her friend and classmate, Annie Lee. This is where Annie told her to wait.

She was the reason Frances came to St. Louis to celebrate her friend's wedding. From the train station, they would go to Annie's family's home above the Asia Café on Market Street in Chinatown. It was only because Frances would stay with her family that her father, Charlie Chan, allowed her to travel to the Midwest alone. As first-generation immigrants, her parents were exceedingly protective of their large family. Particularly the girls.

To fill the time, she impatiently plucked at her white blouse and smoothed out her dark mid-calf skirt. She adjusted her small, close-fitting hat and patted her chin-length, curly hair. As she smoothed her hair, she thought about Pop's displeasure when he saw she had cut and curled her hair.

While he considered her change in hairstyle an act of rebellion, she defended herself, saying it was just hair, and that the style was all the rage. It wasn't an act of rebellion. Nevertheless, she purposely had it done just before her father left for a temporary job with the Secret Service in Washington, D.C.

Her father was famous for his investigative skills and highly regarded in law enforcement across the country, and often sought out to assist in difficult cases. Now, with the war going on in Europe, the Secret Service had pressed him to work with them. Even if temporarily.

As usual, the family stayed behind. It would be too much, and too expensive, to move his large family to the D.C. area. This time, only Tommy, the number three son, went with him. He always allowed one of her brothers to join him on his official travels. Not his daughters. Although her older sisters had managed to connive a way once or twice to be involved with his work, he always discouraged it.

Unfortunately, as a daughter, he thought just being pretty—and compliant—was enough. In this, he was old school. He didn't expect anything else. But, she wanted him to be proud of her, to prove that she could also help him solve crimes. Just like her older brothers.

* * *

Frances craned her neck to look over the crowd. No Annie. Now that she'd arrived in St. Louis, the adrenaline she'd originally felt on entering the magnificent train station was slipping away. She moved closer to the arch's wall and leaned against it.

"Did you bring the documents?"

She turned around. Where had that come from? To her, it sounded like a man's voice with a slight Italian accent.

There was no one near her.

"Yes, don't worry. I have them here in my briefcase. New identity papers. But first, we have to help him escape."

Frances perked up; her tiredness dissipated. Escape? What is this? Escape from what? Where is this conversation coming from? She carefully scanned the people passing by, leaving the station.

"Yeah, easier said than done. I don't know what he looks like, much less what name he's currently using. Do you?"

The conversation was so clear. It was as if the speakers stood close by. But— all of the people walking in front of her were simply leaving the building. From what she could see, no one was engaged in an intimate conversation.

The voices continued. "I've never met him, but I've got a picture of him among his new documents. He's going by Lorenzo Giordano."

"Bad luck that he was captured."

"That, and that he is being sent to a detention camp near Weingarten, Missouri, not somewhere in Europe. Now we have to not only help him escape as they move prisoners through this train station on their way to the prisoner of war camp, but we also have to get him out of the country and back to Italy."

"Why don't we have more people for this assignment? This is a lot for just the two of us."

"Too many people involved could alert the American officials. We can't risk that. The most important job we have is to get him free and out of the country, without drawing attention to us or him."

There was a silence. At that moment, Frances looked past the now fewer people walking out of the main entrance. She caught a glimpse of two men at the other leg of the arch, their heads close together, one nodding.

"Yeah, I know. The Americans mustn't discover his true identity or that he's a spy. He knows too much about our war plans. He's too valuable to the cause."

Excited, Frances immediately decided to call Pop and tell him about this caper. It certainly was an important discovery. She couldn't go to the local police. Since they didn't know her, they probably wouldn't take her seriously.

At the very least, they wouldn't believe her in time to stop these two from carrying out their plans. And, by then, the spy will have escaped prison and fled the country.

Just then, a young man in a page's uniform stepped up to her. "Are you Frances Chan?" he asked.

Startled, Frances flinched. Did the two men hear the page ask who she was? Just as she can hear them. Glancing over, she saw the two men stiffen and glance around.

"Yes, I'm Frances," she said quietly, turning toward the page.

"I have a message for you from Annie Lee." The page spoke loudly and clearly. Too loudly and too clearly.

Frances's eyes flicked uneasily back and forth between him and the two men.

"She's sorry, but she has been unavoidably detained and can't meet you as expected. However, she's arranged for her brother, Wing Lee, to pick you up within the hour. You're to meet him at the ticket counter. He'll be wearing a blue suit, no tie, and a hat with a feather in the brim."

"Oh," she said. "Thank you." Frances glanced once more at the two men. She saw them quickly turn in her direction and stare. They must have heard him. She tensed up. If they heard the page, they must realize that she was able to overhear their conversation.

As she looked over at them, they started towards her.

Without another thought, Frances picked up her bag and plunged into the crowded train station. As she marched quickly across the expanse, she focused on what she needed to do. First, see that their plans were intercepted by alerting Pop. Second, keep track of where these men were for when the authorities arrived—she was confident either civilian or military law enforcement would come because her Pop would certainly send them. And, third, she must meet Wing at the ticket counter.

There was just one tiny complication: how to elude the men when she couldn't leave the station and, at the same time, how to keep track of them. It was paramount that she not lose them and their briefcase full of critical documents.

As she rapidly moved across the floor, she spied the "Women's Restroom" sign. She made a beeline to it, slowing her gait a bit. After a quick, surreptitious glance over her shoulder to make sure they were still following her, she entered.

Once inside, clutching her bag, Frances slipped into a stall and locked the door. Placing her suitcase on the toilet seat, she opened it and pulled out a bright red dress. This was what she planned to wear to her friend's wedding. She shook it out, hoping to get rid of the wrinkles it'd developed from being packed tightly in the suitcase. It didn't help. She frowned, then shrugged. No matter, this was not the time to fuss over a few wrinkles. No one would notice them anyhow.

After quickly changing out of her traveling clothes and into the dress, she twisted her hair into a chignon. Finally, pulling out a slightly squashed large-brimmed hat, she thumped it into shape and carefully placed it over her hair.

Exiting the stall, Frances stepped up to the wall of mirrors. She tweaked her clothing and tucked a few loose strands of black, curly hair into her hat.

With her head down and her face hidden by the hat's broad brim and net veil, she picked up her luggage and strode out of the restroom. She fought the urge to look for the men, to be sure they were still watching the bathroom door.

Next task: head straight toward the phone booths and call Pop.

She picked up her pace and moved quickly through the crowded station. When she approached the phone booths, she was disappointed to see that they were all busy. Pushing down her nervousness, she allowed herself to search the crowd. When she didn't see the two men, she released a long, slow breath. The men must still be watching the restroom door. Relieved and assured, she gave herself an invisible pat on the back.

Finally, a booth freed up. Leaving her suitcase outside the door, she entered the tight space. Once inside, she opened her purse and pulled out a small pile of coins to make the long-distance call to Washington, D.C.

When her father answered the phone, Frances couldn't hide the excitement in her voice. "Pop, I'm in St. Louis, Missouri, at the train station."

"Why waste money calling me from the station? Call when you are safe at a friend's home."

"Pop, I have something vital to tell you. When I was waiting for Annie, I overheard two men discussing an Italian soldier who had been captured and was being sent by train to a detention camp here in Missouri. The soldier is a spy, and they're here to break him out of detention. One of the men has a briefcase with fake identification documents for the spy to use to get out of the country. Apparently, from the sounds of it, he's pretty valuable to the Italian war effort and knows a lot that could be useful to the Allies.

The men are still here. The military train hasn't come in yet." Frances added breathlessly.

"If I tell the authorities what I heard, I'm afraid they won't believe me. At least, not at first. They'll want to do an extensive investigation. By then, the spy will have escaped, and it'll be too late."

Frances moved the phone into her left hand. She'd been clutching it so hard, her hand was going numb. "When you tell them what's happening, WE can capture the guys before they have a chance to carry out their plans—and we'll find out who the spy is, too," she finished.

"My number three daughter is not only pretty but also smart. Smart enough to stay away from foreign agents and stay out of trouble," her father said.

"Ah, Pop..."

"Go to the ticket counter and tell them who you are. I will call the military security at Jefferson Barracks and let them know what's going on. They have a contingent of soldiers at the station and will put you in a safe place until those men are apprehended."

"Pop..."

"A good daughter listens to her father."

Frances sighed. "Yes, Pop."

* * *

Happy that she at least played a part in stopping the spy's escape and catching the men who were to carry out the escape plan, Frances stepped out of the phone booth and reached for her bag. As she did so, a large hand reached out and gripped her wrist. Frances froze

"Don't say anything, and everything will be alright," a burly man said in a low voice.

She looked past him to a second man standing behind the big fellow. He was carrying a briefcase.

"What are you doing? Who are you?" Frances sputtered.

The man holding the briefcase grinned and glanced down at her bag. "It's a good thing you kept your red scarf tied to your luggage." He looked her over. "You do look different. Without the scarf, we wouldn't have found you."

Frances's heart sank as the second man picked up her bag. The first fellow took her arm and began to roughly guide her through the crowd toward the station's doors. None of the people around them seemed to notice anything unusual was going on. Instead, they walked quickly, purposely, around the threesome. All intent on their own business and concerns.

As Frances and the thugs passed the ticket counter, she glanced over at it; however, the pressure on her arm reminded her to be silent.

Just as they were about to turn away, she spied a young man wearing a hat with a feather gaily stuck in its brim. He also caught her eye. He glanced down at her battered, brown bag with the red scarf still attached. Hurrying over and, with his eyes on Frances, said: "Are you Frances Chan? I'm Wing, Wing Lee, Annie's brother."

"No. No, she's not." The first man answered quickly.

"Yes! I'm Frances," Frances said, trying to jerk her arm free.

With confusion written on his face, Wing looked from her to the man clutching her arm.

Her captor swung her around, attempting to steer her away from Wing. Unexpectantly, Frances side-stepped, moving closer to him, her feet just in front of his. He tripped, teetered briefly, and regained his footing. However, in doing so, he had to momentarily loosen his grip. Just long enough for her to spiral out of his hand.

As she lunged away from him, toward Wing, her would-be abductor shouted "Go! Go!" to his compatriot. Immediately, the two men bolted through the crowd and toward the front entrance. Bewildered, people hastily pressed and pushed against each other to get out of the way, thereby raising the level of chaos in the Hall.

"Wing! Don't let them get away!" Frances shouted as she sprinted after them.

The men barged through the double doors presided over by the serene three-women stained-glass window.

"My car's parked out front," Wing called.

They ran out onto the street, just in time to see the two men jump into a black Buick. Wing directed her to his 1934 two-door Oldsmobile sedan.

"It may be old," he said, "but it's still in top shape."

As soon as Frances scuttered inside, Wing took off. He caught up to the Buick as they drove wildly down Market Street. The Oldsmobile rocked violently as he pressed down on the gas pedal while, at the same time, swinging the big car back and forth, from one lane to another, as he tried to avoid the other cars on the road.

Frances clutched the door handle to keep from being thrown against the side window. Adrenalin pulsed through her body.

As they approached Eighth Avenue, Wing surged forward and, coming up on the Buick's left side, forced it to turn right at the intersection to avoid a collision.

"What are you doing?" Frances yelled.

"Taking … them home," Wing replied as he burst forward again, this time on the right of the Buick, forcing them to make a sharp left into a narrow alley.

"They'll never make it out of here," Wing announced, laughing. With a sharp turn of his wheel, he followed close behind.

Once in the alley, the Buick managed to avoid the many pedestrians but not the several deep, long lines of neatly stacked barrels edging—and constricting—the alley. Unable to dodge the barrels, the Buick plowed into them. Amid a cacophony of the sound of hurtling metal, the big car came to a crashing halt. The doors flew open, and the men jumped out and sprinted down the alley.

Wing slammed on the brakes, barely missing the totaled Buick. They leaped out of their car in hot pursuit. As they ran, Wing started shouting in Cantonese. Frances understood that he was yelling for people to stop the men.

Several guys moved to stop them, but then the man not carrying the briefcase started shooting.

The locals all dropped to the ground or disappeared into doorways, seeking cover.

Wing called out to Frances. "Hide! Get inside an entryway, anywhere. Put something between you and that gun!"

"We have to get the briefcase!" she yelled back. She kept on running, quickly jumping into a shelter whenever she saw the burly fellow turn to shoot. Finally, after one more shot, the gun ran out of bullets.

Wing yelled something else in Cantonese that Frances didn't understand. Soon there was a rain of garbage, dishwater, and cans falling on the two men. They covered their heads with their arms and continued stumbling through the alley. However, they couldn't avoid the wet, muddy mess the lane was turning into. Slipping uncontrollably, they collapsed under the continued cascade of garbage thrown out of second-floor windows. Down they went, feet thrashing the air.

* * *

Charlie Chan and Frances sat at the main wedding table with Annie's family.

"What I don't understand is how number three daughter could hear the men discussing the plot. From what she told me, she stood on one side of the train station's entrance, and they were on the other side."

Wing grinned. "That's due to the Union Station's arch's curious feature. If someone stands near one side of the arch's foot, and someone else stands near the wall on the other side, their voices can be distinctly heard. They could talk to each other in a normal, conversational voice. The locals call it "The Whispering Arch."

"Ah, 'Whispering Arch' carried an important message loud and clear in this case," Charlie said, nodding.

"Yeah, that was unreal, Pop," Frances said. "But wait 'til you hear about our amazing car chase." And, she turned to Wing to tell the story.

Wing cleared his throat and began telling Charlie about it. "Union Station exits onto Market Street, and that's where the Italians had parked. Me, too. So, the chase began there. Fortunately, my car wasn't far from theirs. They took off, driving straight east, down Market Street. We managed to stay close behind, weaving in and out of the traffic.

"When we got near Eighth Avenue, I thought 'How lucky could I be?' I could force them to stop, if I could just get them to turn onto South Eighth Avenue."

"The beginning of China Town," Frances interjected excitedly. "It was so scary, but he managed to do it. They turned onto Eighth. As we flew around the corner right on their bumper, I thought we'd crash for sure. But we didn't." She took a deep breath, remembering the feel of the speeding car.

"Then Wing swooped over to the other side of the road and forced them to turn that big Buick left into the alley. They had no choice if they wanted to avoid a collision.

"What they didn't know was that the alley, Chinatown's Hop Alley, was too small and too crowded for a car to get through," she finished with a big grin. "We...Wing had locked them in."

Charlie Chan nodded in approval. "Fast thinking," he said.

"But they still might have gotten away with that briefcase, if Frances hadn't been so insistent on running after them. We didn't know how many bullets they had left and might have given up too early," Wing said.

Charlie Chan sat back in his chair and looked over at Frances. "Number three daughter not just best looking in Chan family but also top of her school's track team. Strong runner but weak student. Didn't learn to stay out of trouble."

At her father's words, Frances concentrated on her Cantonese Poached Chicken. His lopsided compliment showed that he was proud of her, even though he also worried about her risky behavior. It was the closest he'd ever come to praising her.

She was almost embarrassed at his comment. But not quite.

Back to Alcatraz

By J.J. White

I returned to Alcatraz to investigate a breakout that never happened.

On September 12th, at 11:37 p.m., guard Jake Hansen had just ended his shift and was lighting a cigarette outside the main cell house when he saw a ladder leaning against the wall near the prison library. He alerted the captain of the guard, who pulled the alarm and woke all two hundred and twenty-two prisoners, along with the warden and everyone in employee housing. Because of the prevailing wind, he also woke a good number of San Franciscans. The warden locked down the prison and ordered all fifty guards to find out if it was an escape attempt and who would dare try.

Besides the ladder, guards also found muddy prints and cigarette butts in the utility corridor behind the B cell block. Early the next morning, a guard noticed a roof vent cover had been pried open. Later, they found evidence a small boat had anchored near the west side gardens.

Everything pointed to a successful escape, except. Well, except that night the guards did a roll call, checking every cell, and found all present and accounted for. No one had escaped, but someone had gone to a lot of trouble to try.

From halfway across the bay, Alcatraz reminded me of the Parthenon, the prison's white edifice like that of the limestone walls of the temple. My father's heritage inspired him to drag his wife and four boys to Greece to find his roots back in 1924, and as an impressionable ten-year-old, I had been fascinated by the temple. Ten years later, I first noticed the resemblance when I was sent as a young guard to work at the Alcatraz Federal Penitentiary, which had opened its forbidding arms to the most despicable and dangerous criminals America had to offer. I joined the other guards, whose job, like mine, was to keep those criminals there.

The closer the boat got to the dock, the more the prison's true nature revealed itself, industrial and foreboding in the ubiquitous fog that rolled in off the Pacific. It has been four years since I left the penitentiary to take an investigator position with the Federal Bureau of Prisons in '44. I had thought, no, hoped, I'd never have to return to Alcatraz, having had my fill of it. But now I was back to investigate a prison break, though apparently there was none.

The pilot skillfully maneuvered the boat up to the dock without incident. I disembarked along with ten others, mostly employees and relatives of employees, whose only tie to the mainland was through the prison's large boats that traversed back and forth twelve times a day between Alcatraz and the city by the bay. The passengers exited with arms full of goods that were unavailable to them on the island. Most lived in apartments provided by the government, except the warden and his wife, who lived in a mansion.

I was met at the dock by a guard who was there to take me to meet with Warden James A. Johnston, or Old Saltwater, as he was affectionately known. Johnston had treated me well during my stay on the island and had mentored me, hoping to make me a warden someday. After seeing the toll it took on him, I had no desire for the post. I had been made captain of the guard after five years at the prison, and that had its benefits, especially the pay, but I hated the responsibility of watching over fifty guards. When I'd had enough, I left. I work alone now, and I enjoy working alone.

"Warden Johnston is expecting you, sir," the guard said. "If you'll follow me, I'll take you to the warden's house."

"Son, I worked here ten years. I know where the warden's house is."

"Yes, sir. But it's for security."

I moved in close to the kid, almost nose to nose. "I'm an investigator for the Federal Bureau of Prisons. I *am* security. I'll walk to the warden's house by myself."

The guard nodded and stepped back. I was in no hurry. I wanted to look over the Rock on the short walk to the mansion. Warden Johnston was unhappy someone had attempted an escape right before he retired. That's understandable, but I doubt the joker or jokers who attempted that escape took his retirement into consideration. You're not just a fool to try to break out of Alcatraz Penitentiary, you're a damn fool. In the fourteen years the prison had been in operation, there had been thirteen escape attempts, and they had all ended the same way. Badly. Six of the escapees were shot and killed, and the others either drowned or were listed as presumed drowned. There was no presumed about it. When I was captain of the guard, I had two men in a boat follow behind as I tried to swim the one-and-a-half miles to San Francisco. I gave up about two hundred yards out, climbed back into the boat, and covered myself with thick blankets. Nobody, prisoner or Olympic athlete, could swim across the bay to the city from Alcatraz. If you didn't freeze to death, the current would drag you to God knows where, and if those things don't get you, a shark would probably bite you in half. Alcatraz really was escape-proof. It's why the other federal prisons sent their scum there.

An investigation of the escape attempt of a month earlier was the official reason I was sent to Alcatraz, but the real reason was to prove no one escaped. Warden Johnston most likely wanted to shut down any rumors that a con succeeded in breaking out of his beloved prison.

* * *

I took the path around the main cell house to get to the warden's house, a large, three-story, fifteen-bedroom Spanish-style mansion standing proudly, an elaborate oasis in the mire that was Alcatraz. Despite the unlimited free labor available to him, Warden Johnston met me himself at the door. He shook my hand in the foyer. "Henry, how are you? How long's it been? Two, three years?"

"Four, sir," I said. "I wish I could be here under happier circumstances."

"Things couldn't be better, actually. Ida Mae's excited about my retirement, and the prison is as calm as a sleeping puppy. Come in, have a seat." He pointed to the den. "This thing you're here about is at my request. No one escaped. You're here as a formality."

I sat in a high-back velvet chair that I had sat in many times before when having to explain to the warden the myriad events and problems that occurred almost daily in the prison. For a moment, a nervous feeling crept over me. I fought it down with the knowledge I was only there visiting.

A guard brought in some brandy. After a few sips, the warden continued. "Let's get right to it, Henry. You know most of the details. The main guard on duty had just clocked out—"

"Jake Hansen," I said.

Johnston frowned. "Yes, Hansen. Anyway, he was the first to see the ladder. The captain of the guard called the alarm, and we shut down. Roll call was taken immediately after. You don't know how relieved I was to find out no one had escaped or was free of their cells. We didn't need another problem like we had in '46."

The problem he referred to was the Battle of Alcatraz. In May of that year, five armed convicts overpowered the guards on duty, locked them in an empty cell, and eventually shot them to get rid of eyewitnesses. Only two guards died, but after the alarm was given, three of the perpetrators were killed by Marines called in by the warden to quell the riot.

"Yes, sir," I said. "But this one seemed a little odd, don't you think?"

"What? That no one escaped?"

"Yes, sir. It seems that if someone took all that trouble to climb up from the utility corridor to the roof, then have someone meet them with a ladder and a boat, you'd think they'd at least try to break out."

"Well, thank God they didn't." The warden finished his brandy. "My fourteen years is nearly over, and I want to leave with a clean record. There have been no successful escapes on Alcatraz since it opened, and that's with the worst of the worst populating the prison during my term. No one has escaped, not Capone, not Kelly, not Barker, despite their notoriety. I have an impeccable record, and I want it to stay that way. What I'm hoping you can do, Henry, is find out who the culprits were and if at all possible, bring each and every one involved to justice."

"I'll do my best, sir."

"Yes, I know you will. You were the best captain of the guard Alcatraz ever had; there's no denying it. From what I heard, you're the Bureau's best investigator. One thing, though."

"Sir?"

"If you don't solve this riddle, the outcome is the same. No one escaped."

"Yes, sir. I understand. Now, I'll need access to the inmates' records and someone to show me around and take me through the events of that night."

"I'll have Captain Rodgers escort you."

"If you don't mind, sir, I'd rather have the guard in charge that night, Jake Hansen."

"Hansen. He was your friend, wasn't he?"

"Still is, though it's been four years since I've seen him."

"I suppose we can call him in. He's also leaving, you know."

"I heard that, sir."

"Yes, retiring like me, though he would have had to leave, regardless. The man is self-destructive. I know he's your friend, but that's how I see it."

I nodded. "I was a little like that myself when I was here, sir."

"Perhaps," Johnston said. "Anyway, Henry, thank you for coming on short notice. Now you understand it's important you complete this investigation quickly."

"That's my intention, sir."

"Good," he said. "I'll have Hansen meet you near the prison."

We shook hands, and I left the mansion, wondering if by telling me to complete the investigation quickly, Johnston meant for me to drop the investigation quickly.

* * *

Jake Hansen met me by the lighthouse. Like me, he was six feet tall, but unlike me, he was losing most of his hair. He kept what was left groomed and shiny with too much tonic. I left my hair dry and unkempt. Like my suit. Like my life.

Jake proffered his hand. It was rough and callused, the hand of a prison guard. "Six grand a year and you can't buy an iron to press your suit?" he said, then straightened my tie. "Anyway, Hank, how are you? How's Peg?"

"Peg's great now that she's married to someone else."

Jake looked embarrassed. "Sorry, pal. Sorry."

"It was inevitable. So what's this about retirement?"

"Yeah," Jake said. "It ain't the same as it was when you were here. You crack a head now, they shove *you* in the Hole instead of the convicts."

Jake was talking about the D block. Five cells the inmates call the Hole. A sink, a toilet, and no light or ventilated air. Fifteen days in the Hole, and you were lucky to have any sanity left.

"Anyway," Jake said. "I'm outta here about the same time as Johnston, but I'm heading for Miami Beach."

"On your pension?"

"I got a little put away if you know what I mean."

I did know. A few guards tried to benefit from having rich thugs in their prison, and I wouldn't be surprised if Jake was one of them. There were rumors Capone took care of guards if they made life a little easier for him.

"Well, congrats," I said. "Let's talk about September twelfth."

"You probably know most of it," Jake said, lighting a Camel. He offered me one. I shook my head.

"Got my own," I said and lit a Lucky from my pack. "I read about it in the brief, but I want you to show me. Now don't get upset, but the Feds want me to find out why no one saw the ladder before you did."

"What does that mean?"

"They think you might have set this up to be the hero who stopped the escape right before he retires."

"Really?" Jake took a long drag on his cigarette. "You think I'd pull something like that?"

"No, I don't think you'd pull something like that."

"Well, good. Because I didn't. I came outside after my shift and stopped for a smoke. It was a lousy night, lots of wind. I heard something banging up there." He pointed to the top of the cellhouse. "That's when I saw the ladder leaning against the wall. I went to the captain of the guard and had him follow me back. He pulled the alarm and alerted the warden. That's it."

"Hoover's guys also think there was no boat," I said.

"Oh, yeah?" Jake gestured with his index finger. "Follow me."

We walked over to the west side of the island, where the grass dropped off to a sheer rock cliff about fifty feet high. We worked our way slowly down to the water line. Jake pointed to green paint marks about six feet long on the rocks. "What do you think made those, smart guy?"

"A boat," I said.

"A boat," Jake agreed. "So anyway, after the lockdown, we took roll call. Two hundred and twenty-two cells being used, and two hundred and twenty-two prisoners in them. No escape."

"Okay," I said. "Let's head to the corridor, then admin."

We climbed the rocks and walked over to the main cellhouse. Jake told the guard on duty we'd be in the B Block utility corridor that was between the two rows of cell blocks. The only entrance to the corridor was a locked steel door. We stood in the middle so I could get a look at the roof vent.

"You want my theory?" Jake asked.

"I've got my own, but something tells me they're the same."

"Right," he said. "Here's what I think. Some con got word to a friend outside he'd meet him in the corridor at such and such a time." Jake pointed to the small air vents near the floor that lined up with cells on the other side. "Then he was supposed to bust through his air vent under his sink and wait here in the corridor while his buddy piloted the green boat down near those rocks, dragged a ladder to get to the roof of the prison, and pried off the vent cover. Then the guy slid down the rope to the corridor, and when the con didn't show, he climbed back up, left everything, and skedaddled back to San Francisco. You agree?"

"Yeah. Looks that way. Any plaster, concrete pieces around here that night?"

"Nothing," Jake said. "Clean as a whistle, except for rainwater that got in when the bum pried the cover open. Well-planned escape gone to hell."

"So how did the inmate get word to his buddy on the timeframe?" I asked.

"Beats me. They still get a visitor once a month, but we usually listen in on the phones."

"Usually?"

"Yeah, you know how it is. Sometimes it's a good time for a smoke, so you don't always listen in."

"Is that what you did with Capone when he was here?"

"What's the big deal? I'm not gonna retire and spend the rest of my short, lousy life listening to a radio in a small Jersey apartment. I'm heading to Miami Beach with a doll on each arm. Can you blame me?"

"No. I guess not. Okay, I'm going over to admin to look through the cons' files. They still have the names of the visitors and the times they came?"

"Yeah," Jake said. "As long as Old Saltwater's the warden, the place still runs like a clock."

We started toward the corridor door when I thought of something else. "Was there anything unusual after the escape attempt? Hear any rumors? Something I can use when I look at the files?"

Jake rubbed his chin. "Not much really. Denton in 259. Talk around the cafeteria has him bragging he set this up, but he takes credit for everything." Jake threw down his half-smoked Camel and crushed it with his foot. "Oh, and Westbrook in 296. Couple days after the break-out attempt, he started coughing up blood. Never been sick before, so we took him upstairs where the docs kept him a few days. X-rays showed cancer in his lungs. Said he's got four to six months at the most. He's in for a life sentence anyway, so he gets to leave early."

*　*　*

In the administration building, I stared at the file cabinets, trying to decide whose records to go through first. Rather than take it alphabetically, I started with Barry Denton and Timothy Westbrook, the two Jake had mentioned, one a braggart, the other a dead man walking. Denton was a career criminal who had been transferred from Leavenworth for his own safety. Apparently, he talked so much, a lot of his cellmates wanted to permanently shut him up. He'd had two visitors in the last six months, both lawyers who the guards said talked only about petitions for a new trial.

Timothy Westbrook's records showed he had killed two men in a bar in 1932 and had been transferred from the Atlanta Federal Penitentiary to Alcatraz for beating up a guard. He'd had one visitor, his wife, who came to see him two months in a row. There was no transcript of their conversation.

While I was going over his personal information about his family and associates, I noticed a footnote. As I read it at the bottom of the page, I knew Mr. Timothy Westbrook was in big trouble.

*** * ***

When it was time to herd the inmates from B and C block into the cafeteria, I had the guards leave Timothy Westbrook behind in his cell so I could talk to him alone.

Westbrook gazed up at me. "Guard said I had to wait to eat."

I looked around the cell, dark, sparse, a toilet built into the wall, a metal air vent under the sink, a cot, a few bookshelves, empty except for photos of Westbrook's family, his wife and three young boys, backdropped by the Appalachians.

I proffered my hand. He ignored it. "Henry Galanis," I said. "I'm an investigator with the Federal Bureau of Prisons."

"Good for you."

I took out my pack of Luckys and offered him one. His eyes lit up like a kid's at Christmas.

He shook his head. "Can't smoke inside. I take that and I'll be in the Hole for two weeks."

"No, you won't. Go ahead."

He took one, and I lit it.

"These damn things make me sick, but they help some with the pain."

"That's right, Tim. Is it alright if I call you Tim?"

"Call me what you want," he said between puffs.

I nodded. "The guard said the docs only give you a few months."

"Yeah. It's what they say."

"Something funny about that, though, Tim. The guard said up until about a month ago, you seemed healthy enough, then right after the attempted breakout, you started coughing up blood."

"So what? You die when you die. I ain't got no way to know when it's gonna happen. Nobody does."

I lit my own Lucky, took a few puffs, and walked over to the sink. I kicked lightly at the air vent below it.

"Ain't worked in a while," Westbrook said. "Don't care, though. Let the next con worry about it. I'll be six feet under."

"Your file says you're from West Virginia."

"That's right. Outside Sharples, near the mines."

"Yeah, the mines. A wife, LuAnn, three boys—"

"Kerry, Joshua, and Paulie," he said.

"Seems like a nice family. Your mother and father nearby?"

"Pa's dead. Ma lives near some."

"And two sisters and a brother," I added.

"Well, if you know everything about my family, why you bringing it up?"

"Because, Tim, when I was going through your file and reading about your family, I saw a footnote by your brother Clement's name."

"So what?"

"So, I read the footnote at the bottom of the page. You know what it said?"

"No."

"It said, identical twin. Clement Westbrook is the identical twin of Timothy Westbrook."

"Well, I guess I know that since he's my brother. So what?"

I laughed. "So, I'm a smart man. That's why they made me an investigator. When I saw that and heard you didn't get sick until after the attempted breakout, I put two and two together, Tim. Or should I call you Clem?"

"Don't know what you're talking about."

"I'll spell it out quickly since the boys will be coming back soon with full bellies. Somehow, your brother got through to you that he was going to break out and get to the utility corridor at a certain date and time. You got back to him with your details, maybe through LuAnn when she visited him. Then, on September twelfth, you pulled a boat up to the west side of the island, set up a ladder against the main cellhouse, climbed to the roof, and pried the cover off the air vent. Then you lowered a rope into the utility corridor, which Tim used to climb up. You two changed clothes, then you slid down the rope and crawled back into his cell through that vent." I pointed to the air vent under the sink. "Then Tim climbed down the ladder you left for him outside, made his way to the boat, and most likely paddled away from the island before firing up the motor. Meanwhile, you take your brother's place; I'm guessing because you knew you were dying and figured you'd help your brother get back with his beloved LuAnn and the boys. Nobody knew the better since, on paper anyway, no one escaped. How'd I do, Clem? I get it all correct?"

He shook his head. "Ain't no truth to any of that."

"Well, maybe not. Hell of a coincidence, though. You know it's a funny thing about identical twins, Clem."

"What's that? And it's Tim, not Clem. Clem's my brother."

"The funny thing, Mr. Westbrook, is that identical twins do not have identical fingerprints."

When he didn't respond, I continued. "What would you say to having me get somebody to roll your prints and compare them to the ones we have on file for Timothy Westbrook?"

He threw the cigarette to the cell floor, crushed it with his foot, and looked up at me. "How much?"

"How much, what?" I asked.

"Money. I know that's what you want. I ain't got much and Tim's quit his stealing. He's working my job at the mine. If you want some big money to keep quiet, then he's gonna have to rob some banks to get it."

"What makes you think I want money?"

"Well, why the hell else would you clear out the cell block to be alone with me? If you wanted to keep me locked up and have the Feds go after Tim, then you woulda been here with the warden and the cops to be the big hero. You didn't do that, so you want money, and I ain't got none."

"No, Clem. I don't want money. What would I do with it? I don't have any family, I don't gamble. I'm not interested in women all that much. Well, maybe one, but she's not interested in me."

"Well, why then?" Clem asked.

I shrugged. "Who knows? The chase, the satisfaction of solving a puzzle others couldn't figure out. Maybe I want to be part of a happy ending like the ones they have in the flickers. Who knows?"

"Tim didn't deserve to be here," Clem said. "He killed those boys in the bar 'cause they was gonna kill him. Self-defense. Same with that guard in Atlanta. He beat Tim something fierce, every day, so Tim beat him back. They never should have sent him here. He should've been out of Atlanta in five years, not no life sentence here."

"I agree, Clem. That's what I figured from reading his record."

"So, what now?" Clem asked.

"Now, nothing is what happens now. I tell the FBI and the warden what they want to hear: that someone failed in their attempt to free an inmate. Then, in a few months, you die, and your brother continues to take your place back in West Virginia. I assume he'll marry LuAnn after you die, as strange as that sounds."

"That's right. That's the plan. Nothing unusual about a brother marrying his dead brother's wife in the hills. Happens all the time in mine country. That's the way it is there."

"Yes, I guess so." I stood and stepped through the open cell door. "You take care of yourself, Clem. Put in a good word for me when you get there."

"Yes, sir, Mr. Galanis. And God bless you."

I smiled and threw him my pack of Luckys.

Pico And Sepulveda

By Deborah Lacy

1947—Los Angeles

Nothing in life comes easy. I've learned that the hard way. But I'll admit, I did dance around my little house when I first heard that Pete had left me his detective agency in his will.

That sounds callous. I cried when he died. But that was a few weeks ago, and I have bills to pay. I danced because I thought my money problems were over. I'd even have enough to retire. How could I have been so foolish?

I've always found a way to take care of myself. You learn that right quick when your mom is a drunk and you never had a father. But I'm not looking for your pity. God gave me a brain, and I use it.

You've probably heard at least part of my story before. I left Mattoon, Illinois, at sixteen with my high-school sweetheart, driving his beater old Ford, headed for a glamorous new life in Hollywood.

He wanted to be a famous director. I would be a famous movie star. Super original. Right? We barely had enough money to cover gas and a sandwich.

We had visions of a mansion with a swimming pool in the backyard, never mind neither of us could swim.

Of course, he always had a reason to blame me for our many setbacks. Nothing was ever his fault. As soon as reality hit us in the face, he started hitting me in the face.

I handled it the best I could. Nobody knew us in Hollywood, so no one asked me questions when he disappeared.

My money-making options back then were not so great. I didn't have waitressing experience. Never worked in a store. Too short for modeling.

So, I set up shop on the corner of Hollywood and Vine. I worked the street, making damn sure I stayed away from the pimps. Working for them is what you call a no-win situation.

Then my life changed when I met Pete. Good 'ole Pete. His wife didn't understand him, but I certainly did. He loved curvy redheads who laughed at his jokes. Check and check.

He promoted me into the role of professional girlfriend. Many of the work duties were the same for both jobs, but the clientele, pay, and work environment were much better in the professional girlfriend business.

Pete put me up in an apartment, gave me gifts, and money for food and utilities. He could only see me three nights a week, and being an enterprising businesswoman, I realized that left me four more nights for another generous boyfriend.

It didn't happen often, but if anyone laid a hand on me, I knew what to do.

Being a professional girlfriend worked well for me until the past few years, when I turned 45. Even after taking make-up lessons and dyeing the grey hair away.

The small house that Pete bought me is paid for, and that is something, but I've sold most of the jewelry and other gifts, and once again, I am down to my last few dollars.

Before this fancy lawyer phoned, it never occurred to me that I might inherit anything, much less a detective agency. I put on my most modest dress and a pair of high heels and marched down to the fancy lawyers' office.

The meeting did not go well.

First of all, Pete's angry wife threw things. She almost hit me in the head with a stapler. The shrewish woman had no business blaming me for Pete wanting to take care of me in my old age. It's not like I asked to inherit the detective agency. Heck, I wasn't even sure what to do with it.

Second of all, the agency wasn't worth much. Pete didn't own the building, so I couldn't sell it. The furniture, the lawyer said, was also rented. The monthly rent of twenty-three dollars, which I absolutely didn't have, was due in ten days. I looked at that lawyer with his beady little eyes, "How am I supposed to get any dough out of this?"

"Get clients and solve their cases."

Then that bastard laughed out loud.

I walked straight from that stupid lawyer's office down the street, the three blocks to Pete's detective agency.

Correction, MY detective agency.

The high heels hurt my feet with every step. How was I going to solve cases?

When I reached the office, I found the door that said, Pete Hearts Detective Agency. His last name was Hearts. I always loved that last name, even if I never came to love the man. I certainly liked him very much.

"Sorry, Pete." I said it out loud. "A girl's gotta do, what a girl's gotta do."

I took a quarter from my handbag and gently rubbed his first name from the door.

Now the sign said Hearts Detective Agency. It's not my name, but maybe it's better if people think the agency has a man running it and I'm the secretary or something.

I'll figure the rest out later. The word Hearts wasn't centered as the words Detective and Agency, but it would have to do for now. I don't have any money to change that sign to make it look perfect.

The key fit in the lock as promised, and the knob turned easily. I opened the door half expecting a man to jump out of me, but no one did.

I saw a secretary's desk, a chair with a phone, and a typewriter. There was a large half-dead plant. I couldn't sell a dead plant. The inner office, Pete's office, had more stuff—filing cabinets, filing folders. On the wall next to the portrait of President Truman hung a painting of a woman with red hair. She looked like me. But then again, Pete had a thing for redheads. Many men do.

My next order of business was to search for cash in the desk drawers and the filing cabinets. Look for a bank book or something. Although I am pretty sure that slimy lawyer already rifled through everything.

No cash in any of the drawers.

I'd have to learn how to be a detective or invent some other kind of business I could run out of here.

The phone sat there on the desk, daring me to call someone. So, I dialed a cop I knew, not because he was a good cop, but because he liked to talk, and he liked to give advice. Right now, I needed advice. This cop had unwittingly helped me on a least two occasions to make my problems disappear.

I told him about inheriting the agency.

"Now, Red," he always called me Red, "You already know how to be a detective. I don't know who's going to hire a dame, but if they do, you can solve their case. Just put yourself in the other person's shoes. Detecting is mostly about recognizing human nature. You got that in spades."

How ironic that he had used the word spades. He was right. I did know an awful lot about human nature.

I had no sooner hung up the phone when my office door opened.

There stood a woman.

Neat appearance. Too much makeup. Bland dress, but well-made. Clean gloves. Expensive handbag.

I knew the price of the handbag because I used to have one before I sold it to pay the electricity bill.

She looked nervous, "I'm looking for Pete Hearts." She stuttered a bit on Pete's name.

"He ain't here," I told her. This woman couldn't have known Pete. Every single newspaper in Los Angeles had an article about his death. He had a heart attack in the middle of a fancy restaurant, and he wasn't with his wife. Good thing I wasn't there.

"I need a detective," the woman said. "Are you a detective?"

I thought about how that lawyer had laughed at me when he suggested that I get clients and solve cases.

I said, "We can help you."

Honestly, I didn't know if I could help her or not, but I could try. I opened the desk to pull out a pad of paper and a pencil. There was a pad of receipts. Pete used to say you always had to ask a client for money up front or you might not get paid. Pete liked to drone on about work. Good thing I listened.

"Fees are ten dollars a day, plus expenses." I was a little shocked at my own boldness, but the woman looked like she could afford it. "There's a four-day minimum. So, we'll need forty dollars upfront. What name should I put on the receipt?"

"Mrs. Wilbur Pennyman."

The name sounded familiar. I wondered if I had ever seen Mr. Pennyman professionally. There were more than a few short-term jobs that didn't pan out.

The woman opened her handbag and handed me the cash. She didn't bother to ask me any other questions. I should've asked her for more money.

I filled out the receipt and made sure the carbon recorded what I had written on the second page. I handed the woman the original. "Now, Mrs. Pennyman, tell me why you need a detective."

"My husband is missing. He runs a big movie studio."

Movie studio? Shoot. I should have asked for more money. How am I ever going to retire if I don't get paid enough for my services?

"I'm afraid he's having an affair. Sometimes he says the name Miranda in his sleep, but we don't know anyone named Miranda. He's been gone a week. What if he's left me and the kids for good?"

I hid my excitement. My talents include determining if a man wants to have an affair or is already having one. This skill of mine has been honed during years of on-the-job training.

"We specialize in cheating husbands," I said and pulled out another chair. "Tell me about your troubles." It was the same phrase I'd used with my boyfriends. While they talk, you fixate on them like they are the only person in the world. It's all part of making them feel amazing about themselves; it works every time, whether it's tethered to reality or not.

"He told me he was going to scout a movie location. It should've only taken him a few hours, but it's been a week. He's been gone for a few days before, but never this long."

"Do you know where he went?"

"What do you mean?"

"The movie location, the one he was scouting. Where is it?"

"Oh, the movie location. Um. I think he said he was going to the corner of Pico and Sepulveda."

"You know, some guys I met at a party a few weeks ago were writing a song about the corner of Pico and Sepulveda. They sang it that night. It's a silly song about the streets of LA. The party crowd loved it."

"Yeah, I heard the song at a party too. Real catchy."

"One guy at the party said there's nothing there."

"Nothing where?" Mrs. Pennyman said.

"At the corner of Pico and Sepulveda. Nothing there but tumbleweeds and dust."

"I haven't gone there or anything. Why would I go there?"

I wrote down Pico and Sepulveda in my notebook, mostly because serious people take notes, and I thought it would make me look more like a detective.

"Don't they miss your husband at his job at the fancy movie studio? Anybody I know, their boss would fire them if they're gone for a week."

"He's the boss. He runs Earthwide Movie Studios."

Head of a movie studio? I really should have asked for more money. While the woman's clothes were nice, they didn't say rich wife nice. Perhaps Mr. Movie Studio Big Shot was cheap with his wife's allowance.

"If your husband runs the place, why is he scouting movie locations? Don't the movie scouts do that?"

"When I phone his office, his assistant just says she'll tell him I called when he comes in. She's worked for him for years. I've never liked her. I know what you're thinking, I'd be thinking it too if she wasn't nearly sixty. Definitely not Miranda. Miranda. Miranda. I'm so sick of that name."

Mrs. Pennyman wasn't answering my questions. Preoccupied by this Miranda woman. I wrote down the name Miranda. Mrs. Pennyman smiled when I circled it.

I used to know a Miranda in the professional girlfriend business. Younger. Blonde. I'd lost Ricky the cop to her. I had been furious at the time. I was figuring out my combination revenge deterrent strategy when I heard Ricky beat her. That was revenge enough. Besides, Miranda had saved me a lot of trouble. It's almost impossible to make a cop disappear.

I wondered where the Miranda I knew was now, and if she knew this Mr. Wilbur Pennyman.

"What can you tell me about Miranda?"

"I don't know anything more than what I told you."

Her face told me she was hiding something. "What do the cops say?" I asked her.

"What do you mean?" She opened her fancy purse again and pulled out a stick of gum. She held the packet out to me in case I wanted one. I shook my head no. I never chew gum.

"When you called the cops to report your husband missing, what did they say?"

"I haven't called the cops. I came to you."

"But why did you come to us before you called the cops?"

The woman hesitated just enough before she started talking again, "Why do the cops care if he left me?"

"Right. Why would they care? It's just that you said he was missing when you walked in. Not that he'd left you. You said he was missing."

The woman became agitated. "Missing. Left me. What's the difference?"

I considered the question. "The difference is if he's missing, we don't know what happened to him. But if he left you, we do."

"Either way, he's gone."

"If he's missing, he could come back."

"He's not coming back."

Mrs. Wilbur Pennyman didn't want her husband to return. Also, something I know well. One of my boyfriend's wives called me up once and paid me to get him out of the house on certain nights. I assumed at the time the wife wanted to have her own affair. I was only too happy to pocket the money, and both the husband and the wife were much happier. So, if this wife didn't want her husband back, what did she want?

She forked over the forty dollars quick enough to someone she didn't know.

I heard the repetitive lyrics of the Pico and Sepulveda song in my head.

What a ridiculous song. What movie could they possibly film at that street corner? I know the streets were named after people—Pico was a former governor of California and the Sepulveda family at one point owned all of Palos Verdes. I wrote a note to track down the two guys who wrote the song; maybe they wrote it for the movie studio. I scratched out the note. That song had nothing to do with the case. I wonder if the library has a book that I could read about being a detective.

"Are you listening to me?" the woman asked her.

"Oh, sorry, I was thinking about the corner of Pico and Sepulveda, and what possible movie they could film there," I said. "What do you want from this investigation? Do you want us to find him? Do you want us to bring him back?"

She started to cry. "I don't know what I want."

"Lady, you gave me forty dollars; you must want something."

The woman continued to sob. She pulled a handkerchief out of that expensive purse. That's when I saw the bruises on her arm.

I reached over and gently pushed the sleeve of her dress back. The big bruise went past her elbow. I could tell the arm had been broken and not healed right. I looked at her face. The make-up covered a fading bruise under her eye. Why hadn't I seen it earlier?

This was all starting to make sense…her story, the song. This woman was more like me than I thought. I can help her through her troubles and solve my problems while I'm at it.

Mrs. Wilbur Pennyman had already done the first part of the job. But now she needed help with the hard part and didn't know how to ask. Now here is a business where I can charge top dollar.

"Coming here was a mistake," Mrs. Pennyman said as she wiped her eyes with the mascara-stained handkerchief.

"Best mistake of your life. Listen to me. We can get you sorted. But the fees, well, they are much higher than the usual fees. Because of the nature of the work that you need. I'll need a deposit of one thousand dollars."

"A thousand dollars?" The lady sobbed harder, "But my husband only made three thousand a year."

"Look, we can get you out of this mess. You'll do the work, but I'll guide you through it. Understand? But you've got to get yourself together. And you've got to give me one thousand."

The woman stopped crying and straightened her dress.

"This won't be easy, but you can do it. I need to know one more thing."

Mrs. Wilbur Pennyman took a deep breath. "What? What on earth do you need to know?"

"Did you kill Miranda, too?"

The Dame in the Doorway

By Jeff Tanner

Remember: When there's danger, call for Granger. Johnny Granger.

Opening Lines,

"Call for Granger" Radio Show, 1947

After finishing a rehearsal for my show, *Call for Granger*, I quickly said goodbye to everyone and left Mutual Broadcasting's Hollywood studio. On the sidewalk, a few gals waited with autograph books or magazines.

"There's Johnny!" cried one of the dolls, the rest surrounding me with their books out.

"Bill," I said. "I'm Bill Lane, but I play Johnny." The girls didn't seem to care, just pushed their books at me. With a tough guy smile, I took a *Radio* magazine and penned my name next to my photograph.

"Can you make it to Babs, please?" Babs looked to be sixteen, sweet, all spun sugar.

"Of course, cookie. To Babs, love Bill Lane," I muttered as I wrote. The flock tittered, but they were already looking for the next so-called star to leave the studio.

I walked toward my apartment. Alone. Just as I had for the past three weeks.

A sudden clap of thunder warned of coming rain. As the storm raced down the street, I took shelter in a dark store's recessed doorway, the heavy rain blanketing the street.

I lit a cigarette and listened to the rain. My spirits were low. Gloria, my wife, had left for Chicago after our final argument. Her faith in me had died when my movie career ended, even as my new radio show, *Call for Granger,* was picking up listeners. My producer told me that evening that the edge of melancholy in my voice made my character, Johnny Granger, more convincing, and to keep it up. Like I had a choice.

As fast as it came, the rain passed. Misty steam rose from the pavement, still hot from the now-gone California sun. Footsteps of a dame in heels echoed off the few pre-war cars parked for the night, or, maybe, forever. The click-clack sounded in a hurry and coming my way.

After a final drag on my Lucky Strike, I tossed the cigarette toward the gutter. The still-burning cigarette pinwheeled in front of her. She looked at me, then glanced behind her before jumping into the entrance recess. The sound of two more pairs of feet, more like men's, were coming from the same direction.

"Help me get out of this coat," she ordered in a whisper. She threw her hat on the ground behind me and shrugged out of the coat I held. "Drop it behind you."

I did as she ordered. The footsteps got louder as the men got closer, the staccato rhythm growing faster. They were almost even with us. She grabbed me in a tight embrace.

"Kiss me," she said. Her lips came to mine. What the hell, I could pretend she was Gloria. I closed my eyes and obeyed her command.

The footsteps stopped. I tried to enjoy her lips on mine, but she trembled, and not due to the ecstasy of a kiss. I opened my eyes. Two men stared at us, their lascivious grins visible in the dim light.

"Keep moving," I growled over her shoulder. One man snickered.

"C'mon, Lucky, we need to find her," said the other man. He walked on, and after a couple of clicks with his mouth, Lucky joined his friend.

When their footsteps had died away, the doll stepped back. Though the darkness hid her face, I decided that she had to be beautiful with her long hair and full figure.

"Thanks, pal. Well, so long." She picked up her hat and coat and started to walk back in the direction from which she came.

"Wait! What's your name?" I asked.

"Better you don't know." She giggled, hysteria creeping into her laugh. "I thought I was going to break you in two." Her steps clacked off into the dark.

Break me in two, she said. I'm naturally a skinny guy, and I still hadn't filled back out after more than a year of living on the cheap. But I didn't think I was that bony.

I chuckled. Was she real, or did we step into an episode of *Call for Granger?* I shook my head and began walking home.

Footsteps sounded behind me. Perhaps the funny boys were back.

I never found out. Instead, I was spun around by a twisting shove, and a meaty hand came out of nowhere, my face exploding as the fist made contact. I fell back against a car, the back of my head smacking the door's drip rail. The night grew darker, the pool of light from the streetlamp fading into black, and I drifted out.

When I came to, I sat, legs splayed, on the sidewalk, and my back against the car. Someone put something heavy and hard in my lap—a revolver. I stared at it and wondered how it got there. The gat looked like the .38 police special we used for sound effects. I held it as I got to my feet, leaning on the car.

I staggered a few steps, my gait getting stronger as I walked. Something lay on the sidewalk ahead of me. As I got closer, the features of a body lying next to a raincoat and a hat became clear.

Her head hung off the curb. The dame whose lips tasted so sweet, who trembled in my arms, not knowing she had only seconds before eternal sleep, lay with a bullet wound in her back.

I stared down at the sleeping angel before covering her body with the raincoat. Flooded by overwhelming despair at the lost promise of a young woman's life, I couldn't cry or pray. I didn't even know her name.

I pocketed the revolver to give the cops and called them from a payphone inside an all-night diner around the corner. Count Basie performing "Blue

Skies" from a jukebox accompanied my call. Odd background music to report a murder. When I left the joint, the door closed, shutting out the serenade.

My head pounding, I turned back on the street with the dead girl. Nothing moved on the otherwise empty street. I sat next to the body and waited for the police.

"I'm sorry, angel," I said to the woman under the coat, anger rising at whoever did this. "I'm sorry you didn't make it, didn't get away. But I'm not going to be made a patsy."

Several police cars pulled up. Uniformed and plainclothes police started their job of processing death. Eventually, two plain-clothed detectives took me to the station and, after getting my statement and dipping my hands in hot paraffin for a gunshot residue test, decided I was innocent and released me. They couldn't release the overwhelming feelings of having failed to protect her.

Then the newshounds had their turn. They hammered me for details. I repeated the story, without mentioning Lucky's name, several times before escaping. I didn't need him to come calling.

When I got home, I laid a cool slice of cheap bologna on my bruised face, as I couldn't afford to own a steak. I awoke the next morning, the smell of warm bologna assaulting my nose. My head pounded with the rhythm of hot jazz. I opened my good eye and realized it wasn't jazz; someone was knocking nonstop on my door. Tossing the bologna onto a table, I got up and answered the door.

I almost fainted. There she stood, the dame in the doorway from the night before.

"Johnny? Johnny Granger? I'm Clarice Simpson. My sister..." She struggled to speak. Her eyes were puffy, as if she had been crying, but she was still beautiful. She took a deep breath. "You found my sister, Lynne, last night. Please, may I come in?"

Her sultry whisper jarred me wide awake.

"Sure, angel. Only I'm Bill Lane," I said.

So it wasn't her. I ran my hand along my neck, unreasonably ashamed at my failure to prevent her sister's death, and suppressed my desire to hold her close. You're a married man, I reminded myself. But Gloria's gone, I retorted.

The doll didn't respond to my correction of my name, or my nerves wrapped tightly around desire. Instead, she sauntered past, her soft figure held in check by a tight red and white sundress. I followed her Chanel scent into my small den and offered her a seat. She glanced at it, but didn't mention the bologna curling up at the edges as it dried on the table next to her.

"Tell me," she whispered, "what happened?

I gave her the full story. Every lurid detail, straight and without blinking, including the reason for the bologna. I held out the comment about breaking me; I'm not that skinny. She never moved. Not until I finished, her large doe-like eyes staring off into the distance. Then those eyes looked around until they focused on me.

"Can you help me find who did this?" she asked.

"Why not let the police...?"

She interrupted. "I couldn't tell them everything. It's too dangerous."

"Okay." I drew the word out. "You know I'm just an actor, right? I'm Bill Lane, not Johnny Granger. I just play him on the radio."

"I suppose. But I don't have anyone else."

I very much doubted that. The way she looked and with her pillow-soft voice, any red-blooded man would jump at the chance to play Sir Galahad.

"What couldn't you tell the police?" I asked.

"Her boyfriend is...was Joey Ritani. He runs..."

I interrupted. "Campisi's. Yes, I know."

She told their story from the beginning. They were from Pocatello, Idaho, and their parents had died the year before. The sisters came to Hollywood, stars in their eyes and celluloid in their dreams. They found jobs as waitresses, Clarice at the Brown Derby, Lynne at Campisi's.

I knew both places, though only by reputation. The Brown Derby, where the elite meet to eat, I couldn't afford. Campisi's, though, was one of the mob's top night spots, run by Joey "the Rat" Ritani. He got his nickname, the story goes, when a victim's last words were, "The dirty rat shot me."

According to Clarice, Ritani fell for Lynne. She began singing at Campisi's, no longer waiting tables. He paid for a better apartment and bought her better clothes and jewelry. Some mug, claiming to be a producer, had promised her a screen test. Ritani found out. The mug disappeared.

"I suppose I could go to Campisi's, snoop around a little." At my offer, she lit up like the fireworks over Santa Monica Pier.

"I'll go with you. I can't pay you," she said. "But I'd do anything to find my sister's killer."

"I've only got an hour for *anything*," I said, hoping she'd get my intention. "I have rehearsal, then the show later tonight."

She didn't take the hint, which was just as well, said Gloria's husband to me. But before she left, we made plans for her to accompany me to the studio to watch us do the show. I spent a lonely hour smelling bologna and staring at the ceiling, then showered and dressed for rehearsal. I walked to the studio to save a buck for our night at Campisi's.

After rehearsal, I hoofed it to the apartment she shared with her sister. When Clarice opened the door, I was too stunned to even let out a whistle. Her black dress hugged her figure the way I wanted to, and her lips were cherry red. I idly wondered if the dress belonged to her sister, paid for by Ritani.

Clarice sparkled, excited about meeting a producer and the actors as if nothing had happened last night. We cabbed over to the studio, even though it wasn't that far, for the pre-show run-through and then the show.

Heads turned when we entered, and not just because she wasn't Gloria. My agent slobbered an offer to represent her. He'd already finagled an audition with my producer. When Clarice said yes, he patted my back and thanked me for bringing her. I wanted to pull her to me in a display of ownership, but somehow that didn't feel right.

I played Johnny extra tough that night. The cast were regulars, actors who played different roles from week to week. During the run-through, I'd catch glimpses—newfound respect, fear, or some other response to the strength of my acting. Was my performance for Clarice? I hadn't given her any thought nor planned about how to act, instead feeling the part growing into me.

Afterward, outside the studio, I opened the cab door for her. She pulled me to her and kissed me. "Thank you." Her husky whisper made me want a second round.

"For what, babydoll?"

"For getting me these breaks."

"You being you got you the breaks," I said. Reluctantly, I let go of her so she could get into the cab.

"You know, it was really Lynne's dream to be in the movies," she said. "I only came along for the adventure. I suppose now it's up to me to live her dream." I worried she would cry, but I needn't have. Instead, she took a deep breath and, after I had gotten in, slid closer to me.

At Campisi's, the host recognized Clarice and pointed us out to Joey Ritani. Ritani saw her, emotions of surprise, sadness, and hope taking turns on his face. He stopped by our table, welcoming me effusively, calling me Johnny. I didn't correct him. He looked like an ordinary guy; that is, until you saw his eyes. There was a hardness to them. They were the eyes of a killer.

He offered his condolences to Clarice. She smiled sadly. For the second time that evening, I resisted the urge to move closer to her, to show that she was mine.

"I understand you found Lynne?" he asked.

I nodded. "Do you know someone named Lucky? He was one of the two men who followed her last night." A jazz trio played a dance number, a warm-up to the big band coming later.

"I don't know a Lucky. But he won't be so lucky if I find him."

As he spoke, two vaguely familiar men entered from a backroom, silhouetted by the light behind them—silhouettes I thought I recognized. Through the open door, I caught a glimpse of well-dressed guys and dolls standing around a craps or roulette table.

"Interesting," I said.

Ritani, following my lead, looked the two men over but showed no reaction. Instead, he proceeded to examine Clarice and, apparently, liked what he saw. "Clarice, I need a singer. Can you sing like her? Could you fill in for your sister?"

"Tonight, Mr. Ritani?" she asked. She brightened at his request.

"Joey. Tonight or tomorrow night. Up to you."

A platinum blonde draped herself over Ritani's shoulder. "Hey! I'm singing tonight, Joey. Remember?"

"Lay off, Madge. You only look like a torch singer. You sound like an alley cat." He removed her arms from his body. She slapped his shoulder, drawing a look of ire. "How about it, Clarice?" Ritani asked.

"Tomorrow is fine. I know all her songs; we practiced together." Clarice smiled sweetly. Madge stood ready to claw out her eyes.

"Great," Ritani said. "You can both sing tomorrow night. We'll let the audience decide who's the best."

At Ritani's pronouncement, Madge stomped off, her gold lame gown shimmering in the romantically lit room. She sat at a table against the far wall. With the two men.

"Who's that with Madge?" I asked Ritani.

"That's Falcone, her boyfriend. I don't know the other guy. I hear he's out of San Fran, though."

San Quentin seemed more likely, I thought. "Falcone. He the one with the curly hair?" Ritani nodded. "What's he do? For a living, I mean."

"He's in business."

The way he answered, I presumed Ritani meant that he's in the mob, Henkel's mob, the same Henkel who owned Campisi's.

A man came up and whispered something in Ritani's ear. He excused himself and led the man to the gambling room to take care of something.

I must have been staring at Madge, as Clarice asked me if I preferred to sit over there.

"I like where I am very much, angel."

Angel, an endearment from the language of Johnny Granger. The tough fix-anything man whose name rhymed with danger. Clarice may have looked like an angel, but I began to suspect that any resemblance stopped at the surface. She didn't act as though she had just lost her sister, more like a dame on the town. Then again, I wasn't a hard-boiled detective either. We were both acting out a script that felt like something someone else had written.

What was this show all about? Perhaps a jealous Madge convinced her boyfriend to rub out a rival? Or did Lynne see something she shouldn't have, and Ritani disposed of her? And how did Clarice mix in?

I wasn't sure whether Falcone was the other man or not, but I was growing confident that the one Ritani didn't know was Lucky. A hitman brought in by Falcone for the job? But why bring in a hitman just for taking out a doll?

Clarice, though, distracted me from simply sitting and thinking. We danced a little, talked a little. After a while, we ordered dinner. Ritani comped us a bottle of champagne to go with our oysters and steaks. Madge came on at eleven. She had some talent, but she wasn't as good as the food or champagne. By midnight, we had the place almost to ourselves, and Ritani didn't look happy. He stopped by the table.

"You see why I need you?" he said to Clarice. "Madge couldn't empty the place any faster if she yelled fire."

He sent the bandleader over with Lynne's song list and the two talked shop while I sat on my hands, the odd man out. They set up a brief rehearsal for the next day.

"C'mon, babydoll, let me take you home," I said sometime later to a swaying Clarice. Madge was butchering a ballad. Francone watched her with moon eyes while Lucky seemed disgusted. Her singing would do that to any man who wasn't tone-deaf.

"Aw, let's have some more bubbles. I like bubbles."

"I can see you do. We'll take a bottle with us. Unless you have some at home?" I asked.

She flicked an eyebrow up and down. "Oh, I think I can find something suitable," her voice sultry, her words slightly slurred. She leaned against me, and I steadied her as we walked out.

She may not have gotten the hint earlier, but there was no need for subtlety when we got to her apartment. I left her hours later, my body crying out for sleep. I had a commercial to make the next day, or rather, later in the same day, and a script to read through before we would go back to Campisi's for her singing debut.

I got up at the crack of noon. A cup of java wasn't quite rinsing the cobwebs out of my brain. Squinting at the bright sunlight streaming through my kitchen window, I grimaced. Ordinarily, I'd be happy at the tourist-bureau-perfect weather, but I had no time to enjoy it. Instead, Johnny Granger had a commercial for Sparkies cereal to record. "When you get in the chair in the morning, ask for Sparkies! They'll give you a jolt to start the day!" Maybe they'd have a sample at the studio.

The night before, Clarice had seemed disappointed or perhaps frightened when I said I'd meet her at the club rather than take her. I didn't tell her that I'd seen enough rehearsals. Nor did I tell her that Lucky was probably the man with Falcone. I convinced her to go on her own because, individually, perhaps one of us could find something out about the killer.

I also didn't tell her I packed a gun, a .25 caliber I inherited from my uncle. I hadn't fired a gun in years. When the war broke out, I tried to enlist but they wouldn't take me—too anemic. But now I was tough-guy Johnny Granger; no way I'd go unarmed. The smaller .25 fit in my pocket without the bulge of a .38 or a .45. Maybe no one would notice.

At the club, I sat at the bar and watched each girl alternate songs with the band, throwing in a few dance numbers in between. Clarice's gown was designed for the spotlight, a pale blue brocade with gold highlights. She didn't need anything too sensuous to show up Madge. Madge's gown, however, looked ready to fall off at the first vigorous shimmy. Every man's eyes bugged out in vain hope.

Couples danced to a rhumba version of "Heartaches" when a waiter handed me a note from Clarice. The note read to come backstage and help her into a gown for the next set. Being a gentleman, more or less, I did as the lady requested, passing by the table where Falcone and Lucky sat with Madge.

The dressing room was little more than a closet with a make-up table. The two of us were alone.

"Here, help me out of this dress."

"Sure, baby." I unzipped the dress, my hands lingering on her waist. She took a half-step forward, as far as the little room would allow. Reluctantly, I let go.

She stepped out of her dress and hung it carefully. Her Chanel scent filled my senses; she was less than an arm's length away, and her satin slip and silk stockings were shining in the lights. I couldn't help myself; I pulled her to me and kissed her neck. She turned around and put her arms around me.

"Just a kiss for now," she said. "I need to fix my face before I go back out."

"There's nothing about you that needs fixing." We kissed, and then kissed again, holding each other tight.

"I want to hold you so tight; I could almost break you in two." She pushed me away and sighed. "Now, help me into this dress."

She slid on a blue gown with puffy sleeves and turned around so I could zip her up. She gave me a peck on the lips, then pulled me close again for a deep kiss. With another peck and a slight push on my chest, she said, "That's all for now. I have to get ready."

I reached out for the doorknob but stopped.

"Break me? In two? That's what the dame in the doorway said." As I said those words, I could see the truth. "You weren't wearing lipstick, but she was. It wasn't Lynne they were following. It was you."

Her face melted as if she were about to cry. The truth, if that's what I heard, came tumbling out.

"Oh, Johnny, I didn't know Lynne was there, honest, I didn't." She called me Johnny. I didn't correct her. "I heard the gunshot and then a car tore past me. I hid in the shadows. They couldn't see me. I ran back to Lynne. You were starting to moan, so I tossed the coat and hat down and leaned back in the shadows until you went into the diner, then I ran off."

"But why were they following you?" I asked.

"That's just it. They must have thought I was Lynne. She'd been so jumpy for a few days, I figured something had happened. She asked me to go to the diner to buy cigarettes from the machine there while she got ready to go to the club, but those men followed me. They scared me." She clutched at my arms. "I think she sent me out as a, a, a decoy or something. She must have followed to see if they were there. And when they came back, they shot her."

If the truth, that story didn't add much, except that Lynne knew someone was after her. I began to suspect Ritani was behind it. Maybe she saw or heard something she shouldn't have.

"Okay, baby. It's okay." I took Clarice in my arms and vowed to keep her safe.

A knock at the door followed by someone saying, "Five minutes," put her into a panic. She pushed me away and sat at the makeup table. I saw her reflection in the mirror. She blew me a kiss. I left as she went to work, fixing her makeup.

I didn't know what to make of her story, except it didn't change my belief that Lucky had killed Lynne. My nerves jangled like car keys carried by a drunk, but I managed to bump into only one chair on the way to the table where Falcone sat between Lucky and Madge. They warily looked up as I approached.

"Let's see," I said, in my best tough-guy voice, "you're Falcone and you're Lucky." I sat down.

Lucky's eyes squinted with menace. "What do you want?"

Were it not for the liquid courage I had poured down my throat, I might have walked away. I was afraid they could hear my knees knocking together with fright. Instead, I clicked my tongue the way Lucky had on the street and took a seat. That tipped off Falcone, too, at least as to my identity—that man with the dame.

"Oh, not much." I ran my hand along the table, my right hand. I hoped it gave them a sense of security, however false, for I held the gun in my left under the table because I'm left-handed. "Just want to know why."

"Why what?" Menace dripped off Falcone's voice. He narrowed his eyes, his face reminding me of a serpent's.

"Why'd you do it. You know, plug Lynne. Was it for Madge?" I looked directly at him.

Everyone's heads swiveled toward the door. Someone had entered the room, and the two mugs in front of me were on full alert. Falcone nodded curtly to Madge. She slid out of her chair and ran as fast as her tight dress would allow, bumping into Clarice coming out for her next number.

I craned my neck to see who had come in. It was the big man, Henkel himself, walking in with all of the confidence of a mobster with a machine gun escort. Except this was his place, and no rods were visible.

Until suddenly, rods were everywhere.

Lucky waited until Henkel was only steps away. He pulled his revolver out and fired twice, hitting Henkel in the stomach and chest. One bullet exited and lodged in the henchman closest to Henkel. The other three men with Henkel were reaching for their pieces, but it was too late. Henkel lay dying on the floor.

Falcone stood, hands up to show they were empty. "It's over, boys. Put 'em away."

"That why you killed Lynne? Because she knew you were about to take down Henkel, to take over the mob?"

As I spoke, Henkel's gunsels were looking from Ritani to Falcone and back. From the way Ritani's men were not reacting, I gathered that the only ones not in on the job were the four men who came in with the dead man. Most of the patrons watched silently, frozen with fear at the tableau before them. The band had cleared the stage at the first shot, taking their instruments with them.

Lucky started toward the backstage door when Ritani stopped him.

"You're not going anywhere," shouted Ritani. "You killed Lynne, you bastard!" He swung at Lucky, knocking him into the wall.

Lucky brought his gun up on Ritani. This was it, the moment when I had to decide. Would I let him shoot an unarmed Ritani? In a split second, I weighed the consequences, to my career, to my life. The Rat probably deserved to die, but to be slain unarmed didn't feel right. Johnny Granger wouldn't allow that.

I fired, the gun surprising me with a kick. The bullet shattered the table and hit Lucky in the groin. Lucky, his mouth falling open in surprise, fired wide.

He slid down the wall, his eyes and mouth still open but lifeless.

Falcone and Ritani, the only unarmed mobsters in the joint, stared at each other. I didn't know how mob takeovers worked, but the two men were probably in on it together. But not Lynne's murder. Her death divided them.

I stood, my heart pounding so strongly that I thought I was seeing my blood pulse through my eyes. I put the gun back in my pocket and searched for Clarice. She stood next to Madge, looking grimly satisfied, her chest heaving with each full breath. I turned my back on the bodies on the floor and walked over to her.

"You did it, Johnny, you did it. You found the man who killed my sister." She wasn't looking at me. Her eyes were focused in the direction of the dead man slumped against the wall.

"Let's sit down, baby, and wait for the police."

I'm not Johnny. I'm Bill Lane. I just play Johnny for the radio.

And for the dame in the doorway.

Captain Bligh's Sword

By Nina Wachsman

One of my best business decisions was going blond. It allowed me to get past the security guard with just a casual wave, and merited a smile from the parking attendant instead of a scowl when I tossed him my keys.

From the sounds of laughter and splashing, the party was in progress at the pool, and to find my new employer, I'd have to walk around the house in my new heels. Luckily, a flagstone path leading to the patio would spare them. The bushes along the side of the house rustled as I passed, as if someone was hiding in them. *Not my business to investigate—yet.*

The patio was bright with lanterns, the glitter of jewels, and gleaming white smiles from cosmetically enhanced teeth. The dashing figure of my new employer was not in evidence. Stopping a sweaty busboy carrying a load of dirty glasses, I asked, "Where's the boss?"

He pointed a thumb towards the open French doors. "By the bar."

I followed a trail of glasses and drunks to reach Mr. Errol Flynn. Elegant in a white open-collared shirt, his famous pencil-thin mustache stretched across his smile, he was playing bartender to a pair of gossamer-clad lovelies. His glance was swift and savvy as he took in my proportions, but he was smarter than I expected since he pegged me. "You must be Dorothy Dent."

"What gave me away?"

"You're the only one wearing a suit." His grin reminded me of the Big Bad

Wolf. "Come along and we'll talk in private."

He led me down a corridor to a pair of double doors, which he unlocked with a key he pulled from his pants pocket.

"The scene of the crime."

"Nice," I said as I entered, and I wasn't lying. Definitely a lion's den, but airy and open, with large windows, a lot of open space, and fine craft furniture. There were even books on the bookshelves that looked like they might have been read.

Over the fireplace was Flynn's portrait. He posed beneath it and pointed to the opposite wall, where a long glass case was noticeably empty.

"Captain Bligh's sword. *Mutiny on the Bounty*. Like in the Charles Laughton movie? My mother's a descendant of one of the mutineers, who seized it as a trophy."

"I thought you were Irish." Was he lying? No tics, no shiftiness to signal nervousness.

"Tasmanian. That sword's my little touch of home."

"Is it valuable?"

Flynn shrugged. "I guess it would be worth something to collectors. But its real value is to me, which is why it was taken."

"Why? Have you been touched already?" I went to the case to examine it closely. Solid oak, latched, with sturdy brackets and no sign of forced access. "Does this thing lock?"

"No, since the room is always locked, I didn't think it was necessary. Besides, any thief could just break the glass to take it. And no, I have not been contacted with an offer to redeem it."

Flynn came up behind me, leaning close while putting his hands on my shoulders. The smell of his alcohol-overlaid-with-mint breath was overpowering. I angled my elbow purposefully, forcing him back.

Pointing to the desk and the chair beside it I gave him my orders. "Have a seat. We have some business to conduct, and I'm supposing that's where you'll do it."

He obeyed, pulling out a leather folio from the desk and uncapping a pen. I gave him my rates, and he didn't protest. Within a few moments, I was slipping his nice, fat check into my purse.

The door burst open to admit three men, who paused at the sight of me, taking a few extra moments to ogle. I recognized them: Errol's movie and real-life sidekicks, Bruce Cabot, Freddy Hall, and the Brit, David Niven. They'd been partly responsible for Flynn's former beach house being known as *Cirrhosis-by-the-Sea*.

"Help yourself," said Flynn, gesturing to the bottles of scotch at the sidebar. Then he leaned back and asked me, "Now that you are officially my employee, tell us what's next."

"Us?" I raised my eyebrows and tilted my head towards the other three men.

"Errol doesn't mind if we're here, right?' said Freddy, lighting a cigarette and blowing smoke at the ceiling.

"Who are you anyway?" said Cabot, circling me, with a drink in his hand, trying to look tough. I would have loved to knock the drink out of his hand and perhaps break one of his fingers.

"She's a fixer for Jack Warner," said Flynn, adding, "he's loaned her to me to help me out during my recent troubles."

Flynn didn't need to elaborate. Thanks to the tabloids, everyone knew about his trial for statutory rape. Yup, Errol Flynn liked them young. Not necessarily innocent, but young.

Evoking their boss's name had its effect. Cabot backed away as if I had the plague, and Niven raised his glass to me in a mocking toast. Freddy tapped his foot and blew out some more smoke.

"What's she doing here?"

Flynn pointed to the empty sword case with his drink. "She's here to find out who stole Captain Bligh's sword. Any of you know anything about that?"

Niven gave us a face of mock horror. "That treasured family heirloom? Why would they take that, of all things?"

I nodded to Niven. "I couldn't have said it better. Feels more like a prank than a theft to me."

"Now who would do such a thing to our good buddy, Errol?" asked Freddy, smirking as he stubbed out his cigarette in an ashtray.

His buddies may be taking the theft as one big joke, but Flynn *did* look worried. I perched on the edge of the desk, crossing my legs. Distracts men, so when I lob my first volley, their guard is down and they may reveal something I want to know.

"Mr. Flynn, you wrote a pretty substantial check to me just now, to find a sword that probably isn't worth much."

Flynn's smile faded along with his cockiness. "The sword has deep emotional ties—"

"Save your acting for the screen. You want me to find more than the sword." I stood and folded my arms across my chest, confronting him.

Flynn glared at me before ordering his buddies out. None of them protested or complained.

Once the door was securely locked behind their departing backs, Flynn turned to me. He had regained his composure and, despite all the scotch he'd tossed back, seemed stone-cold sober.

"Jack Warner told me you were the one who dug up all the dirt on those girls at the trial. There's more involved than you can imagine about this whole case. Two girls suddenly coming forward at the same time, just when I'm the highest box office star for Warner? Not a coincidence." He pulled a cigarette case from his pocket, and as he lit one up, his hands were shaking. "Taking the sword was a message. Whoever took it got access to this room, which was supposed to be secure. This theft is a threat, and I am taking it seriously."

"It sounds like you've got a suspect in mind."

He blew out a long stream of smoke and looked at me, as if he was weighing how much to share. "Well, there's Lilli."

"Your ex hates you; I get that. She has opportunity because she probably kept a key to the place, and she would want to take something personal to send a message. But Lilli doesn't scare you, does she? Unless she's got something more than child support over you."

Errol sighed, giving me the 'poor-me' look designed to gain motherly sympathy from most women, but I haven't a motherly bone in my body. I got up from the desk and sauntered over to the empty case.

Flynn continued, "Lilli wants two things: my money and to discredit me in the film industry. Hence, the theft of the sword. Quite a joke for the Great Swashbuckler to have a sword stolen from right under his nose." He snorted and stubbed out the rest of his cigarette emphatically. "As if this stupid court case isn't enough to do that on its own."

"It could be the theft of the sword may have some bearing on the court case." I looked around. Besides the door, there were some tall windows that were bordered by bushes, the same ones I heard rustling as I came in. "I assume you keep the windows and the door locked when you leave. They're the only ways into this room."

Finishing off his drink, he put the glass down with a thunk and went over to the fireplace. His hand traveled under the ledge of the mantlepiece, which swung sideways, opening a door to a passageway. "Not exactly. Shall we?"

The stories of Flynn's notorious voyeurism and the secret passageways with peepholes into the bedrooms and bathrooms seemed to be true.

"Where does this go?"

He shoved his hands into his pockets and looked up at me with a sheepish grin. My God, this guy was always acting! Now he's playing the naughty boy caught with his hands in the cookie jar.

"The corridor leads to a doorway behind the bar. That's where I'm headed."

"Anyone who knows how to open the passageway could slip in here without notice." I scratched my head. "Getting into this room doesn't seem too difficult. But carrying a large sword, that would catch someone's attention, even at the bar."

Three ways to get in and out: the locked door, the latched windows, and the 'secret' passageway. Anyone who knew how to access the passageway at the bar could get into the room. Once I was sure Flynn was gone, I headed through the passageway but stopped before a rectangle of bright light.

It was the vanity mirror from the ladies' powder room. A blond was touching up her lipstick a few inches from my face. A dark-haired beauty appeared beside her, leaning over to push a false eyelash firmly in place.

There was a hidden microphone in the bathroom. "Which one do you want? David, Bruce, or Freddy?" asked the blond.

Flynn and his boys would not enjoy this conversation. Despite their reputations, from these women's assessments, movie stars apparently weren't the lovers they were supposed to be.

Time to move on. I was feeling my way along a length of the dim corridor to a small circle of light, a peephole into a bedroom. A young girl sat on the bed, her arms in her lap, an older woman beside her. The older woman reached over and squeezed her shoulder. "Come on, honey, don't mope. Mr. Manzilli promised he would take care of everything after this. Just one night, that's all it is."

"I'm scared," said the young girl in a small voice.

"Why? Because he's a big star? You should be excited, not scared. You loved him in his movies, now you'll get the chance to be with Captain Blood in real life." The older woman put her hand to the young girl's chin and turned the girl's face towards her. "Come on, this isn't like your first time, and he likes young girls."

"The whole thing makes me feel...it's not right."

The older woman removed her arm from the younger girl's shoulders. "Enough of this. You got a job to do, and Mr. Manzilli expects you to do it. You know we can't disappoint Mr. Manzilli, right?"

There was a brief sigh from the girl, and she rose and smoothed down her tulle skirts. "Okay."

"Come on, just follow me. I'll get you in front of him."

I left the peephole before they left the room. I knew enough from the work I was doing for Jack Warner that this was another attempt to set up Flynn for a fall. This was a bad time for another young girl to complain about Flynn's advances. I had to get out there and warn him.

I hurried forward to a large square of light. It was the mirror behind the bar. I felt around until I found the mechanism to slide open the door. It was hidden in a shadowy corner behind the bar, but with a few steps forward, anyone standing there would be obvious. Especially if he or she were holding a 3-foot-long sword.

Food for thought as I headed towards the sound of clinking ice in cocktail shakers.

Flynn was doing the shaking, and Bruce and Freddy were leaning on the bar in anticipation. The young girl in pink tulle and her older escort were approaching, heading in Flynn's direction. I leaned in close to him and muttered, "Incoming."

Flynn followed the direction of my eyes and tugged at the collar of his shirt as if it suddenly felt too tight. Before the lethal young lady and her mother could join us, I loudly announced, "Errol, we need to go over some plans for tomorrow. Jack's expecting a response, so perhaps Bruce and Freddy will excuse us?" I gestured towards the study.

Flynn's eyebrows shot up along with his curiosity. He must be wondering if I'd found something. "Yes, mustn't keep Jack waiting now, should we?"

As we passed by the young girl in pink, the older woman scowled. As soon as we were inside the door, I warned Errol about the conversation I'd overheard from the peephole.

"Manzilli's one of the thugs after Jack," Flynn said, as he locked the door behind us. In two steps, he was at the drinks tray, pouring another whiskey.

"Imagine what happens if a third girl goes to the press just before you're ready to face the jury."

Flynn gulped down his drink. "Thanks for the warning. Anything more you'd like to share?"

"One more question: the last time you were here and the sword was in place, was anyone else with you?"

Flynn shifted his weight from one foot to the other and raised his eyes to the ceiling. "Yes, I was having a drink with Freddy, Bruce, and David."

"Did you leave the room at all while they were here?"

Flynn shifted his weight again and avoided my eyes. Why was he so uncomfortable with my questions? "Maybe I went out for a moment."

He didn't offer a reason why, and since I didn't need to know, I moved on. I was beginning to get an idea of what might really be going on.

"Bring your friends here, now," I said, "Time to put this thing to bed. But remember, not with young blonds in pink tulle."

Flynn's jaw tightened. "Maybe I should have had her escorted out."

"Not a bad idea."

Though I wasn't waiting long, it did seem longer than expected. Niven sauntered in, acknowledging me with a nod, followed by Bruce, who did the same with a leer. Freddy leaned against the wall by the fireplace and burped loudly. Flynn distributed drinks while I took my seat at the edge of the desk.

"A locked room, an empty case, a missing sword, and me, a private female private detective hired to get to the bottom of it. Mr. Flynn said he heard of me when he hired me, but since you're both such good friends of his, you must have known about it too. Correct?"

After a quick glance at each other, David, Freddy, and Bruce nodded.

I shot my first question at Flynn. "Which of them recommended me?"

Flynn blinked a few times in succession, as if trying to recall. "Niven."

Next shot. "Whose idea was it to steal the sword?"

I stared down the other three. Surprisingly, it was Niven who broke and murmured. "Bruce."

Flynn blew out an air stream of dismay and then shook his head. "Really. Some good friends you lot turned out to be." He shifted his attention to me. "You really are as good as they say. I may have lost the sword, but I did win the bet."

"Bet?"

Niven gave me a half smile. "Word on the Warner lot was that you're a Jack Warner favorite, but we figured…"

I wanted to slap him. "I get it. You all bet I wouldn't be able to solve the case, and that one of you could get me in the sack?"

None of them could meet my eyes.

Errol Flynn raised a hand in denial. "I bet you *would* find the sword and the culprit. I thought someone had broken into this room and taken it. I never dreamed these three would pull a stunt like this."

"It was just a joke, Errol. Don't get your panties in a twist over it. Like she is." Freddy pointed a thumb at me. "How did you figure it out?"

"I realized right away that taking the sword wasn't the problem; it was leaving with it. That was the challenge, and it narrowed down the suspects. You three practically live here, and your reputation for high jinks practically ensures that no one would challenge *you* if you were seen carrying a sword.

Any servant, waiter, or other guest would have been stopped or questioned immediately."

I shot a look at Niven and Bruce. "Flynn let you in, as he always does, and left for a short while. My guess is that one of you took it, the other unlatched the window, and dropped it outside into the bushes."

When Bruce's mouth dropped open, I explained, "I heard noises coming from the bushes earlier, beside this window."

"Stupid sword fell deep into the bushes," muttered Bruce, "Niven refused to climb in and get it, and so I had to. Had the devil of a time until I found it."

"It was supposed to be a prank, a joke on Errol who likes to show off the silly prop sword from Captain Blood." Errol started to protest, but Niven cut him off. "Come on, you don't think we really believe the Captain Bligh story?"

"My mother is a direct descendant of the mutineers," said Flynn, like a mantra, his face reddening.

It was time for me to get to the heart of the matter. "It wasn't the sword you were worried about, was it?"

"Not the sword," Flynn repeated.

I slapped my hand on the desk. "It's what you had hidden in here that's missing, isn't it? Photos, I'll bet. It's always photos your type loses and requires fixers like me to get back. Photos are the last thing you need being made public right now. If the tabloids got them, they'd sell papers faster than hotcakes."

Freddy was inching his way towards the door. Unfolding my arms, I pointed my nice little gun at him. "Well, Freddy, time to come clean. What did you do with the photos?"

Flynn's expression had turned from mildly amused to deadly furious. He torpedoed his glass at Freddy, missing him but smashing against the wall beside him. Freddy winced as he brushed away bits of broken glass. "I don't know what you're talking about. Why are you blaming it all on me? Niven was in on it, too."

Niven flicked a match and lit up a cigarette. He blew out smoke in a stream and raised one eyebrow, looking barely perturbed.

"Niven doesn't have gambling debts like you do. And Bruce doesn't have the proclivities you do, which takes lots of cash to cover up."

I caught a skeptical look from Flynn. "How do I know? Well, Jack Warner's favorite investigator had to clean up a few of Freddy's indiscretions, too."

I kept the gun steady, aiming for Freddy's belly button, and I confess, would have liked very much to shoot him. It was I who had insisted Jack pay the bills to restore the girl's teeth Freddy had knocked out.

Freddy's eyes were focused on the gun. He appealed to his buddy, my boss. "Errol, you won't let her shoot me, will ya? It was all a joke, no harm done."

Flynn poured himself yet another drink and turned away from Freddy as if he couldn't bear the sight of him. "Give me back the photos and the sword, and I'll keep Dorothy from shooting you in the leg. You've only been shot on screen, but I've experience with bullet wounds. In real life, they hurt like hell. If I were you, I'd talk before she decides to shoot you somewhere else."

"She's Jack's favorite fixer, and every cop in this town wants a chance to be in a Warner Brothers picture, so they'll be on her side," Niven reminded Freddy, "if I were you, I would certainly tell her what she wants to know."

Freddy Hall wiped his sweaty forehead with his hand. "All right. First of all, the sword's still in the bushes. I didn't have a chance to get it out earlier this evening."

"And the photos?" asked Flynn.

"I already gave them to Manzilli."

I clicked back the safety and pointed my gun just where he'd be most afraid of getting shot. "If that were true, Manzilli wouldn't have needed to send another sweet young thing for Mr. Flynn tonight. So I'll ask you again: where are they?"

Freddy's lips were trembling, and his eyes were wild. "All right, all right. I wasn't going to give them to Manzilli, I swear. I was going to offer them to you, Errol, I promise."

"How much do you owe?" asked Errol.

"20 grand. But it goes up every day I don't pay."

"Where are the photos?" I repeated, and I didn't lower the gun.

"In the glove compartment of my car. I can go get them."

"Hand Mr. Flynn your keys. Errol, go and get your stuff back. I'll keep Freddy company here with my gun, just in case." My gun hand was getting a little tired, so I propped my elbow on my lap. Freddy was still standing flat against the wall, but Niven and Cabot had moved to the long window.

"Where do you think you're going?" I called out to the two of them. "The window is now latched, so you can't make it out that window as easily as the sword did. How much do you owe Manzilli?"

"Not a dime. I don't go in for gambling," said Niven, with that high-class accent.

"No, but you're in some of those pictures, aren't you?"

"You are a clever girl. Why else would I be looking to partner with that one?" He jerked his head towards Freddy. "It's not like we're boon companions."

"That's what put me on to you in the first place. Strange bedfellows, and all that. I figured it had to be someone who knew about the photos and the sword and was recently in this room. Only the three of you wouldn't be stopped for skulking around the house or carrying a big sword." I gestured with the gun. "Take a seat, you're making me nervous rolling your eyes like that. You too, Mr. Niven. I like my targets smack in front of me."

The two men complied, Niven crossing his legs, carefully minding the crease of his trousers. "When Flynn finds the pictures, we burn them," I said.

"The best course of action, for certain." Niven turned to Bruce and Freddy. "We had best keep quiet about all this if we want another contract from Warners'—I'm sorry, am I stealing your lines, Miss Dent?"

"You are, but no matter. Saves me some breath. As soon as those photos are toast, you'll be seeing the last of me."

Niven looked me up and down. "Another part of the bet was that one of us could get you."

I gave him the same once over. "Funny thing, I overheard three lovely ladies talking about the three of you. Except they were drawing lots about which one they'd be getting stuck with."

This time, it was Niven's eyes that grew wide, and his lips trembled. "You can't be serious."

The door burst open with Flynn holding a sword in one hand and a smaller packet in the other. "Got them both!"

"Stoke up the fire, Mr. Flynn, and toss it in. Then, I'll be collecting my final check, and I'm out of here."

Niven was still plaguing me with more questions about the ladies' room conversation, Freddy was still moaning about his debts, and Bruce held his head in his hands. When I left, Flynn was ever the gracious host, pouring each of them another scotch.

Piano Man

By Nicky Nielsen

Comic actor crushed by falling grand piano. It sounded like the sort of absurd storyline the world had come to expect from one of his flicks. But Giovanni Comiso's death had been entirely real. A freak accident on a poorly managed set. And 'Comical Comiso', one of the legends of Tinseltown, had taken his final curtain call.

I'd read the headlines, just like the rest of LA. And then I hadn't thought anymore about it. Not until there was a knock on my door one early morning in the summer of '34, less than two weeks after Comiso's final scene. Miss Belanger hadn't made it to work yet, not surprising given her aversion to timekeeping. I had to open the door myself.

The man waiting outside was taller than me by nearly a head. With his expensive suit, meticulous side parting, and the cloud of Bay Rum orbiting him like a moon, he wasn't the kind of guy who usually wandered into my rickety office in Sawtelle.

"Adison Palmer," the man said. It wasn't a question. He already knew who I was. And I knew him.

"Mr. Lesatz. Can I offer you a drink?"

"A little early, don't you think?" he said, following me into my office. I dropped into my chair, opened the bottom drawer, pulling out a bottle of bourbon and two glasses.

"I'm still toasting the end of Prohibition," I said, filling the glasses and pushing one across the desk towards him. He didn't crack a smile, but did pick up the glass and incline his head.

"Your health," he said.

I threw back the liquor and looked at him curiously.

"What's a big-time producer like you doing in the rough end of town?"

Lesatz sniffed at the contents of his glass before fastidiously taking a small sip.

"Got some business for you," he said. "Looks like you need it."

He glanced around the cramped office, his deep-set greyish-blue eyes taking in the peeling paint, the smudged windows, and the filthy curtains.

"I do just fine," I lied, trying not to think about the angry letters in the wastepaper basket.

"That business with the emerald tiara brought you a bit of attention in certain circles. Some people were mightily impressed."

I winced.

"That business also got me shot," I said, feeling a stab of pain in my leg at the thought of the bullet tearing through flesh and muscle.

"The job I'm offering's a lot less dangerous," Lesatz said. "You've heard of Giovanni Comiso's tragic passing?"

"Who hasn't?"

"Then you'll know he died on my set. On a film produced and directed by me."

I nodded. "I also heard his grieving widow's throwing around some pretty serious legal threats. Something about criminal negligence, wasn't it?"

Lesatz glared at me, his lip curling.

"Very astute," he said eventually. "Yes, there're rumors that Mrs. Comiso's planning on taking a run at the studio."

I leaned back in my chair. I found Lesatz objectionable, though I couldn't quite figure out why. The thought of him getting taken to the cleaners by Mrs. Comiso was pretty entertaining.

"I'm a PI," I said. "Not a lawyer."

"I've got plenty of lawyers," Lesatz said. "What I need from you is a bit of nosiness. And a lot of discretion."

"Oh yeah?"

Lesatz didn't reply. Instead, he pulled a folded-up piece of paper from his jacket pocket and spread it out on the desktop. I glanced at it. It was a typed note. Four words. I glanced up at Lesatz.

"I don't read Italian," I said. His cryptic manner was starting to annoy me.

"It reads: *We warned you, Giovanni.*"

I stared at Lesatz.

"And? Is that supposed to mean something to me?"

"The coroner found this note in Giovanni's pocket during his autopsy. He must have received it after changing into costume for the last time." Lesatz paused, looking at me intently. Then he cleared his throat.

"How much do you know about Giovanni's background?" he said.

"About as much as everyone else," I said. "Came over from the old country as a young man. His father was a farmer in some nowhere-town in Sicily. Giovanni had a talent for comedy, so he joined a circus in New Jersey as a clown, and that's where you found him. You brought him out here and built his career. Ten years ago, he seemed to be in half the flicks made in this town."

"But recently, fewer and fewer," Lesatz said. "Giovanni's talent was physical comedy. As soon as talkies became the fashion, his career was pretty much done."

"Why was he filming at all then?"

"*Piano Man* was going to be his last great hoorah," Lesatz said. "I didn't want to do it at first, but he persuaded me. One last movie, low production costs, and maybe the nostalgia would pull in enough audiences to get a nice payday for both of us. Then he could vanish into happy retirement with his wife."

"I read that he hated your guts," I said. Lesatz was getting a bit too comfortable. I like keeping people on edge. "That's what the papers say, anyway. You made big bucks on him during the good times, and then ditched him as soon as his star began to fade."

Lesatz looked visibly annoyed.

"This is a business," he said. "Giovanni knew that. Didn't I just say that he came to me?"

"Sure," I said. And that was odd enough. "So what's the note got to do with anything?"

"Giovanni's father wasn't just a farmer," Lesatz said. "He was a low-level member of the Cosa Nostra."

At the sound of those two words, I leaned forward in my chair, interested despite my growing dislike of Lesatz.

"You don't say."

"Giovanni did some work for them as a younger man, but he didn't like to talk about it. Truth be told, I think one of the reasons he emigrated was to get away from them."

"Out of the frying pan and into the fire," I said. "There're as many of them here and in New York as back in Sicily."

Lesatz sighed.

"Sometimes he'd receive visitors on set. Visitors connected to the old country in some way."

"Ghosts from the past coming back to haunt him," I said.

"You could say that."

"But Giovanni's death was an accident."

For the first time, Lesatz looked uncomfortable. He bit his lower lip and glanced at his empty glass. I recognised the unspoken request and refilled it.

"We rehearsed that scene a dozen times," Lesatz said. "Over and over and over again. Giovanni was serious about safety on set. All those pratfalls and crashes and whatever else he did on the screen. They were choreographed like a ballet. And dropping a full-size grand piano right next to him. Well. He knew it was dangerous. We tested the pulley system, we dropped pianos next to a dummy, we even put a big fat X on the ground in white tape so he knew exactly where to stand to be safe."

"So why did the piano hit him?" I asked.

Lesatz drained his glass.

"That's what I don't know," he said. "And what you need to find out for me."

I smiled, finally seeing the reasons for the producer's visit.

"Because if I can prove that someone sneaked onto set and messed up the stunt, something perhaps that links to that threatening note and Giovanni's past, then his death wasn't an accident."

"If Giovanni was murdered, his widow deserves to know."

I scoffed.

"And if Giovanni was murdered, then her lawsuit against you falls apart before it's even been put together."

"How much do you want?" Lesatz said irritably.

I thought for a long moment. I didn't want to help him out of the pickle he'd gotten himself into. But then I thought about the letters from the bank.

"Five thousand," I said with a sigh. "And not a dime less."

I half-expected him to argue, but he just shrugged and pulled out a chequebook.

"You get a thousand now," he said. "And the rest, when you bring me proof Giovanni was murdered. If anyone at the studio hassles you, give them this," he said, passing me his business card.

* * *

After a greasy breakfast at Hal's Café, I hopped in a cab and rode across town to Silver Screen Studios. The guard wasn't the friendly sort, so I showed him Lesatz's business card. He rolled his eyes, but let me into the lot, a vast expanse of sandy scrubland filled with sheds and fragments of set.

I started by walking through the set. There weren't many people around. I guessed that the death of a movie star had put a damper on production. It looked like the set hadn't been struck since the day Giovanni died. It was set up in the middle of the lot: Six shopfronts, a couple of fire hydrants, and some slabs of concrete to make up a fake street. A heavy-looking pulley was affixed to the second floor of the central shop front. I could see the scene play out as if I'd been there. A heavy grand piano, dangling above the street. Giovanni taking his position on the mark, Lesatz calling "Action!" And in front of the rolling cameras, the piano would drop exactly where it had dropped, according to Lesatz, half a dozen times before in rehearsals.

111

But this time, Giovanni would be a little too far to one side. But a little bit was all it took to turn comedy into tragedy.

"Pretty grim, isn't it?"

I whirled around. A nervous-looking young man was peering at me through heavy spectacles.

"I'm Ron," he said, walking forward with his hand outstretched. "I'm the camera operator. The guard told me Lesatz's investigator had come calling."

"My reputation precedes me."

The young man smiled.

"Kinda," he said. "We all know the old man's terrified of a lawsuit. Mrs. Comiso could take him for all he's worth."

"You're not afraid of getting caught up in all this?"

Ron shrugged.

"I just run the camera," he said. "It's all way above my pay grade."

"Were you behind the camera the day Giovanni died?" I asked. He shuddered despite the warm summer day.

"I wish I hadn't been," he said. "But at least Giovanni went instantly."

"Never knew what hit him, you might say."

"That was pretty tasteless."

"Sorry, it's been a long day, and it's not even lunch."

I looked appraisingly at the young man.

"There's footage of Giovanni's death?" I asked.

"Sure," Ron replied. "But you won't find it here."

"What do you mean?"

"Mrs. Comiso sent someone down to secure the footage a few hours after the accident."

"Smart move," I said. Pretty quick thinking for a grief-stricken widow.

"I guess she didn't want to risk it getting lost."

Mrs. Comiso immediately went up in my regard. I like a woman who can think on her feet.

"Were you also at the rehearsals?"

"Yep," Ron said. "Every one of them."

"Did you notice anything different about Giovanni on the day of the accident?"

Ron pursed his lips and narrowed his eyes.

"Na," he said after a few long moments. "Nothing really. We did the rehearsals on Tuesday afternoon, and then we started the shoot first thing Wednesday morning. I guess Giovanni seemed a bit nervous. Usually, he liked to joke around with the crew, but he kept to himself that day."

"And right before the accident?"

"I was checking the camera," Ron said. "I wasn't really paying attention, I'm sorry to say. Giovanni stood on his mark. I started rolling. Lesatz called action. Then the piano fell..." he trailed off.

"You're sure Giovanni stood on his mark for that final take?"

Ron hesitated, but only for a moment.

"Yes," he said. "Yes, I'm sure of it."

"Who's responsible for security here during the night?" I asked.

"That'd be the Captain. Sorry, that's what we call him. He's a bit full of himself. His name's Schwartz. You'll find him over in the guard shed." Ron pointed in the direction of the gate I'd come in through. I thanked him and left him standing in the middle of the fake street.

If Giovanni had stood on his mark during the last take, that only left one possibility in my mind. Someone had moved the mark. Moved it just enough to ensure that the falling piano clipped the actor. Maybe Lesatz was right after all.

Schwartz was an elderly gentleman with a stern face and thin grey moustache, and, as Ron had warned me, a rather pompous manner.

"My men and I take the studio's security seriously," he said grimly.

"How many men do you have?" I asked.

"Six in total."

"Not many for a lot this size."

"That's for Mr. Lesatz to decide," Schwartz said. His pencil moustache twitched.

"Do your men stay in the shed during the night?"

"Oh no," Schwarz said with a note of pride in his voice. "I got 'em doing rounds every thirty minutes. They patrol all the outdoor areas of the set."

"And the buildings?"

"They're all locked up after the crew goes home."

"You didn't notice anything out of place the day Giovanni Comiso died?"

"Not a lick," Schwarz said dismissively. I stared at him for just a few seconds too long. He cracked.

"Look," he said, lowering his voice and stepping closer. "I've heard the rumours. Mr. Lesatz thinks someone murdered Mr. Comiso. But trust me when I tell you that no one came in or went out at any point the night before he died."

I nodded and thanked the old man. Outside the small guard shack, I paused for a moment to gather my thoughts. Then, on a hunch, I headed back into the maze of buildings that made up the production offices of Silver Screen Studios.

It took me a while to find what I was looking for. But Mr. Lesatz's business card was like a magic wand. I just waved it, and everyone I met became the very picture of eager helpfulness. I met cinematographers and gaffers and catering staff and all kinds of production people. No clue what half of them did, but none of them had what I was looking for. Eventually, I was shown to a large tin-roofed shed filled with aisles and aisles of clothing of every type, cut, and fashion imaginable.

A harried-looking young woman with a mouth full of pins and a measuring tape slung around her shoulders met me at the door. I introduced myself, and she removed the pins from her mouth, sticking them into a small cushion tied to her wrist. She nearly jabbed herself with the pins a couple of times, and more than once she scraped them against the glass of a small rectangular wristwatch she wore next to the cushion. Pretty nervy. But maybe that was just her way.

"How can I help you?" she said.

"I'm just snooping around," I said. "Occupational habit, you might say. This the costume shop?" I asked. The girl raised her eyebrows. She glanced around, her gaze taking in the racks of clothing. I grinned.

"Guess it is. You in charge in here?"

"No, that's Mrs. Adler, but she's not in this week," she said. "I'm just a tailor."

"You made all of these?" I asked, impressed despite myself.

"I mostly repair the costumes. Sometimes design and make new ones if we need something specific that can't be brought in."

"Must be a rewarding job," I said, smiling encouragingly. The girl blushed and looked down.

"I guess," she said. I took in the state of her clothes. They were clean and well-maintained, but nothing to write home about. She wore a cheap scent with an acrid overtone. "A girl can do worse for less."

"I'm sure," I said. I tipped my hat to the young tailor and walked out of the costume shop, leaving her to her pins and measuring tapes.

* * *

The mansion squatted on the top of a sheer ridge. The owners had an unimpeded view of Downtown and the "Hollywoodland" sign from the terrace. Swanky place, all Carrara marble, stucco, and stained-glass windows. A testament to the fortune that Comiso's pratfalls had generated.

Mrs. Comiso was not exactly what I'd expected. From the papers, I knew her only as the beautiful, stylish dame hanging on Giovanni's arm. She always seemed to be swathed in mink and decked out in jewels like some Russian Empress.

The woman who greeted me in the mansion's downstairs library that evening was certainly beautiful. But she was simply dressed in baggy light-grey trousers and a deep maroon blouse. Her curly hair was still jet-black despite her encroaching middle age. It was held back from her forehead with a thin green hairband.

"Mrs. Comiso," I said, standing from the armchair the maid had deposited me in. "Please allow me to offer my condolences."

"If you're just here to snoop on behalf of that ogre Lesatz, you can clear out," she said in a strong New Jersey accent. She ignored my proffered hand.

I hesitated.

"I am being paid by Mr. Lesatz, sure," I began, but trailed off at the dangerous look in her eyes. This was one fiery lady. I cleared my throat. I'd have to handle this carefully.

"Cards on the table," I said, deciding that honesty might after all be the best policy. "I'm no fan of Lesatz, but if life gives me a chance to make him a little poorer, then I'm gonna take it."

The corner of Mrs. Comiso's mouth twitched.

"Bourbon?" she asked, walking over to a globe of the world that stood by the ornate marble fireplace. She pushed a button, and it opened, revealing a well-stocked drinks cabinet.

"Sure, if you're offering," I said. She brought two glasses over and sat down across from me.

"I'm guessing you have questions," she said matter-of-factly.

I swirled the bourbon in my glass. Then I threw it back.

"I do," I said. "But first, I'd like to use your restroom."

She blinked.

"Up the stairs, third door on the left," she said hesitantly. Always keep people on edge.

I returned ten minutes later. Mrs. Comiso sat where I'd left her, staring plaintively into the fire.

"I ask again," she said, a little annoyed now when I'd sat down. "What do you want? I assume you didn't come all the way up here just to use my powder room."

"I know your husband's death wasn't an accident," I said. "I knew that from the moment I spoke to Ron, the camera operator at Silver Screen. He seemed a nice fella. Got no reason to lie to me. Someone went onto the set the night before the shoot and moved the mark Giovanni was supposed to stand on. Moved it just enough for everything to go wrong."

"If that's what you think, then I'm afraid you'll have to leave," Mrs. Comiso said sharply. "I'm sure my lawyers wouldn't like me talking to you if you're planning on taking the stand for Lesatz."

"Hang on," I said, raising a hand. "I know your husband's death wasn't an accident. But I don't think he was murdered either."

Mrs. Comiso didn't react much. Perhaps a tightening around the lips, a slight crease on her forehead.

"I went to visit the costume shop on the set," I said. "Met a young girl there, one of the tailors. I noticed something a bit off about her."

"Oh?"

"I'm guessing a costume tailor don't make much money. She didn't look like she was rolling in it by the state of her clothes and shoes. But she was wearing a swanky Cartier watch. The kind that costs hundreds of dollars. It was new, too, not some heirloom. Do you know how I know that?"

Mrs. Comiso shook her head slowly.

"Because she kept jabbing it by mistake when she used that pin cushion strapped to her forearm. She isn't used to wearing the watch, see? So, either it was a new purchase or a new gift, and as I said, she didn't look like the kind of gal who can blow hundreds of dollars in a Cartier shop."

"What does any of this have to do with Giovanni's death?"

I walked over to the drinks globe and poured myself another bourbon. Mrs. Comiso didn't protest.

"Someone waited in the studio the day before Giovanni died. Waited for everyone to leave and for the guards to lock up the buildings. That costume shed's pretty roomy. Good place to hide. I'm guessing someone gave the girl the watch to make sure she kept quiet."

Mrs. Comiso leaned back in her chair and took out a packet of slim cigarettes. She fished one out and struck a match.

"At first I thought you did it," I said.

The cigarette stopped halfway to her lips.

"Did what?"

"Murdered your husband," I said. "I never really bought into Lesatz's Cosa Nostra idea. Oh, I'm sure Giovanni was involved with them. And I'm sure they were threatening him. I'm guessing he received quite a few threatening notes through the years. But those kinds of men, well. They don't really make murders look like an accident. They like murders to send a message."

"You speak from experience?"

I grinned.

"No one's gonna let an Irish lad like me into the Cosa Nostra," I said.

I took a sip of the bourbon. It really was good stuff. Better than the rotgut I keep in my office drawer.

"I nipped into your boudoir while looking for the restroom," I said. "Rude of me, I know, but I had to make sure. The newsreels always show you wearing those big, expensive furs. And you know what, I couldn't find a single one in any of your dressers. Lots of mothballs to protect the furs, sure. But no furs at all."

"And why do you think that is?"

"I think it's because you sold them all. You and Giovanni. His career was going down the drain. He was funny, but only in silent films, and silent films are old news these days. How much did he have to pay his former friends in the Cosa Nostra for them to leave you two alone?"

Mrs. Comiso looked straight ahead. The cigarette smoldered in her hand, sending up a thin plume of smoke.

"Too much," she said quietly. "Every year, they wanted more. We were together for twenty years, you know. And not a month passed without a demand for more money."

"I guess they didn't mind him skipping out on them when he was just some small-time circus performer. But when he became a big shot…"

"… they came for their pound of flesh," she completed my sentence. "They made it very clear what would happen to us if the money stopped."

"So, when Giovanni's star faded, you sold the furs."

"We sold everything we could," Mrs. Comiso said. "But they kept coming back."

"Right up to his dying day," I said.

"Cruel bastards."

I nodded slowly.

"Your husband could only see one way out in the end, I'm guessing," I said.

For a long moment, there was no sound but the heavy ticking of the grandfather clock in the corner.

"Giovanni went to Lesatz and persuaded him to fund one last film for old time's sake. Despite their history," Mrs. Comiso said. "It took some doing, but Giovanni won him over in the end."

"How much would you take home from a lawsuit against Lesatz and Silver Screen?"

"As a grieving widow of a beloved star of the flicks? Way more than the movie would ever have netted us. Enough to pay off the Sicilians for good," Mrs. Comiso said.

"Who came up with it?"

In the firelight, tears sparkled in the corners of her eyes.

"Giovanni," she said. "He was a showman at heart. I begged him not to do it. I told him we could just run away together. Disappear. But he knew they'd find him. He knew it would put me in even greater danger. He told me flat that he was going through with it whether I liked it or not."

"And he took your wristwatch to give to that young tailor?"

Mrs. Comiso nodded.

"We needed her to look the other way when he sneaked into the costume shop, and out again the next morning. There wasn't much else left to give her," she said. "This house. The cars. It's all mortgaged to the hilt. Not long now until the bank starts claiming it all back."

"Giovanni stayed behind after the rehearsal. Hid out in the costume shop while the studio closed down and waited for dark?"

"Yes," she said, tears now rolling down, leaving shallow trenches on her rouged cheeks.

"He moved the mark himself."

"Yes."

I cursed inwardly. Sometimes this job was a bitch.

"And the footage? The footage that shows your husband's last moment?"

"I had to get it," she said. "I needed to make sure that there wasn't anything on the film to give us away. I needed to make sure Giovanni didn't hesitate, or look as though he knew what was coming. It had to look like an accident or there would be no lawsuit against Lesatz."

"And is there?"

She shook her head and smiled through her tears.

"His acting was perfect," she said. "Right to the end."

I reached over and took the cigarette out of her hand. I took a drag on it and crushed it in a mother-of-pearl ashtray. Then I drew out the note Lesatz had shown me.

"Then it seems to me," I said. "That Lesatz's idea of a murder plot stands and falls on this."

I looked into her deep brown eyes for a long moment. Then I crushed the note in my hand and threw it into the fire, which accepted it with a grateful crackle.

The fog was rising as I drove back down the hill to Sawtelle. The lights of the city had a ghostly quality to them, like reflections seen through an old, clouded mirror. A city of dreams. A city of hopes. A city of a thousand stories. At least I could make sure this one would end the way it was supposed to.

Another One

By C. C. Guthrie

As a cub reporter, I was inspired by pioneering investigative reporters like Nellie Bly and Ida B. Wells, and the dozens of women who'd followed the GIs into battle to report from the front. I was sure I could make a difference. Every reporter believed that, or they wouldn't put up with the crap.

On a day that tested my resolve, I waited with my colleagues in the LA *Dispatch* bullpen for Norm-the-jerk to arrive and start the assignment meeting. Every few minutes, one of the guys checked the wall clock and lit up, adding a new layer of smoke to the room. They sat up front, most talking quietly about cars and sports. The trio, known behind their backs as the three stooges, loudly discussed a Hollywood party they'd attended the previous weekend and punctuated their comments with raucous laughter.

"She could have been pretty if only she'd smiled more," Stooge One said.

"Yeah, I don't get why girls can't just be happy that a guy shows them some attention," said the second one. "What's with all the serious looks and butting into conversations?"

"No one cares what girls think," the third stooge said.

Then Frank Tierney entered the room and conversations screeched to a halt like a '35 DeSoto in need of a brake job. He was the classic crime-beat newshound. With sources all over the region, he didn't need no stinking assignment meeting.

In the six months I'd been on the job, I'd never talked to him and rarely saw him in the bullpen. He bypassed his desk and joined me at the back.

"Solid story, kid," he said in a loud voice. "You've got good instincts. *The Times and The Examiner* are playing catch-up. This paper needs more reporters like you."

Against the odds, the day before, I'd had a front page above-the-fold story in the Sunday edition about a brewing scandal in a little east LA County town. The reaction from the other reporters in the room? Bupkis. Radio silence.

I wanted to be accepted by the guys, so I didn't react to Frank's compliments. Instead, I tucked away his words like a squirrel hoarding nuts for the winter. The next time my self-confidence took a dive, I'd dig up his comments to get me through the rough patch.

Frank paused for a lung-aching cough before he continued. "Ruth, not everyone would know a crime story if it bit them on the ass." He paused, possibly to make sure everyone in the room was listening. "Never let a dickhead tell you that you aren't doing a good job." He looked to the front of the room where the three stooges sat.

A decade earlier, when Frank left for Europe to cover the crime of the century, he was already a Southern California legend. Those who'd known him before the war said he'd been lithe and graceful. Now he was painfully thin with a gaunt face and haunted eyes.

The old-timers at the paper said he was different after he'd reported on the camps and the trials. Elsie, the editor of the Women's Section, insisted he'd changed after covering the notorious Black Dahlia case.

I figured both were true. Constantly reporting on murder had to take a toll. It didn't matter if the victim was an aspiring Hollywood actress or more than six million Europeans.

Frank settled back in his chair and paged through his notebook, occasionally checking off an item or scribbling a comment. The other reporters went back to complaining about the delayed meeting. Elsie, who sat off to the side, neither up front with the guys nor at the back with me, looked particularly irritated.

She was the lone female section editor, and Norm-the-jerk insisted that she attend every assignment meeting. When she demanded to know why the male editors were exempt, he said they had other responsibilities. The same ones, Elsie said to me later, that she had. She was a war widow with a kid to raise, so there was a line she couldn't cross without risking her job.

If she irritated Norm-the-jerk, I set his teeth on edge. I'd been hired without his knowledge when he was out with a broken leg. Officially, my time was split between the women's section and the news desk. He'd have been happy if I worked for Elsie full-time. He frequently said, and always when I was near, that women weren't cut out to report hard news. I hoped that my front-page story gave him heartburn.

The three dickheads resumed talking about their weekend party, ranking the girls they'd met, before comparing them to movie stars who were blonde and buxom.

Dickhead One looked back at me. "Too bad you don't have those attributes going for you, Ruthie. But you do have legs. Is that how you got your little story? You flash one of those one-horse-town officials a look at your gams?"

Frank stubbed out a cigarette with one hand and used his other to reach for the pack of Lucky Strikes in his shirt pocket. "Such catty remarks. Are you jealous of Ruth's writing talent?" He tapped the bottom of the box, and a fresh cigarette popped out. After he lit up, he checked his watch and stood. "As much as I've enjoyed this little get-together, I've got stories to write and deadlines to meet."

I pushed back my chair and rose, ready to follow when Norm-the-jerk walked in and gave me a scathing look.

"Where do you think you're going, Ruthie?" He asked. "You aren't exempt from assignment meetings."

I gave an exaggerated look at my wristwatch. "Needed a seventh-inning stretch after sitting here so long."

Muffled snorts in the room suggested my colleagues agreed. I sat down, and surprisingly, Frank did too. Norm-the-jerk handed out assignments, and none came my way, which was fine. I was nearly finished with a second-day follow-up to my scandal story. Just when I thought I'd escaped Norm-the-jerk's attention, he smirked.

"The LA County Fair starts next week," he said. "I think the sewing and craft events will be a nice challenge for Ruthie. Roy will take over the small town city council story. Ruthie, hand over your notes."

Elsie's reaction was swift. "No, Norman. I've made the assignments for the fair. I'm not making changes."

He didn't respond to her refusal, but his eyes bulged, and there was a loud pop after his jaw moved in an unnatural direction.

Emboldened by Elsie's defiance and Frank's earlier praise, I jumped into the skirmish. "Roy had his chance with the story when you first assigned him to the council meeting. Only after he objected did you dump it on me. I found the corruption angle. It's my story, my notes, my sources."

It was obvious from the petrified look on Dickhead Two's face that Roy didn't want my story. He and his two pals weren't real reporters. Their jobs were courtesy of high muckety-mucks on the paper's Board of Directors. Until Hollywood called with PR jobs at one of the film studios, those three were killing time, doing as little as possible, which Norm-the-jerk frequently allowed.

Elsie took advantage of Norm-the-jerk's silence to circle back to the fight like the cavalry to the rescue. In a soft voice, she said, "Don't forget, Norman, Ruth developed her story from an assignment that you gave her."

But it was Frank who ended the battle. He stood, scanned the room, and issued an unspoken threat to the other reporters. "Norman, when this meeting is over, everyone here will join me at Leo's desk to tell him that you tried to take Ruth off of her story without cause. As shop steward, he'll be forced to file a grievance with the union."

Norm-the-jerk wasn't the paper's brightest member of management, but even he saw that his mission to sideline me was doomed.

This time.

He shifted his jaw, gathered his papers, and stalked out of the room.

Frank sat back down and leaned close. In a voice that he didn't want overheard, he whispered, "Friendship Café. Noon," and left the room.

For the next thirty minutes, I worked the phones. When I wrapped up my follow-up story about alleged municipal mismanagement, I had a barrage of "no comments" from the little town's department managers and a balanced set of quotes from citizens and county and state officials.

I ripped the copy from my typewriter that had more bent keys than I'd had birthdays. Confident that all eyes were on me, I walked to the chalkboard, added my story slug, completion time, and dropped the pages in the wire basket. As a reward for my efficiency, I went for a coffee refill on a different floor to avoid Norm-the-jerk. When I returned, I found a piece of copy paper on my typewriter from Frank.

Sorry, kid. Off to a story. Maybe we can meet tomorrow.

The broken cross bars on the ts and the misaligned b on his note were as familiar to me as the squeak of my chair. Frank had typed his apology on my machine and signed it with an oversized F.

With a hole in my day, I went down the hall to Elsie's office, where she mimed a toast when I walked in. "Congratulations on your first front-page story. Other than Frank, did anyone else in the bullpen say anything?"

"No, but he's the only one who would dare oppose Norm-the-jerk's campaign to freeze me out, so I'll quit."

"True," Elsie said. "It's not as if women need jobs to pay rent, or buy groceries…"

"…since we only use our salaries for fur coats and flashy jewelry," ending our running gag about why Norm-the-jerk thought that women worked.

"I hate to spoil the mood," she said. "There's been another one."

Those words had special meaning for us. In the last decade, there'd been dozens of LA County women who'd gone missing, and some were later found murdered. Elsie had known one of the early victims and tried, unsuccessfully, to convince the police that the girl was not a runaway. Because of Elsie's interest, I began to follow the stories, too.

"Where did they find the new victim?"

"In front of a crypt at Hollywood Memorial Park."

Without knowing the details of the new case, there was nothing for us to discuss. Elsie returned to choosing the next round of bridal photos privileged to appear above the fold in the women's section, and I left for the little burg facing a big city scandal.

When I reached the town's city limit sign, I turned off Main to avoid the feed store in the next block. The last time I'd passed by, a gaggle of old men on benches hurled catcalls and jeers. I was in no mood for another round of dickhead behavior.

Little did I know.

I made the rounds in the sad little cinderblock city hall and discovered the mayor, the vice mayor, and the budget manager were unavailable. While the lone municipal secretary politely explained that she didn't know when the officials would return, I pointed to my wristwatch. She nodded and held up an index finger.

Buoyed that she might have more explosive information for me, I took a shortcut down the alley to my car. A mistake I wouldn't have made in LA. Two old men who might have been the president and vice president of the Feed Store Spit and Whittle Club followed me. One was a querulous old-timer who claimed to have prospected the entire San Gabriel Canyon. His skinny pal wore faded bib overalls that looked older than I was.

The old miner called out, "Hey, girlie, why are you back?"

"You didn't like what I wrote?" I braced to hear that I'd gotten something wrong in my reporting.

"Nope, you got those town crooks on the run. Everyone's waiting to see what happens next."

"That's why I'm here, following the story."

"A fella woulda been better," he said. "Like that reporter who wrote about the big land swindle. Named Henry, or maybe Oscar."

I mentally ran through the list of *Dispatch* reporters and came up empty. "You must be thinking of a different paper. We don't have any reporters with those names."

"What about Frank Tierney?" The prospector's friend asked. "He wrote about a bank robbery last week. He's a good reporter."

"He is, but I'm writing about your town."

The men shared a look and took a step forward, which forced me to back into the rear wall of city hall.

"Missy," the old miner said, spraying a mist of spittle across my face. "We appreciate that you wrote about the shenanigans here."

His fellow complainer pushed an index finger into my shoulder. "It's time you let a fella take over the story so more folks will read it. They see your name and figure you don't know everything you should."

The men were so close that I could have taken them down with a one-two knee thrust that would have left them writhing in the muddy alley. Before I could eenie, meenie between them, another citizen came to my defense.

With waving arms, a solidly built woman scurried up and shouted, "Move away from her, you old goats. Shame on you. Get on now. Leave."

The pair backed off, casting anxious looks at my rescuer as they retreated down the alley. The woman was equally distrustful and watched until they turned down the first side street.

Then, like a snake, she turned on me. Wagging a finger under my nose, she said, "There's more going on here than you know. This isn't the place for you."

She stomped off before I could ask what she meant. It wasn't the first time I'd been warned off a story, but I'd known why the other times.

Down but not out, I left for my meeting with the city hall secretary in a different town just over the county line. I waited thirty minutes, but she was a no-show, so I left. On the positive side, I spent the drive back to LA composing another story that I knocked out ten minutes after I returned to the bullpen. Frank walked into the room as I pulled my copy from the typewriter.

"Sorry about ditching you earlier," he said. "Will you be around tomorrow?"

Hell, yes!

The next day, Elsie called me into her office, where Frank was waiting.

"Kid, I gotta proposition for you," he said. "I need someone to be my legs for a few weeks while I look after a friend who's getting out of the hospital. I'll share my byline in exchange for you doing my rounds to check sources, follow up on leads, and write a first draft of the stories. Since my name goes first, I get final copy approval."

I hesitated, trying to read the look on Elsie's face. Frank must have thought that I would refuse his offer.

"Ruth, you're a good reporter, but you're green and still have a lot to learn," he said. "I can help you."

"Norm won't approve this arrangement."

"He won't be a problem," Frank said.

"What about my city council story? You and Elsie fought for me yesterday. I hate to let him win that battle."

"Will he win?" Elsie asked. "Norman will probably reassign the story to one of the stooges, and we all know how that will go."

Frank waved his hand dismissively. "Doesn't matter. That story is running out of steam. Until there's an official investigation, all you've got are accusations, speculations, and opinions. Without evidence to back up the rumors, that story is only worth a brief recap every few weeks."

He looked at Elsie and then back at me. "The top floor has already signed off on this deal, but if you aren't interested, I'll get someone else from the bullpen, and no, not a dickhead."

"I accept."

For the next week and a half, Frank introduced me to everyone who mattered in the city, county, police, and sheriff's offices, and to many of his street sources. We covered three murders, all men, two bank robberies, an insurance scam, and a series of cat burglar cases that had wealthy Hollywood homeowners up in arms. We followed leads and interviewed the police and witnesses to the crimes. One day, in between our stops, I suggested a story about the missing and murdered LA women.

"Been covered," Frank said.

"I know there have been stories on each of the murder victims. What about a story that highlights all the missing women, some of whom turned up murdered, and the many that haven't been heard from since?"

"We don't know there were crimes associated with the missing women," he said.

"We don't know that there weren't."

"You have facts for that story?"

"No."

"Then you have an idea but not a story."

Yet, I muttered.

"Good attitude. Research it and see if it has legs. But that will have to wait because you won't have time while you're working with me."

He was right.

Frank disappeared to look after his friend, but managed to call me nearly every day. When another woman, a girl really, disappeared, Elsie took the brunt of my frustration. I paced the length of her office, which only took eight steps in each direction.

"The police said this one was another runaway. I met the mother and saw the daughter's room. Her walls were covered with pictures of actresses, and the mother said her daughter wanted to study drama."

"Do you know if the policeman who took the missing person's report saw the girl's room?" Elsie asked.

"The mother said he did."

"Jeez," Elsie said. "Girls who want an acting career run *to* Hollywood, they don't run *from* it."

"And this girl only lived four blocks from Santa Monica Boulevard." I collapsed in Elsie's extra chair. "Frank said a runaway story wasn't worth a write-up."

Elsie looked thoughtful and then said, "He's had a lot on his mind lately."

I didn't disagree with her assessment. Often when we talked on the phone, Frank sounded exhausted and said he'd been up all night with his recovering friend. Mostly, he approved what I'd written without too many changes. A few times, though, I'd gone toe-to-toe with him. One witness's quote that I'd fought to include in a story led the police to reinvestigate the cat burglar cases and make an arrest.

Frank was gracious in admitting that he'd been wrong. I ribbed him about that until the end of his life, which was the following month when his heart gave out. Turns out he didn't have a sick friend. He'd been put on bed rest.

I continued to cover his crime beat, provisionally, according to Norm-the-jerk. When another missing woman was found dead, I again suggested a story exploring a possible connection between the two groups of women. Armed with facts about the similarities and differences between the cases, I was sure my idea was compelling.

Silly me.

"Ruthie, stop," Norm-the-jerk said when I finished my pitch. "The subject is closed."

Until it wasn't.

Two weeks later, Norm-the-jerk came to the assignment meeting and held up the front page of the competing Hearst paper with the blaring headline, ARE MISSING AND MURDERED WOMEN CASES CONNECTED? "Ruthie, why isn't this our story?"

Elsie shot to her feet. "If you'd read the article, Norman, you'd know that the anonymous letter raising those questions was only sent to a Hearst reporter. And if you remember, Ruth suggested similar stories more than once. You rejected each of her ideas."

Norm-the-jerk's jaw popped with a loud crack. He ignored Elsie's pointed rebuke and started the meeting.

Later, when Elsie and I met in her office, she propped her feet on the edge of her trash can and said, "Isn't it amazing how competition can make a story more appealing?"

"Hmm, yes. Today, the other paper only has hints about the cases. My story will be better because of my research."

"Who do you think sent the letter?" She asked. "The killer? Is he taunting the police?"

I almost confessed. At the last minute, I offered an alternative. "Could be a victim's family, angry about the lack of progress."

With Frank's last piece of advice, "Never apologize for fighting for what you believe," echoing in my head, I'd sent an anonymous letter to the *Dispatch's* competition, typed on Dickhead One's typewriter.

I didn't offer up a suspect, a solution, or even suggest a connection between the cases. My letter only posed questions. Questions that I hoped would inspire action.

Do I regret what I did?

No.

When it came to life and death, rule-breaking was necessary.

In the end, it didn't matter. The disappearances and murders continued. There was always another one.

The Last to See Him Alive

By Greg Herren

It took me a few moments to realize the loud pounding was not inside my head but someone at my front door.

Groggily, I opened my eyes and sat up on my couch. I hadn't made it to the bedroom when I'd staggered in at whatever time it had been, just collapsing in the living room. I reckoned I should be grateful that I hadn't just passed out on the floor.

Still in the clothes I was wearing last night and smelling of stale alcohol and sour vomit, I got up and staggered to the bungalow's front door. I peered through the slats on the door blinds. Maybe I wasn't as sober as I would have liked, but I was sober enough to know that waking up to Sam Atchison pounding on my door at—I looked at the clock—just before eight on a Saturday morning was never a good thing.

I needed my wits about me.

He saw me looking through the slats and raised an eyebrow.

I opened the door and forced a smile on my aching face. Best to play it off as a social call, I decided. "Sam. What a pleasant surprise. What are you doing out and about so early on a Saturday morning? Come on in and I'll put some coffee on." I yawned and gestured to my rumpled clothes. "Had a night last night, but come in and have a seat." I shut the door and wandered into the kitchen, both my heart and head pounding.

Sam Atchison didn't show up on your doorstep on a Saturday morning to have a cup of coffee and wish you a good weekend.

I needed to be able to think clearly.

Sam's official title was Executive Vice President of Publicity, and everyone at the studio knew the kinds of things he did. He was a fixer—made scandals go away, made sure blackmailers left town with their lips sealed, arranged abortions for the girl next door types, forced "unmarried" male stars to find a convenient wife—whatever he needed to do to make sure Transco's secrets were safe so the studio could keep churning out pictures rubes all over the country paid their quarters to get in to see.

You didn't want to be on Sam's bad side. He was a big man, and he carried himself with the air of someone who knew he could hurt you in ways you couldn't imagine. He knew gangsters and had invested money in a mob-fronted casino in Las Vegas. He could make your problems go away…but he could also be your worst nightmare. Sometimes he'd be in the gossip columns, seen squiring one of the bigger-name stars around to dinners and parties and openings and awards ceremonies, but those women lived on a much higher plane than I did. I'd done my own fair share of escorting starlets and Oscar winners around to throw the papers off my trail—but had never married.

He didn't come to my bungalow this early on a Saturday morning to tell me to find a wife, though. Transco had made it clear they were done with me.

So why was he here?

I put the coffee on and splashed water on my face. "Let me brush my teeth," I called back into the living room and headed into the bathroom. I gobbled down a piece of Wonder bread to soak up any gin still left in my stomach. I brushed my teeth and examined the damage in the mirror. Eyes red and swollen, check. Stubble in need of shaving, check. Hair stiff, matted, and standing up? Check. I ran a comb through it and arranged it with some Brylcreem to lay flat. I didn't like that greasy look, but it was better than before.

I was a far cry from the photo shoot currently on the newsstands in *Hollywood Stars* magazine, but it would have to do.

"You feel the earthquake last night?" Sam asked as I carried the coffee tray into the living room. He drank his black. I put cream and sugar in mine and sipped.

"I did, right when I was getting home, I think?" It hadn't been much, just a slight sway that had somehow knocked my signed poster of Karla Weiss off the wall, but the glass hadn't even shattered. I'd slept through any aftershocks. "Where was the center?"

"Out in the desert near Barstow's what I heard on the radio." He took a slug of coffee. "That's good coffee."

"No matter how many years I live here, I'll never get used to the ground not being stable." I said lightly. Nothing in California was stable, especially the picture business.

"Yeah." He looked at me. "That what you were wearing last night?"

"Yes."

"Do you want to change into something else?" He gave me a sly grin. "You look like how I usually feel in the morning, and that's not a compliment. I'll just have some more of this good coffee while you make yourself—" he waved a hand. "Presentable."

I could smell myself and wondered if he could, too. "Give me a second." I walked back into the bedroom and stripped off the cream-colored dress shirt and the string T-shirt I had underneath. I caught a glimpse of myself in the mirror when I grabbed a MUSCLE BEACH sweatshirt.

I looked worse than I had in the bathroom mirror. There were two enormous bruises on my chest, just below the nipples. Deep, rich Phoenician purple outlined by sickly yellow-and-orange discolored skin ran down my right side from the lower ribs to the pelvic bone. My face had looked better, but besides the red eyes and the drying sick in the corners of my mouth, overall, not too bad.

I wasn't camera-ready by a long shot, but nothing some Vaseline on the lens and some make-up wouldn't fix.

The magic of Hollywood.

I examined the bruises on my torso more closely. I touched them gently. A little tender, but could be worse. I was breathing okay, so no broken ribs, and probably no internal damage, either.

"Is this better?" I asked, walking back out and sitting on the couch. I reached for my coffee. "Sam, you didn't come over here to see what I was wearing and to drink coffee, did you?" I smiled at him. "I didn't think we had that kind of relationship."

He made a face when I said *relationship* and put his cup back down on the table. "No, but ain't I always played square with you, Logan?"

Logan Perry was my screen name. My real name was buried and long forgotten, left on a railway station in the middle of nowhere in Kansas on a snowy night with big, fat, heavy flakes falling as the Missouri Pacific train heading for the coast pulled in just before midnight.

"You did me a good turn with those nudie pictures, sure." I sipped my coffee. When I was getting started and trying to make a quick buck, I'd posed for some of the more unseemly photographers in the city. I didn't care if anyone saw them. I wasn't completely naked. I'd worn a G-string with just enough cloth to keep my privates private. The rest was just a string around the waist and running up the crack of my ass. I looked good in the pictures—better than I did in some of Transco's publicity shots, for that matter. But I was a heartthrob and big with the teen girls, and the studio felt they'd damage my image. I was never sure what exactly Sam did, but I never heard from the photographer who'd "fallen on hard times" again.

Which was even scarier.

Sam had come to me after I'd gone directly to the studio head, Isaac Rothstein, even skipping my agent. I didn't need his lectures or shaming. He was losing interest in me—Transco dropping my contract and not picking up the option probably had something to do with it. Rothstein told me to expect a visit on set from Sam—and I told him everything.

He gave me a set of the pictures as a souvenir.

Transco Pictures no longer gave two shits what I did anymore.

Any trouble I got into was *my* trouble.

So why was Sam here?

"What's this—about?" I asked. My voice sounded raspy, and my throat was still raw from puking.

"I got to say, Logan, sorry about your contract." He took off his gray Fedora and placed it on the coffee table next to his cup.

"Ah, well, that's the way it goes sometimes, Sam, you know that better than anyone else, right?" I smiled crookedly at him. His face was completely impassive. "One more picture and Transco is done with me. Unless they don't want me on the picture? Is that why you're here?"

Sam waved his hand. "I don't get involved in casting decisions. Ain't part of my job, you know, and I don't care." He smiled, his eyes glittering. "I'm a problem solver, and that's what I like to do. Solve problems, make everybody happy."

Sam was a big guy. There were a lot of rumors about him around the lot. Some said he'd been a professional wrestler, others insisted he'd been muscle for the mob when Isaac had hired him away from some big timer who'd had some interest in the business for a while. His voice was a deep baritone that rumbled up and out from his chest. The scariest thing about him was how pleasant and friendly he sounded. People around the lot were afraid of him. He always seemed cordial, but there was something cold and reptilian about his eyes.

He also had no problem using his fists or whatever was handy to get what he wanted.

I'd have to play this very cool. The studio had dropped me, so this wasn't about me.

It was about something I might know—which could be more dangerous.

"So, what's the problem?" I asked, reaching for the coffee pot, and winced as the bruises on my side reacted to the stretch. "What can I do for you?"

He noticed the wince. He noticed everything. "Something wrong?"

I smiled as I refilled my cup. "I fell down a flight of stairs." It wasn't a lie, but it wasn't where the bruises were from. The bruises were none of *his* business. That's not why he was in my house this early in the morning. The bruises were my problem, something I'd have to take care of myself. "I had a little too much to drink last night and slipped on the stairs at the after-party."

"Go to the emergency room?"

"For some bruises?"

"Could have cracked a rib."

"Nah, it looks worse than it is. I've always been an easy bruiser. I stub my toe, it bruises."

I'm not a great actor. I'm not even a good actor. I know my limitations. I look good on screen and with enough takes a director can coax something not too jarring out of me. The Western is the last picture on my contract, and the studio's not going to offer me another.

My prospects were pretty limited.

My agent told me all this yesterday. On set. Before the wrap party.

Why he chose then to tell me is a mystery.

But that was part of the reason I drank so much last night.

It's why I went to the after-party.

And why the night unfolded the way it did.

I don't know if I'm a good enough actor to convince Sam. He was used to actors, stars, people who pretended to be other people, and lied. The eyes are the windows of the soul, and Sam could read them better than most. People like Sam aren't on the studio payroll because they're easily suckered by professionals. I knew if and when he wanted, he could be at my throat before I realized he was moving. He thought I knew something he needed to know. Sam wasn't a dealmaker—unless I could make his job easier.

I just had to play along until he started putting his cards down on the table.

"You happen to see Dirk Robinson at the wrap party last night?"

Dirk? This was about Dirk?

"He wasn't there," I replied carefully, my mind working, running through the mist of the liquor fog. What the hell had Dirk done now? He was getting desperate, and desperate people do stupid things. "He finished his work last week."

"He's the star of the picture, isn't he?" Sam looked at his nails nonchalantly, checking his manicure.

I could almost hear his rattle.

"Yeah. But we finished principal photography with him last week. This week was all scenes he wasn't in, you know? Reshoots and scenes with the rest of us. I guess the studio wanted to free him up? He's doing that Bible picture next? Playing David? They needed him for costume tests this week." Nothing that wasn't in Hedda Hopper's column yesterday, and certainly nothing new to Sam. He knew all this already.

Every actor at Transco and some from other studios had wanted that part. I had, too, but knew I didn't have a shot. I looked good on camera, and from what I'd heard, some of David's costumes were scanty. But it also required more acting skill than I had. At least they let me shoot a screen test as well as some costume tests. There was one costume that was barely more than what I'd worn for those pictures Sam had gotten back.

Some little bit of irony there, wasn't there?

Bible pictures have more nudity and sex in them than most pictures.

"So, how was your evening? Have a good time?" He crossed one ankle over his knee and I could see the dagger strapped to his calf. I hoped he didn't have plans to use it before leaving.

He'd mentioned Dirk.

"So, this is about Dirk?" He didn't answer, and his face was expressionless, so I went on. "He wasn't at the wrap party. I don't know where he was or why he skipped it." Because the picture was a stinker and he knew it was what I'd thought, but Sam didn't care about my thoughts. "The party started breaking up, and Lara invited anyone who wanted to keep the party going over to her place." Lara Walters was the female lead, a party girl who got her roles on her back and had no discernible talent. She was stacked, though, and sizzled on film. She looked like she was always ready to not only get laid but hungered for it. She had three facial expressions: laughing, romantic, mad. Rumor around the lot said Lara was also on her way out, some kind of shift in studio politics. She was almost forty and hadn't hit big, was still making B pictures, probably destined to wind up on television or making movies in Europe, where she could show her tits.

That was the only way Lara Walters was ever going to be a star.

My agent was trying to sell me on some Italian studio that specialized in sword and sandal pictures…where most actors with more muscle than talent wound up.

"How well do you know Dirk Robinson?" Sam steered the conversation back to the path he wanted. "Didn't he live with you?"

"Yes, for a little while. We share an agent, and he was new in town, needed a place to stay." My heart was pounding, but I managed to keep cool. "Was about six months before he got his own place, give or take. Was glad to have the place back to myself."

"You'd say you know him pretty well?"

"We've worked together a few times." To say the least. "Since he moved out. We don't really move in the same circles." That was a lie, and I was sure Sam knew it. How he responded to the lie would tell me a lot.

"And you didn't see Dirk Robinson yesterday?"

"No, I didn't see him yesterday." It wasn't a lie. It wasn't the truth he was looking for, but it wasn't a lie.

It was after twelve when I saw him last night. So, not yesterday. Today.

A technicality to be sure, but not a lie.

"I got a call from a buddy of mine at the LAPD," Sam said casually. "He wanted to let me know they'd found a body on the beach in Santa Monica. Drowned, it looked like. They recognized him, and so he called me to see how the studio wanted it handled." He smiled, baring large crooked yellow teeth. There was something stuck between his front tooth and his left canine. He pulled out a pack of Tareytons and lit one without asking.

I took the ashtray off the side table and set it down in front of him. I held out my hand and he shook one out for me. I had a carton stashed in the kitchen, but his were more convenient. I'd heard that smoking with someone was a ritualistic method of bonding with them. Dirk had told me that, come to think of it. He said it his first night in my bungalow, when he bummed one of mine.

"Dirk?" What he'd said started sinking in. I exhaled, and my cigarette shook in my hand. "Are you telling me he's dead?" My mind was racing, but I arranged my face right, the features looking the way they were supposed to look when hearing such news, the way I was supposed to look in one of my first pictures when someone told me my dad was dead. I had that look on my face, but my mind was working.

Dirk wouldn't have committed suicide. Not after landing the lead in *Star of David* and the big boost in his weekly salary, the studio star build-up he was getting. No, Dirk was finally getting everything he'd ever wanted out of Hollywood.

Someone killed him.

"Like I said, found this morning by some fisherman on Santa Monica beach in the surf." Sam flicked ash into the ashtray, shaped like a drunken green mermaid with TIJUANA written down her tail. "Looks like he drowned. You don't know how he got there, do you?" He crushed the cigarette out decisively.

"How would I know?" I coughed a bit, excused myself, and wiped at my eyes with my sleeve. Dirk was dead.

This changed everything.

"You can't think of anyone who might want to see him dead?" Sam took out a small notepad out of his jacket pocket and started writing things down, not looking at me. "Word around the studio is he's made a lot of enemies lately."

"What are you asking me for?" I could have bitten off my tongue when his eyes flashed back up at me before looking back down. "Sam, you know more about what goes on around the lot than I ever could, and you hear everything, don't you?" Everyone knew this at Transco. He had the Boss's ear and knew where the bodies were buried because he'd put them there. Who knew what was in his files?

He gave me a sardonic half-smile. "I want to hear what you know, what you've heard."

"Yeah, I mean, there's always bullshit going on at the studio—all that backbiting and jealousy." I'd noted more than once that the studio was way worse than the little town in Kansas I'd grown up in. "But I can't think of anyone who'd want to—who'd actually—no, I can't." I was acting, giving a performance. Maybe I was better at it than my directors and the critics thought because Sam seemed to be buying it. Actors would sell their mother down the river for a part; everybody knew that. The wonder was more of them didn't wind up dead. "Wow. I mean, wow." I gestured to the two bedrooms in the back of the bungalow. "I mean, Dirk could be a bastard when he wanted to be, and it was smart not to get in his way when he wanted something." I buried my face in my hands. "But he moved out of here years ago, you know, when his star started rising and he started making money. We weren't exactly close." A lie, but if Sam didn't know about my history with Dirk Robinson, I wasn't going to enlighten him.

Especially with him dead.

"That bother you?" His lip curled. "Dirk coming in after you and getting a star build-up instead of you?" Sam asked, watching my face, a nerve jumping in his left cheek. He'd cut himself shaving right near the chin, a small pimple of dried blood just above the cleft in the middle.

"If other people getting star treatment bothered me, I wouldn't have lasted in pictures this long," I shook my head with a humble smile. "And you know they aren't picking up my option. The western is my last picture for Transco." I paused. "Wow, Dirk's dead. Dead. And so young. What a waste of talent." I didn't think Dirk was talented. Dirk's acting skills were as negligible as mine. But if I lit up on camera, Dirk came alive on screen in that way the big ones—Gable, Davis, Flynn, Stewart, Hepburn—did. When he was on screen, you couldn't take your eyes off him. *Star of David* was going to shoot him into the stratosphere. You could have knocked us all for a loop when *Variety* announced he'd gotten the lead in *Star of David* since Brick Warren was the fresh young male pretty face and body around the studio. He got bags of fan mail per week. Transco had even somehow managed to get him a supporting Oscar nod for his second picture.

Everyone just figured it was the next step up the ladder for Brick.

"Who do you think will get his part now?" Sam asked idly, lighting another cigarette. "You tested for it, didn't you?"

I kept my face immobile. *Star of David* was a big-budget Biblical extravaganza, the kind of thing the studio thought would bring audiences back into the theater and get them away from their televisions.

"Yeah. Everyone on contract at Pacific did, you know that, Sam." I waved my hand. "And since they're dropping me, I don't think I'm in the running to replace him. If they don't, just cancel the whole thing."

Sam shook his head. "Too much money spent on pre-production already.

The bankers are already getting nervous." He looked back at me and licked his lower lip. Yes, there was something reptilian about him. "Did you ever wonder how Dirk got the part in the first place?"

I crushed out my own cigarette with a shaking hand. I somehow managed to sound calm. Maybe I was a better actor than the critics gave me credit for. "I just figured he had the best test."

"You've been around too long to be that naïve." Sam leaned back in his chair. "What would you say if I told you that some things came into Dirk's possession that the studio wanted kept private?"

I took a deep breath and sat back myself. "Oh?"

"Cut the shit, Logan." His words cut like a lash. "I know you and Dirk weren't just buddies, and he wasn't someone you just took under your wing as a favor to Victor." His eyes gleamed. "What I want to know now is if you were involved. Now that Dirk's dead…" he shook his head.

"I wasn't involved with anything Dirk was up to." I managed to inject the right amount of bitterness into my voice. "After Dirk moved into his own place, we didn't really talk much." That was a lie and a risky one. Some people knew, but not many.

How much did Sam know?

"I know you left Lara's party last night with him." Sam's voice lowered, so I could barely hear him. But I could hear the menace in his voice clearly. There was the dagger strapped to his calf. He probably had a gun in his shoulder holster. He might have backup waiting outside. I was nothing to Transco. My part in *Guns of Old Tucson* was a supporting part anyone with a pretty face could play. If he messed me up or killed me, I could easily be replaced. Pretty boys with lean, muscular bodies were a dime a dozen in this town.

Maybe I shouldn't have disdained Victor's Italian work idea.

"He gave me a ride home," I replied evenly. "You also probably know I was so drunk I could barely stand. Victor told me about me getting dropped yesterday. I was feeling a bit sorry for myself." I rubbed my temples. "I barely remember the drive home."

"He never mentioned anything to you about any leverage he might have on the studio?"

"No." I rubbed my temples again. "Probably afraid I'd steal it from him."

Sam laughed. "Would you have?"

"No," I replied. "I'm tired of the games, to be honest. The studio politics. The backstabbing." I hugged myself and shivered. "Maybe I'll just give it all up and go home to Kansas." I'd rather die than go back there, but Sam didn't know that.

At least I hoped not.

"What if I told you that the studio would pick up your contract if you find it?" He examined his fingernails. "But you need to find it this weekend. And if it falls into the wrong hands…"

"What am I looking for?"

He leaned forward. "You know it was Dirk who discovered Brick, right? And brought him to Victor and everything that followed? Not the bullshit story in the trades, but what really happened?"

Victor's boys all followed the same path. Victor's casting couch, nearly nude photos, and then Victor carting his pretty boy all over Hollywood, getting people to talk about him and wonder who the new handsome young man was.

The pictures.

"I can guess."

"Remember that problem I fixed for you a couple of years ago? Same kind of thing, but a little worse."

"Worse?"

He nodded. He reached inside his jacket and tossed a bundle of twenties onto the coffee table. "A gift from the studio for your help."

I picked up the bundle and fanned the money. "I'm looking for pictures? Negatives?"

"And a film." He stood up and placed a business card down next to the coffee pot. "Keep me posted and call me the minute you find anything. Don't make me come looking for you, you understand?" He got up and walked to the door. "And if you have any big ideas about finding the stuff and using it yourself….well, it didn't exactly turn out well for Dirk, did it?" He opened the front door and looked back. "I am not someone you want to fuck with, Ezekiel." The door shut behind him.

Ezekiel.

My real name.

I locked the front door with shaking hands and put the chain on, leaning against the door and catching my breath, trying to calm down and get a handle on everything.

I wasn't surprised that Dirk was dead.

I'd always figured it was just a matter of time, and when I saw him last night, he'd been scared.

I remembered that much through the drunken fog. He'd shown up at Lara's after midnight, after she and some of the other girls and some of the younger studs went skinny dipping in her saltwater swimming pool. Frank Sinatra was still playing on her turntable, and there were a couple of us left inside when he showed up. He was in a tux, the bowtie undone and hanging around his neck. His armpits were wet with sweat, and his blond hair was slicked down, but beads of sweat dotted his forehead, too.

"Logan, I need you to come with me," he'd whispered in my ear when he sat down on the sofa next to me, after making his hellos and making small talk with the others.

I was bored, and I knew where he wanted to go. I couldn't blame him, so I followed him outside to his Cadillac and I piled into the passenger seat. I slumped down in the seat while he backed out of Lara's driveway.

"You're making a mistake," I said as he turned onto the road leading us back to Beverly Hills.

He just smirked at me.

I walked back into my bedroom, got down on my hands and knees, and pulled the bag out from under the bed.

It was a night deposit bag from a bank, the kind made from metal mesh and locked. It couldn't be cut open. I felt both sides of the bag. I felt the film canister. It was small, the kind of film you used at a stag party. And there were rolls of film, too.

He not only had the film but the negatives, too.

No, it wasn't a surprise Dirk turned up dead. He worked the angles, made enemies, did things he wasn't supposed to do. No one ever thought he'd amount to much, you see, and so no one stepped in and told him not to do the things he was doing. He wanted it all and didn't care what he had to do to get it.

In this town, that's liable to get you killed someday.

Or make you a star.

Dirk's gamble hadn't paid off.

Now we'd see if mine would.

No Way Out

By Wendy Harrison

"What the hell? You're a girl?"

The name on the door of my small office said, "Chris Falconi, Private Investigator." It was 1950, and the first thing to spring to mind was not that Chris might be short for Christine.

The man who had pushed open the door without knocking was pissed off. I couldn't be sure how pissed off, so my hand crept under my desk toward the .45 I had on a magnet-attached holster.

I looked up at him. "Chris Falconi, at your service. What can I do for you?"

I watched as his good-looking mug worked through whether he should turn and leave or give it a shot. Lucky for me, his shoulders relaxed, and he lowered his six-foot-plus into the chair in front of my desk. Lucky for him, too, since it was only then that I let go of the gun.

We looked each other over. I knew who he was. You couldn't live in my world without recognizing Harry Harmony, second in line to the boss of Newark's Delcante family. No one dared to talk about how a guy named Harmony managed to rise in the ranks of the local Italian mob, but I knew the story. He was born to Mary Harmony on the wrong side of the mattress. When Harry was old enough, his father, Stefano Rogerio, took him into the Family without a peep from Beatrice, his wife. She knew better.

We sat without talking at first, listening to the sounds of the boxing gym downstairs rising through the floorboards and floating through the open window. It was the music of my life. You wouldn't know it to look at me, but I had put in my time in the ring. I was all muscle and good enough back then to keep my face protected while I did the women's boxing circuit, unbeaten in flyweight and bantamweight. The money was okay. Not like for the men, but good enough for me to buy the creaky old building that housed my gym with its upstairs office and apartment. I didn't fight anymore, but I did keep a close eye on the boxing operation downstairs. The P.I. thing was an accident, but it helped pay the bills.

I got tired of waiting for Harry to make up his mind about answering my question. "Let me guess. A dame?"

Harry snapped out of his daze. "Who told you?"

"Relax. That's the usual reason guys end up sitting across from me." He really was a treat to the eyes. They didn't call him Handsome Harry for nothing. He could've been a movie star. He was a lot prettier than the ones who played gangsters on the screen. I wouldn't mind going a few rounds with him myself.

"This is just between you and me, right?"

"Your secrets are safe with me. I'm guessing you got my name from someone you trust? So you can trust me, too. First off, did they tell you about my rules?"

He shook his head. I wondered what they did tell him, since you'd a thought my being a dame would've been high on the list.

"Okay. Here they are. First, no rough stuff. I'm not muscle for hire. Second, nothing too illegal. I don't mind snooping around, but nothing to land me in handcuffs. Last, I charge by the day, and you pay in cash, three days upfront, minimum. Got it?"

"Got it."

His lips twitched with a smile he tried to stop. I could tell he was reacting to hard-nosed words coming from a lush mouth made more for sex than a boxing ring. At least, that's what I'd been told about my looks back in the day.

I pulled a pad from the drawer and the cap off my Waterman fountain pen. "Who's the dame?"

His smile died. "My wife. Rose. Rose Harmony. I think she's steppin' out on me." His voice trembled. Anger? Pain? Jealousy? Whatever it was, I knew Rose would be in a world of hurt if his suspicions panned out.

I stopped taking notes and put the cap back on the pen. "Sorry. Can't help you."

There was fire in his eyes, but he got a grip on his voice. "Why would that be?"

Could I tell him I wouldn't be an accomplice to whatever he had in mind for Rose? But I didn't have to decide. Harry was a step ahead of me.

"I don't blame Rose. I know I haven't been the best husband. I've done some stuff. But I love her. Whoever is taking advantage, it needs to stop."

I'd turned down cases before, askin' me to step outside my rules. But this one was different. If he was telling it straight, I didn't have to worry about him hurting his wife. But what was he going to do to the guy she was cheatin' with? If I didn't take the case, someone else would. And maybe that someone else wouldn't think twice about droppin' a dime on Rose's fling. So I'd be doing him a favor, taking the case and making sure no one got hurt. I had no idea how I'd do it, and I wasn't sure I'd be thinking this way if Harry weren't so damned easy on the eyes.

"Please." He reached across the desk and put his hand on mine. "I have to know. I swear this ain't gonna go back on you." I've been lied to before by experts, but I wanted to believe he meant it. I set aside the question of how he'd keep his promise. He moved his hand to my pen and gently removed the cap. I held my breath as he placed the cap on the back of the pen and offered it to me, his eyes locked on mine. Was Rose crazy? Who could she be sleeping with who could compete with Handsome Harry?

I knew I'd kick myself later, but I couldn't stop the words. "Okay. Don't make me regret it."

Harry filled me in on what I needed to get started. A photo of Rose, who was as beautiful as I expected. Home address. Rose's usual schedule. He claimed he had no idea who the guy was, but he could tell she was lying to him. He took a fat roll of hundreds out of his pocket and peeled off enough for three days of my time with extra for expenses. No signed contracts in my business. None of my clients wanted a paper trail, but I'd never been stung. At least, so far.

We shook hands, and Harry left. I watched out the window as he climbed in the back of a black Lincoln Continental. I couldn't see the driver, but I had a good idea of what he'd look like. Nothin' like Handsome Harry, I'd wager.

* * *

Rose and Harry lived in a large, elegant house, set well back off the street with gardens in front, all enclosed by a sculptured iron fence and a gate that didn't open unless you were buzzed in. Harry was well protected, especially if you count the two beefy guards just inside the gate. I got there at nine o'clock the next morning and parked at the end of the block. Nothing happened until just before noon when Rose's car left the driveway and stopped at the gates. Rose smiled at the guards. They smiled back. Their boss's wife was either naturally friendly or knew which side her bread was buttered on. They were protecting her as well as Harry. I was surprised she didn't have someone driving her. I wondered if Harry had offered, but she refused. Maybe she didn't want him to keep track of her.

It wasn't hard to follow Rose. My old Ford looked like a piece of junk, which meant no one would think twice about it. She was in a new Jaguar convertible, red and easy to keep in sight. She drove to a restaurant downtown, one of those places with white tablecloths, good silver and china, and a check at the end of the meal that would've paid my bills for a year. She sat at a table by the open front window. I saw the maître d' remove the Reserved sign. No ordinary waiter for Harry Harmony's wife. After a few minutes, Rose was joined by a short blond who gave her a hug. I snapped a picture of them from across the street. The more I looked at the two of them, the more convinced I was they were sisters. Other than the blond's bleached hair, they had the same features. Even their laughs sounded alike. They lingered over salads and white wine, and when they finished, they left together. Another hug, and the woman walked to the car parked behind

Rose and drove off. I jotted down the plate number.

The rest of the afternoon, I trailed along as Rose went in and out of the high-end clothing stores along Main Street. She didn't buy much, and by the end of the day, she had only two small glossy bags with upscale names on them. This was a woman who had too much time on her hands. Was she having a fling to offset boredom? Seemed like a dangerous fix, considering who her husband was.

I staked out her house the first night until all the lights went out around eleven o'clock. I'd done this kind of thing often enough that my car was filled with ways to pass the time. After parking half a block away to keep from agitating the muscle at the gate, I had settled in with my portable radio playing big band music, my bags of snacks, and a cooler with drinks. I went easy on the liquids. The guys in this business could always find a tree to pee on. Not so easy for me. For absolute emergencies, I kept a wide top jar to use, but so far, never had to find out if it would work.

Day two went pretty much the same. Rose drove out in the early afternoon and then spent hours wandering around the Newark Museum. It was getting harder to keep her from noticing she was being followed, even though I dressed different each day.

I found a pay phone and called the number Harry gave me. I told the guy who answered who I was and that Harry was expecting my call.

He yelled, "Harry. You know a Chris Falconi?"

"Gimme the phone. Chris? Got something?"

I told him what I'd seen so far. When I described yesterday's lunch, he said, "Yeah. That was her sister. You sure there's nothing else?"

"I'm being straight with you. How long do you want me to keep this up?"

"I'll tell you when you can stop."

I didn't like the sound of that. "You paid me for three days. That's what you'll get."

I held my breath. Harry wasn't the kind of client who would let me call the shots.

"I'll check in with you in a couple of days. But call if you see anything I should know about."

That night, a limo left the house at nine o'clock. I could see enough of the driver to recognize the muscle from the gate. I assumed Harry and Rose were in the back. He had told me they liked to go clubbing, so it was no surprise, although I wondered why he hadn't mentioned it when we talked earlier. Was it a test to see if I was doing my job?

I followed them to The Piccadilly, a jazz club I'd been to many times. Their bouncer boxed at my gym and always let me into the club for free. I was happy to see him on duty.

"Bruno. How you doin'?"

He grinned, showing the gap in his teeth from when his mouthguard had been knocked loose by a punch that got past his raised gloves. He faked a jab toward me.

"Doin' good, Chris. How about you?"

"Not bad, my friend. Who's playing tonight?"

He looked around to see if anyone was listening. His voice low, he said, "A special attraction. Harry Harmony's wife. Rose."

I didn't expect that. Why hadn't Harry told me? "She any good?"

"I'd be afraid to say if she wasn't, but she's the real deal. Her maiden name was Rosemarie Clarey."

I knew that picture Harry showed me looked familiar. Rosemarie Clarey was a terrific jazz singer who had dropped out of sight a few years ago. Now I knew why.

"And she's singing tonight? What's the occasion?"

"Favor to her husband. It's his birthday. He don't usually want her singing in public. The guy is head over heels for her and jealous as they come. He ain't someone to mess with, you know."

He was right. I did know. And none of this was making me happy about agreeing to follow her. It sounded like she was his prisoner more than his wife.

I went inside and took a seat at the bar. Soon, Lou Vicarra, the owner of the club, took the stage. Mic in hand, he announced, "And now, a surprise for you. The Piccadilly is happy to present the one and only, Rosemarie Clarey."

The applause was enthusiastic as Rose walked onto the stage. I watched Harry. He looked like a proud daddy until a drunk at a back table yelled, "You're still lookin' good, baby. Sing it for me."

Harry looked toward Bruno, who was standing a few feet away from me. Bruno heaved his muscled body into motion and made his way to where the drunk sat. Rose stood frozen at the mike.

It didn't take long. Bruno lifted the loudmouth out of his chair and pushed him to the exit. I didn't want to think about what was happening outside.

Rose turned to the band behind her and nodded. They began playing "I Got it Bad (and That Ain't Good)." I wondered if she had picked the song or Harry did. It was the story of a woman who knew she was being destroyed by her love. Odd choice for a birthday celebration.

When she was done, everyone in the place stood and cheered. The goosebumps on my arms were still there even after she ended the song. She turned and left the stage. I saw Harry start to follow her, but stop when she turned into the hallway where the bathrooms were. I headed after her, not sure if he saw me.

Rose was standing in front of the sink, staring into the mirror. She had a tissue in her hand and dabbed at the tears on her cheeks. Her makeup came off, and I saw the bruised skin around her left eye. She pulled a gold compact from a small beaded purse and began to cover the black and blue skin.

"Are you okay?" I realized she hadn't seen me because she jumped at the sound of my voice.

She turned. "You scared me."

"I'm sorry. Didn't mean to." I repeated my question. "Are you okay?"

She saw me looking at her eye. "I'm fine."

I took a chance. "Did he do that?"

She went back to putting on her makeup. "I don't know what you're talking about."

"Yes, you do."

She returned the compact to her bag. "I don't know who you are, but I'm telling you to back off. My life is none of your business."

I started to explain, but she pushed past me and slammed the door as she left.

What had I been thinking? Harry wouldn't think twice of getting rid of me if he thought I was on his wife's side. There wasn't anything I could do to help her. Maybe she didn't even want help. I tried to find comfort in that thought since there wasn't anything I could think of to save her anyway.

Harry was back in my office the next day. He sat and pulled out a wad of cash. "I want you to keep it up. You're doin' a good job. I saw you follow Rose back to the toilets in the club. Did she say anything to you?"

"Not a word. Just fixed her makeup and left." I hoped he didn't ask for any more. There was no doubt in my mind that he was the cause of her black eye. He would've killed anyone else who laid a finger on her. "Harry, there's no sign at all she's seeing anyone. Take the win."

He tossed the money on my desk. "Not yet. This should take care of another week. Keep me posted."

Before I could refuse, or try to refuse, he left. I watched out the window again as he came out of my building and wished he'd never shown up at my door.

The next few days were a rerun of the first three. One day, lunch again with her sister, another day exploring antique shops, another at a movie matinee. That was a strange one. "The Damned Don't Cry" was all about a New York socialite who finds a life with rich gangsters wasn't really what she wanted. I saw it when it first came out. It didn't end well. I wondered if Rose would take it to heart.

I decided to give it another few days and then call it quits. I was feeling sorrier for Rose each day and had the feeling she knew I was following her, no matter how careful I tried to be. Maybe she was playing me. I couldn't tell until day nine, when it all turned around.

It started out like the other days. I spent the morning in the car, watching for Rose to leave. It was just noon when she drove out and headed for The Piccadilly. It seemed strange since I didn't think they opened until five o'clock. I pulled into a space a few cars down from her and twisted in the seat to see her go inside. No Bruno at the door this time, and no one else around.

I waited a few minutes and decided to follow her. The door wasn't locked. I was quiet as I could be. No one was around. Then I heard sounds coming from the office near the bathrooms. There was no mistaking what was going on in there. I wished I had never met Harry Harmony because now I knew he was right. His wife was cheating on him with Lou Vicarra.

I had a couple of choices, all of them bad. Tell Harry, knowing that he probably would take it out on Rose. Her black eye made him a liar about how he would never hurt her. Or lie to him, knowing that if he found out, I would be toast. There was one other way I thought would have at least a chance at getting me and Rose out of this.

I walked down the hallway and knocked on the office door. It took a minute for Lou to open it a few inches, blocking my view.

"Yeah? The club is closed. Come back later."

I ignored him and called past him. "Rose? I know you're in there. We need to talk."

"It's okay, Lou." She sounded defeated. "Let her in."

He stepped aside. Rose was buttoning her dress. No mistaking what was going on. She stared at me. "I figured it was just a matter of time. Harry hired you to follow me, didn't he?"

I nodded. "I don't like this any more than you do. But if you give it up now, I promise I won't tell him."

Lou put his arm around her shoulders. "I can take care of this one, Babe." He tilted his head toward me. I should've expected his reaction. It was the one alternative I didn't consider. Take me out, and there's no one to tell Harry what was going on.

Instead of telling him it wasn't an option, Rose thought about it and then said, "She's not going to tell Harry. Are you, Chris?"

I felt like a fool. She knew my name and knew what I'd been doing. Some P.I.

"You're not going to," she continued, "because you know what he'll do to me. You don't have it in you."

Before I could tell her she was wrong, she stopped me. "I knew it when you asked me about my eye. I tried to warn you off. I'm not going to give up, Lou. He's the best thing that ever happened to me. I can handle Harry. He already feels terrible about popping me. He won't do it again."

I shook my head. "He's a dangerous man. I don't have to tell you that."

"So is Lou. He won't let anything bad happen to me."

She was dreaming. I knew it. Lou must've known, too. This couldn't end well for them. But she was also right. I couldn't tell Harry.

"You get one chance from me. I won't tell him about today. But if I catch you again, I won't risk my own life for you. All bets will be off."

Lou looked at Rose. "Got it. It'll be like this never happened."

I left them there, knowing they weren't going to stop but hoping they would hide it well enough that I didn't have to choose. I decided to give it a week with innocent reports to Harry and then insist I was done with the job. Maybe I could get out of this with my life.

* * *

Since Rose never left the house in the morning, I asked Harry if I could show up closer to lunchtime. He was okay with that. Everyone on his payroll at the house would let him know if she took the car out earlier, and he'd call me. I liked having those hours to get things done in the gym. I was running a business that needed my attention. I wasn't used to having a P.I. job last this long.

Things went smoothly for a few days. Harry checked in with me every night by phone. Lucky for me, Rose was behaving during the time I spent following her. She even waved to me when she spotted me. No sign of Lou. Maybe she came to her senses. I was trying to decide when Harry might agree to give it up. The sooner the better. The extra money was nice to have, but my nerves were shot, wondering if my luck was going to run out.

Then came the morning when I opened the door to my office and saw someone had torn it apart. Drawers were pulled open. Even the cushions on the chairs were thrown on the floor. The one filing cabinet that had paperwork for the gym was lying on its side, papers tossed everywhere. My first thought was relief that my P.I. job was paperless. Nothing for anyone to find if that's what this was about. My second thought didn't turn out as good. The gun I kept hidden under the desk was missing. No way I was going to call the police. They hated private investigators. I was afraid to answer questions about what I was working on that might have caused someone to break into my office.

I cleaned the place up and thought about telling Harry what happened. But I couldn't risk him starting to put two and two together. If this somehow tied to Rose and the secret I was keeping, it could go south in a hurry.

I got to Harry's house the usual time. The guards were used to seeing me now. Sometimes we shot the shit until Rose's car started to leave. This time, they called me over.

"How ya doin?"

"Doin' okay," I said. "What's up?"

"The missus said to meet her at your office at one o'clock on the dot, and she was sorry she ducked out on you today."

There was something wrong going on. The guards knew what I was up to, but Rose wasn't supposed to let on that she knew. It seemed careless of her to let it slip like this. Why wasn't she worried about Harry finding out she was onto me?

Gino repeated his message. "Remember, one o'clock. No earlier, no later. That's what she said. Got it?"

"Don't worry. I got it."

With time to kill, I stopped off at the nearest deli and treated myself to a sandwich. It sure beat the stuff I'd been eating in the car every day. The more I thought about Rose's message, the more uncomfortable I felt. Even if she wanted to tell me she and Lou were calling it quits, I couldn't tell Harry he didn't need me anymore. Something was off, but even I didn't know how bad it was going to get.

I walked upstairs to my office and opened the door on the dot of one o'clock. From the doorway, the place looked like I left it. All cleaned up after the break-in. I stepped inside and closed the door behind me. As I walked toward the desk, I jerked to a stop. Harry Harmony was on the floor, on his back, a growing red hole in his starched white shirt. I could hear the sound of sirens coming through the windows. Feet pounded up the stairs. Before I could react, I saw the gun, my gun, lying a few feet from his body. I knew my prints would be on it. A single red rose lay on my desk, a parting message from the real-life Rose, who'd left me with no way out.

Garbo's Ghost

By M.E. Proctor

Murderers that messed with their victims' bodies held a special place in Tom Keegan's vision of Hell. The torturers, mutilators, and collectors that his Homicide colleagues bundled together as *Crazies*. For Tom they were more and less. More vicious and less human. He'd seen soldiers freak out in Bastogne, and he'd been close to losing it when their jeeps entered the camps. He knew there were more kinds of crazy than there were varieties of apples.

The *Chronicle* would slap a nickname on the killer that disemboweled Seaman 1st Class Jerry Larson from Cudahy, Wisconsin, at the Mt Davidson cross, Saturday night—monster, ogre, goblin. Mythical creatures.

This horror was only too real.

"It needs to stay out of the newspaper, Tom," the medical examiner said.

"The people that found the body talked to reporters."

"The boy was alive when he was cut open."

Tom turned his back on the butchered flesh on the slab and fumbled in his pockets for his smokes. The doc took him by an arm and steered him toward the hallway.

"He can't have been alive for long," Tom said.

"Too long. The killer was proficient with a scalpel."

"How can you tell, in that mess?"

"The edges are clean cuts." The doc's voice was strained. "The boy was tied to the cross. Standing. Fibers are embedded in his wrists and ankles. I'll test for narcotics."

Tom lit a cigarette. "It's a hike to the cross. He didn't carry the kid all the way."

"There might have been more than one aggressor."

That was even more disturbing, somehow.

* * *

Tom went back to the Mt Davidson park. The scene was cordoned off and uniforms stood watch. It was raining and the November wind discouraged the gawkers that tended to congregate near disasters.

"The rain will wash it all off in no time," one of the officers said.

The blood stains on the lower part of the monument were consistent with the medical examiner's observations. Jerry Larson had been propped up, then cut loose and left to crumble in the grass. His uniform, cap, socks, and undergarments had been found in a pile nearby, no blood stains on them. The shoes were missing. The rope used to tie him up was nowhere to be found.

Tom sneezed. Water ran in a steady stream from his soggy fedora down his neck.

* * *

The young sailor had come to shore with a gaggle of shipmates. They hit the bars closest to the harbor, then made their way into town for more exotic entertainment. They scattered all over the International Settlement, swarming the Pacific Street cabarets, dance halls, and gambling parlors. In the smoke of cheap cigars and the vapors of harsh liquor, none of the boys could tell when or where they'd last seen Jerry Larson. They didn't remember where they went, all that neon blended together after six in the tank.

Tom talked to the MPs who patrolled the perimeter. He showed Larson's picture in every watering hole on the Street and got no bites. In their blue uniforms, all these kids looked the same. He asked if anybody had noticed anything unusual, and the laughter he got in response made clear that when the boys were in town, the definition of *unusual* had to be seriously amended.

Millie, a dancer at the Bird of Paradise, was on a break when she saw a sailor get in a blue Chevrolet sedan. She noticed because her boyfriend drove the exact same car and she wondered what he was doing in San Francisco when he was supposed to be in San Diego.

"It wasn't Roy behind the wheel." She smiled, relieved she wasn't two-timed. "That guy was bigger." She puffed on the cigarette she bummed from Tom. "The woman was a knock-out."

"What did they look like?"

She tilted her head. "Not being mercenary and all…"

"I'll buy you a drink or a slice of pie, Millie."

"I wouldn't mind a steak," she said, practical.

They went to a corner restaurant, sticky table tops and crooked chairs.

"It's hard work on that stage," she said. "Girls drop like flies."

She had a healthy appetite. Tom sprung for a red wine that came in an anonymous bottle.

"I didn't see the guy's face." Millie wiped her mouth before taking a generous swallow of wine. Her cheeks colored. The plonk was the kind of vintage that dissolved cooking grease. "I had a good look at the woman when she talked to the sailor. She had a perfect face, classy. Just like Greta Garbo. An expensive broad." A chuckle. "For sure, my Roy wasn't in that car!"

"What did the sailor do?"

"Whaddya think? He hopped in the back."

Tom pushed his dinner plate to the side. The congealing steak juices made him queasy. "You ever saw her before?"

"Not in real life."

"Meaning?"

"As I said, she was a dead ringer for Garbo, like she was in *Camille*, so romantic." There was mist in Millie's eyes. Might have been the wine…

* * *

The investigation spun its wheels. A blue Chevrolet sedan, a Garbo look-alike. Nothing came of it. Jerry Larson's body was shipped back to Wisconsin. New cases piled on Tom's desk. Christmas was chilly. January was one long wet misery.

An officer poked his head through the door. "Keegan? The Chief wants to see you."

Tom grabbed his jacket. He wasn't worried about a summons from upstairs. It usually meant more work was heading his way.

"I'm concerned about you, Tommy," the Chief said. "You're morose."

"Not my favorite time of year."

"It's the sailor case. It weighs on you."

"It's still open. These creeps are predictable. They'll do it again, or they might have done it before. I contacted other cop shops." The Chief offered Tom a cigar that he declined.

"You're good at closing cases, but there are times in a career when resolution doesn't come. You can't let it get to you, Tom. There's too much work to do." He blew a perfect smoke ring toward the ceiling. "I've decided a change of scenery would be beneficial."

"Now? With my caseload?"

"It'll still be there when you come back. You're going to Los Angeles for a few weeks."

Tom was aware of the changes happening down there, with William Parker taking over as Chief, his zeal for reform creating rolling earthquakes. "Why?"

"Bill Parker needs good officers to anchor the organization."

"You must be kidding."

"Parker wants the best, and you are it, Tom."

Jesus. "Don't do flattery. You don't have the face for it." He bit his lips. Goddamnit! That fast mouth of his...

The Chief was silent for a solid minute. "I'll let it slide because you used to jump out of airplanes and I'm afraid of heights, but don't try it with Parker."

"He'll ship me back with a demerit?" Tom smiled.

"He'll give you a stick and send you to direct traffic."

Tom raised both hands in surrender. "Sorry, Chief, I apologize, but it doesn't make sense. What good can I do in a few weeks? It'll take Parker years to clean the stables. If they don't break his broom. Besides, I'm not a team player. Send Hank Simmons, he's smart and he could charm the sting off a scorpion."

"He doesn't look the part."

"Hank sees more with his one eye than half the squad with both. He's a war hero, for chrissake."

The Chief shook his head. "He'd spend all his time having to prove with his fists he's not an invalid. Three weeks, Tommy. Out of the fog and the rain. Palm trees. Hollywood."

Right. With Parker in charge, Tom would be lucky to have a glimpse of a beach out of a car window.

* * *

The first couple of days in Los Angeles were spent getting a sense of the geography and the people. Chief Parker had been stiffly welcoming before handing Tom over to fellow Army veteran, Freddy Keath.

"I used to be in tanks," the wide-shouldered redhead said, by way of introduction. "Parker picked me because I'm close to you in the alphabet. He loves lists."

And paperwork. Tom's reading materials filled a cardboard box.

"Forget that. Let's go for a drive. There's no better way to understand how this town holds together. Mostly, it don't."

The car was a nondescript Ford. It still sent people scurrying off the streets in the Negro and Mexican areas. In the Chinese parts of town, the citizenry muttered curses.

"You have a problem," Tom said.

Freddy laughed. "Wrong. *They* do."

Tom bit back a comment that was guaranteed to send his stint with the LAPD down the sewers in no time at all. "How do you handle undercover?"

"Informants are a dime a dozen. Want to see where the stars live?"

It was pretty, leafy, and sprawling, and Tom got impatient. "What are you working on when you don't play tour guide?"

Freddy turned the car around with a sigh. "And I hoped to lay down the yoke for a few hours…"

"The mother of all cases is on my plate, Fred. I shouldn't be here catching a tan."

"I heard about that." Freddy winked. "Monroe wants to talk to you."

Glen Monroe was a grizzled LAPD veteran who looked down his nose at 'the kids', meaning anybody under fifty, and that included Chief Parker. He was loud and evil-tempered. He was also a dogged investigator with a solid track record.

The man barked. "You the mick in charge of the gutted sailor? Any leads?"

The Mt Davidson murder had made national news; Monroe's question didn't come as a surprise. The acid-laced tone aimed at a reaction. Tom thought the man tried too hard.

"Clues that haven't panned out yet," he said. "I should be working them instead of perusing Parker's book of rules."

That earned him a grunt of approval. "What clues?"

Tom grabbed a chair. "I'll share if you return the favor."

"What makes you think I have something to trade?"

"You're way too eager."

Monroe cracked a smile. He pulled a file out of a drawer and put a paw on it. "Let's hear it."

"A sailor was seen getting into a blue Chevy the night of the murder. We're confident it was Larson. We talked to all the boys. The only rides they got were with MPs. A man drove the Chevy. No description. A woman was in the passenger seat. The witness says she's a dead ringer for Garbo. The car is a '49 model, 4-door sedan."

Monroe lifted his fist and slid the file toward Tom.

The photographs were on top. It took a moment for Tom to understand what he was looking at. The images were grotesque, like a big insect squashed by a giant's boot. He looked up from the file. Freddy was at the window, and

Monroe was filling three glasses from a square bottle without a label.

Tom turned the pictures face down on the desk. The words on the medical examiner's report ran together. Ribs hacked from the spine with a hatchet. Lungs exposed. Face crushed. Genitals mutilated. Rape. Ligature marks.

Officers' notes. Andrew Mallard, age 19, U.S. Air Force cadet, from San Antonio, Texas. In Los Angeles to visit family. His clothes were found near the body, his duffel bag nearby. Shoes missing. The crime scene was the backyard of a for sale Beverly Hills mansion. Neighbors heard a pack of dogs howling and called the police. Two days ago.

Tom was already in town. "There was nothing in the paper." His voice sounded muffled to his ears.

"We're keeping it in-house," Monroe said. "For once, I agree with Bill Parker. Hush-hush and no interferences. How long are you here for, Keegan?"

"Three weeks. If you're putting a team together, I want in. There are similarities with my case. Our kid's shoes were missing too."

Monroe waved at the glasses. "Have some. You're in, kid. Both victims are soldier boys, their clothes are unsoiled, and they were tied at the wrists and ankles."

Tom took a sip of whiskey. It was smoky. "The ropes and the shoes weren't found at the scene, and the kids were raped. Disembowelment is straight out of the Middle Ages." He pushed the photographs further away. "I don't know what this is."

"I'll tell Parker you're mine for three weeks. You too, Fred."

* * *

Tom resumed his nationwide search for unusual murders and dived into the LAPD crime files. He'd been at it for a week when he unearthed a nugget.

"Ever heard of Leona Palumbo?" He dropped a thin file on Monroe's desk.

It was late at night, the team had disbanded.

"Carmen Miranda's stand-in?" Monroe chewed on a ham and cheese sandwich, a tumbler of rye by his elbow.

"You should stop eating right now."

Monroe wiped the bread crumbs off his tie and reached for the documents. One look at the pictures and he threw what was left of the sandwich in the garbage bin.

"Who worked this? I never heard of it."

"That's the thing," Tom said. "Nobody worked it. A janitor found burlap sacks in a high school gymnasium. Body parts. A couple dicks swung by. They started a file. The end. It happened last August."

The date said it all. The department was in shambles. Bill Parker had just been sworn in. Officers were being reassigned.

"Leona's family is in Mexico. I doubt they've been told." Tom lit a cigarette and stretched his long legs. He'd been sitting in a cramped office all day. "She worked as a nurse at the Veterans' Hospital. Rented an apartment with two other girls. Leona Palumbo fell through the cracks. She might be these freaks' first victim. There was no staging, the chopping was amateurish, and she wasn't killed at the site."

"Or it's a different killer."

"Her nurse's uniform was in one of the bags, shoes missing. Rope burns and rape. Like the others. And quartering is a medieval execution method. I spent some time chatting about that stuff with a professor at UCLA." Tom wished he had a sip of the rye. "The Andrew Mallard case. That breaking of the ribs and pulling the lungs out is called a *Blood Eagle*. Vikings might have executed high-ranking people that way. It's described in some old poetry. The prof told me it could be a legend made up by the Christian rulers, something to make the guys they replaced look like barbarians. Anyway, that's three for three. Somebody is reenacting medieval torture."

"Who would know things like that?"

"History students, people interested in the Middle Ages, nutcases. It isn't narrowing the suspects pool, but Leona Palumbo's case points at the killers being local. When people start acting out their fantasies, they tend to do it close to home."

Monroe absorbed the information. "What's next?"

"We find the blue Chevy. Draw a city grid and start from the gymnasium where Leona's remains were found."

"You sound like Bill fucking Parker," Monroe moaned. "Next you'll want to go house to house looking for the Garbo broad."

Tom smiled. "The woman has a face made for Hollywood. She must have left a mark somewhere. I'll lead the car search. Freddy will have fun doing the rounds of the talent agencies."

Monroe went no-no. "Freddy looks for the car. You look for the broad. Nobody knows you in town. Buy a crisp suit and a sharp hat. Get a taste of the bright lights in hustle city. Undercover. Pitch a movie or something."

Tom burst out laughing. "Pretend to be a studio hack?"

"They might cast you." Monroe chuckled. "As a hotshot detective in one of these murder flicks with Barbara Stanwyck."

"If Gene Tierney stars, I'm all in."

* * *

Suzy Vaughn, one of the secretaries in Monroe's team, helped Tom built his cover. She opened a post office box and had business cards printed. The phone number on them was her grandmother's.

Tom thought it was overkill. "As if anybody would call or write."

Suzy disagreed. "The moment you drop that business card, the calls and the mail will start coming in. And if nobody answers the phone, the word will go out that it's a scam, and you'll be knocking on closed doors. Hollywood is the most gossipy place on earth. You want the grapevine to work *for* you."

"If the woman learns that we're looking for a Garbo look-alike, she'll run."

"She might come to you," Suzy said. "I don't know a single good-looking female in this town who doesn't dream of being in a film."

"Even a crazy killer?"

"The industry consumes beautiful girls by the boatload. We need to put photographers on the interview list. I bet she's had glamour shots taken."

"You'd make a good detective, Suzy," Tom said.

"Maybe after the likes of Glen Monroe finally retire. You think you can sell the story?"

Tom would be pitching a remake of the Garbo comedy *Ninotchka*, transposed to 1951, with Cold War references and military secrets replacing the jewels of the original. The entire project relied on finding the right actress for the role.

"It's ludicrous enough to fly."

Suzy typed a file. One and a half million budget, a UK studio, London locations, a British crew. Lead actress search ongoing in the US and UK.

"Go shopping. Not too conservative, the suit." Suzy held out her hand. "You won't need your service gun."

Tom felt a touch of guilt for looking forward to the assignment. The stakes were high—three butchered bodies, killers on a spree—and he was excited about taking a peek behind the screen. He'd heard stories of undercover cops getting lost in the playacting. He understood how that could happen.

* * *

Suzy had compiled a list of middle-tier talent agencies and photographers. If Miss G., as she was referred to in the police reports, had been signed by a top agent, she would have landed modeling jobs or walk-on roles, but she was nowhere to be seen. Of course, she could be a suburban nobody. The cops gambled that living so close to Hollywood, she must have tried her luck at the dream machine. There had to be a photograph of her in a drawer, somewhere.

Tom's first trip was to the office of one Avery Giles on Wilshire Boulevard. The visit was a prototype for the dozen that followed. Some agencies were better furnished or shabbier than Mr. Giles's, but the ritual was the same. A middle-aged secretary was entrenched behind a desk, movie posters and star photos graced the walls, trade magazines were piled on side tables, and a flock of hopefuls waited for an audience. Mostly female, mostly young, mostly pretty. Tom admired the display of shapely legs and appetizing curves. His entrance caused gasps, eyelash fluttering, bright smiles, hair pats, and a readjusting of positions on the hard chairs. He was different from the hopefuls and hence worthy of interest.

"Thomas Keegan to see Mr. Giles."

The secretary gave him an appraising look and went to report to her employer.

"He will see you now, Mr. Keegan."

Wherever he went, Tom was never made to wait. Did Giles and his colleagues clear their appointment book ahead of his arrival, or, wicked thought, did they rarely see the hopefuls in the waiting room? The purgatory nature of the setting couldn't fail to strike Tom. Add to it a scoop of the absurd. Everything Tom saw in Hollywood during his undercover stint—the over-the-top cocktail parties, the glitzy hotel events, the so-called intimate, friendly gatherings—had that same slightly disconnected feel. There was a stronger sense of reality on screen than off. No wonder nobody ever suspected he was a fraud; they were all made of a glossy immaterial substance.

He went through his script, the search for the perfect new *Ninotchka*.

"Like finding Scarlett O'Hara," said Giles, beaming.

"The Garbo likeness is key."

"A good make-up artist ..."

"Preference will be given to the closest match."

Giles promised to get on the job right away.

"I'll be in Los Angeles this week, then I'm expected back in London with a short list. I hope you find *l'oiseau rare*, Mr. Giles. I want to meet the girl face-to-face, but I'd rather make an initial selection from photographs. My time is short, and I have other appointments."

Having lit a fire under Giles's skinny butt, Tom shook hands and left. Fifteen pairs of eyes tracked his exit.

Party invitations followed. The first one was at a producer's mansion in Beverly Hills, not far from where Andrew Mallard's body was found. Tom had to get fitted for a tuxedo.

"We better find the girl, Suzy, or the LAPD will garnish my wages till kingdom come."

Suzy looked harried. The phone hadn't stopped ringing, and she had made countless trips to the post box. Pictures were lined up on the dining room table. A big poster of Garbo in *Camille* was pinned to the wall, for reference.

"Not even close," she sighed.

Promising candidates' information was sent to Monroe's team for follow-up. Nothing had surfaced so far.

"It hasn't been a week yet," Freddy said over the phone. "We'll keep at it." He cleared his throat. "We have another body."

"Where?"

"San Berdoo. It happened in early October. A National Guard trooper. It's the same set-up, with the clothes, the shoes, and all that."

October. "How did I miss it when I went through the files?"

"You didn't miss it, Tom," Freddy said. "We don't have access to the San Bernardino County files. It's a follow-up from your phone calls. The local sheriff got in touch. He said the kid was crushed on a chariot wheel. That makes sense to you?"

A wheel? Tom felt nauseous. He dropped the phone. "I need to sit down."

Suzy picked up the phone. "Talk to me, Freddy." She listened, nodding. "I'll tell him. Yes, I understand." She hung up.

"What did he say?" Tom's tongue felt too big for his mouth. He had a sip of cold coffee left in a cup, his or Suzy's. The bitterness gave him a jolt. A breaking wheel, how far would this horror go?

"The body was found in an abandoned barn, by a hobo," Suzy said. "Kids coming back from a dance said they saw a car parked nearby. A dark Chevy. The girl said there was an O in the license plate, the boy thought it was a P."

Tom had recovered from his brief spell. "We should go back to the office, Suzy. Help the team find the car. We're useless here." He had been invited to yet another ridiculous party.

"I don't need to be by the phone," Suzy said. "I'll go interview the photographers. We'll cover more ground that way. Grandma can take messages."

The elderly lady stayed out of their way. If the constant ring of the phone bothered her, she didn't mention it. She smiled at the two young people who had invaded her house.

"We can't ask her to do that."

"She'll love it. What's that wheel thing Freddy mentioned?"

"Another horrendous execution method." Tom raised a hand. "Don't ask. And I'm not going to that party tomorrow. I can't take these people anymore."

He'd had enough of drunken orgies, cocaine on bar counters, people jumping in pools, sex behind flower pots, and crying girls loaded in taxi cabs. He couldn't hold in the same mental picture frame the excesses of Hollywood and the image of a boy broken on a wheel in a ruined barn.

"You have to go, Tom. It's the launch of the Oscar season. Everybody will be there. If Miss G. has any connection with the business, she'll attend. People bring their wives, daughters, mistresses. There's no better opportunity to cast a wide net."

She was right, of course.

"Okay, but that's it. We run down the last names on the list, and we close the shop. Monroe needs everybody on the Chevy. If the press gets wind of that piece of information, the killers will ditch the car, and the case is dead."

* * *

The Hollywood elite appeared to be on its best behavior at the Chateau Marmont shindig. But it was still early. With plenty of rooms upstairs and bungalows on the grounds, things were bound to slide given time and alcohol lubrication. Tom roamed the still sparsely populated ballrooms. No Greta Garbo. He took position near the main entrance where ushers collected invitations. Most cartons listed studios or talent agencies. There was no guest list. The stars didn't need an invitation. Their face sufficed. Bette Davis walked in. She was smaller than Tom expected, but made up for it in attitude. Most celebrities were shorter in real life. Not Jimmy Stewart, though. He had a good inch over Tom.

Hours dripped by, and still no Garbo duplicate. The noise level had gone up several notches. Waiters worked the bedazzled crowd. Tom snatched a champagne flute. A smoke lid hovered above the heads despite the garden doors having been flung wide open.

Then he saw her through the haze.

She was exactly as Millie-the-dancer described. The fine porcelain face, the thin, straight nose. The resemblance to Garbo was uncanny. Tom was careful not to stare, letting his eyes glide to the people around her. None of the men and women in her group looked like a partner in murder. They were middle-aged and self-important.

Tom couldn't afford stepping out to make a call. The woman might disappear as suddenly as she materialized. He pulled out one of the bogus business cards and scribbled a few words on the back. He waved at one of the young waiters.

"A sawbuck if you place a phone call for me." He gave the card and the bill to the boy. "That's the number and that's what you say to the person who answers."

She's here.

Suzy would know what to do.

* * *

Tom jumped when somebody wrapped an arm around his shoulders. He was so focused on Miss G. he hadn't seen anybody coming.

A soft voice whispered in his ear. "A dozen plainclothes are on the premises. All the exits are covered."

He turned to face a young, handsome guy who flashed him the kind of smile that could decorate Avery Giles's walls.

"Who the hell are you?"

"Danny Ebel. With Parker's Press Office. I was with Monroe when your girl called."

"Watch your mouth, kid."

Ebel's smile wavered. "Uh, the g...Miss Vaughn said you had eyes on the target."

"Take a gander. Discreetly. At my three o'clock."

Ebel let out a low whistle. "Ghosts exist after all. Who are the people with her?"

"No idea. The bald guy with the red carnation has intentions, he watches her like she's the Koh-i-Noor. He's so close he can taste her. Make yourself useful, kid, find me a drink, and cigarettes."

Ebel trotted away. He was back quickly, with drinks. He'd put a damper on his smile and his swagger.

Guests were starting to trickle out. A ponderousness had settled over the gathering. The big stars had left. People in search of a partner had found a match for the night. Drunks were sprawled over sofas. The ice in the tubs had melted.

"You want to wait till she leaves?" Ebel said.

"We'd have to bag her entourage. It could be awkward. She hasn't danced all night. I might have a shot at separating her from the herd."

Tom dropped his cigarette stub in Ebel's empty glass and walked across the ballroom. He ignored the man with the carnation who tried to block him and bowed lightly in front of the woman. She was lovely at close quarters. "They'll soon tuck away the instruments. It might be our last chance."

She raised her perfect chin. Garbo in *Camille*, like the poster.

"There's always another party, another chance," she said.

Tom held out his hand. "I'm not so sure."

Carnation-guy grabbed her arm. "Carolyn, I warn you."

She shrugged him off and took Tom's hand. He led her to a clear space close to the garden doors. As he put a hand on her waist to pull her close, he caught a glimpse of a big guy in a brown fedora, standing just outside the doors. Freddy.

The orchestra was playing the *Tennessee Waltz*.

Freddy had the good sense to wait for the end of the song.

* * *

In the morning, the blue Chevy was located at Mines Field, Los Angeles International Airport. Its owner, Duncan Battle, was about to board a Pan Am flight to Hawaii.

The cops didn't go to Mines Field on a hunch. They found a plane ticket in Carolyn Lake's apartment. A suitcase was by the front door. Miss G. was packed and ready to go.

If not for a star-studded gala … but as Suzy Vaughn said, nobody wanted to miss the Chateau Marmont party. Stars and killers alike.

* * *

Chief Parker acknowledged the news of Tom's departure with a curt nod. Monroe was more emotional. He offered him a glass of rye.

Freddy couldn't understand why Tom was leaving so soon.

"You don't want to know who they are and why they did it? Why they took the shoes and where they hid them? They'll talk, Tom. It's the only way they can hope to avoid the gas."

"Killers never have anything interesting to say, Freddy. I plan to get so drunk that by tomorrow I won't be able to remember their names."

The evening before, Suzy had emptied the post office box, and they made a bonfire of its contents on the Santa Monica beach.

The *Camille* poster went on top. It was gone in no time at all.

Serious Acting

By Devon Ellington

"That better not be a real dead body," Matty Bauer, the production manager, growled, as we stared at the body sprawled across the cables, blood pooled under him. "We're already behind schedule."

"I don't think the murderer cares about our shooting schedule." I ran a hand through my hair.

"No, no, it can't be murder, Gin," Matty moaned. "An accident. It has to be an accident. He tripped and fell."

"Onto a knife?" I pointed to the knife in his chest. "And then fell backwards? Even if I was writing fantasy, I couldn't make that scenario work, boyo." I sighed. "I doubt he knifed himself. Someone wanted to make real sure he was dead."

"Where are those damned rewrite pages?" Clifford Guest, the director, bellowed. He turned the word "damned" into two syllables, leaning into the second one, to emphasize his British accent. An accent I knew was a put-on.

I looked down at the sheaf of typed pages in my hand, then back to the set. "You have to call the police, Matty. You can't just throw a tarp over him and pretend it didn't happen until we wrap for the night."

"You're right, you're right," Matty nodded. "With the lights, he'll start to smell."

"You're not treating one of mine like that." Wes Millard, the director of photography, joined us.

"He's one a'your guys? You sure?" Matty moaned. "Maybe he just wandered in, when one of the boys went out for a smoke."

"He got that tattoo in the Navy." Wes pointed to the topless mermaid wrapped around an anchor. "We used to joke about it. That's Nicky Johnson. New on the crew."

Something about the tattoo rang a bell in my brain, but I couldn't quite catch it.

Matty groaned. "This is bad. Really bad."

"Call the cops right now, or I will, and I'll tell them you hesitated." Wes glared at the other man, arms folded over his chest. The top two buttons of his shirt were unbuttoned, and the sleeves were rolled up, exposing his forearms.

An impressive chest and nice arms, I thought, *and I should not be thinking like this right now when there's a dead man lying only a few feet away.*

"Why aren't the rewrites here yet?" Clifford raged. "Is everything ass-backwards in this place?"

"I'll deal with the director," I said. "You get the cops here."

"I'll stay with the body," Wes offered.

For a moment, I wondered if it was because he looked after his crew, or if he wanted to hide something because he had something to do with the man's death. But why would I think that? I didn't know either man, although I knew Wes had a good reputation. But, if I was a murderer, or, in my case, a murderess, I'd offer to stay with the body and remove necessary evidence.

"You okay, Mrs. Race?" Wes asked, his tone gentle.

"Thinking too much," I said. "Hazard of being a writer." I looked up, into those deep blue eyes. I hoped he wasn't the murderer, not with those eyes. "Let me deal with Cliff Guest."

"You sound like you know him," Wes said.

"We go way back," I retorted.

"That sounds like a story I'd like to hear. Someday." He grimaced at the body.

Flirting over a dead body? Yeah, Hollywood was weird.

I sighed and trudged back to the set, where Clifford Guest paced.

"Where are those bloody pages?" He raged. "And where's Sherry Anne?"

"You sent Sherry Anne to her dressing room on break until you approved the rewrite." The leading man, Gil Reynolds, sounded bored. He inhaled his cigarette deeply and held it, before an extended exhale.

"The new pages are here, but we aren't shooting any time soon." I held them out to Cliff.

He snatched them away, not looking at me. "Why not? You think they're bad? Or you think Sherry Anne can't learn them? I know she's not the sharpest knife in the drawer, but—" he looked at me. "Ginger Newhouse? Is that you? Are you a PA here?"

"I'm the Race of Gold and Race, the writing team on this film," I said.

"When did you become Ginger Race?" Cliff looked flummoxed.

I grinned. "When did you become—"

"Let's take ten!" Cliff called, and everybody dissipated, although Gil gave me a long, interested look before sauntering off.

Cliff waited and looked around until he was sure they were alone. "How can Ginger Newhouse be Gin Race?"

"How can Clyde Gordon from Coney Island be Clifford Guest, the British director?" I countered.

"It's called re-invention, darling," Cliff said. "What's your excuse?"

"Married a man named Harry Race, who died on the beach at Normandy," I replied.

"I'm sorry," said Cliff.

"Thanks." I would not cry. "He was a good guy. Anyway, I teamed up with Benjamin Gold. Remember him, from back east? He came out here for a job and convinced me to join him. Ginger Natalie Race was too long a name, and too feminine, so I went with G.N. Race for my books and short stories back east, people started calling me Gin, and it stuck when I came out here. Wasser just put us on the picture a few days back, to try and fix it."

"Well, I'm glad they put you on this picture, or it would be hopeless," said Clifford. "The rewrites almost make sense now." He put up a hand as I sputtered. "I'm well aware how little you had to work with. But why can't we shoot?"

"One of the camera crew's been murdered," I said. "We need to stop for the cops. Real ones, not one gussied up by the wardrobe department."

* * *

"Mrs. Race, thank you for your statement." Detective Jeremiah Rove snapped shut his notebook and tipped his fedora in my direction. "Not often we get such a clear, concise report."

"From a dame?" I teased. He had nice eyes, hazel instead of blue. Nice features, too. Man would look good in front of a camera. I could write him such a role… "Sorry? I missed that."

"Just giving you my number, ma'am, in case you think of something else." He handed me a business card. Under the printed phone number for the cop shop was a handwritten number. "In case you need to reach me at an odd hour."

"Thank you." Maybe his gracious manner wasn't just all business after all.

"We done here, Rove?" another detective, this one shorter and rounder, with the stub of a cigar hanging off one side of his lip, waddled up. "How come you got to question the pretty dillies, and I get the chuckleheads?"

"Just luck I guess." Detective Rove stood.

"Is it true you upset that Sherry Anne doll so badly she needed a shot from the doctor?"

"Murder upsets the ladies."

The short detective snorted. "Trust me, that one ain't no lady." He grinned at me. "You, maybe. Her? I gots opinions."

Detective Rove sighed. "Good day, Mrs. Race."

"Good day, Detective Rove."

I enjoyed watching him walk off the set.

"Rove and Race doesn't sound nearly as good as Gold and Race." Ben Gold dropped into the seat next to me. "Too much alliteration."

"Don't worry, I'm not trading you in for a detective." I yawned. "Any chance we're gonna wrap soon?"

"We have to, cuz the doc shot up Sherry Anne and put her down for the night," said Ben.

I sighed. "Someday, we'll work with actresses who can, y'know, act better onscreen than off."

Ben laughed. "We gotta climb the ladder to a better studio for that. All we need to do for the moment is grind out the formulas that bring in the cash.'

"Not a bad way to make a living." I considered. "Why would anyone want to kill this Nicky Johnson? Just a regular guy, doing his job."

"I've been wondering that myself." Wes joined us, pulling up another chair.

"How long did he work here? If we're looking at the usuals, of sex, money, revenge, where's he fit in?"

"Hired him about a week ago," said Wes. "One of my guys quit to move to Manitoba." He smiled at me as I started to giggle. "I know, I know. I don't get it, either."

"Gotta be a girl involved," said Ben.

"Probably." Wes shrugged. "Nicky was new in town, finished his tour with the Navy, war's over, he wants something fresh. What's fresher and sharper than movies? He got some experience behind a camera in the Navy. I looked at some of his work; he had a good eye and understood light and shadow. I could see him working his way up to his own credits one day."

"How'd he get someone mad enough to kill him in such a short time?" Ben mused.

"That tattoo…" I shook my head. "It reminds me of something."

"Nicky was in love with a gal before he went into the Navy, back in Kansas," said Wes. "He told me he described her to the guy who did the tattoo, out in Hawaii, since he didn't have a photo."

"Do we need to get in touch with her? Let her know what happened to Nicky?" I asked.

Wes shook his head. "She dumped him while he was fighting in the Pacific Theatre. Said she had bigger dreams than tying herself to an anchor clunker."

I thought about that. "You think her dreams brought her here?"

"You think Nicky's girl was an actress?" Ben asked.

"Or wanted to be one." It made sense.

"She might have gone on the skids," Wes pointed out. "Depends how long she was in town. How talented."

"And where her talent—" Ben began.

I smacked him. "Stop."

"Gin, you joined me out here six months ago, you know how this town works."

Wes looked from one to the other of us. "How long you been together?"

"As a writing team, not much more than six months," I said. "Although we became friends in college."

"I convinced her to sell out and join me writing movies," said Ben.

Wes tilted his head, regarding me. "Selling out?"

I shrugged. "I enjoy it. I'm having a good time and making decent money. I like my apartment."

"Your apartment, or your," he pointed from one to the other, "apartment?"

"I live alone," I said. "Ben and I are writing partners, not a couple."

Wes grinned at me. "Glad to have that information."

* * *

"Gin! Come have a cocktail!" Marsha Bryant waved as I arrived at the apartment complex. Her curly blonde hair was held in place with oversized sunglasses, pushed up on top of her head because it was well past sunset. She wore a silk robe with large red flowers over her red swimsuit and was stretched out on a lounge chair.

"Don't you have an early call?" I asked, walking over to join them.

"They're running behind. Johnny Kempe keeps forgetting his lines." Marsha poured clear liquid from a pitcher into a martini glass. "I'm pushed back to the afternoon."

"Someone's here to see you." Betty Harris, sitting beside her, gestured to a chair farther in the shadows. Her brown ponytail swung as she looked from one to the other of us.

As my eyes got used to the dim light, I recognized Detective Jeremiah Rove.

"He asked us not to tell," Marsha teased.

"I'll take that drink." Marsha handed it to me as I passed her chair, and I sat in the nearest empty chair to Detective Rove. "I hope my friends have kept you entertained."

"They're delightful," said Detective Rove.

I thought his tone was a little dry. *I* certainly found Marsha's exuberance and Betty's quieter approach to life entertaining. "How can I help you, Detective?"

"Why didn't you tell me you know Clifford Guest's real identity?"

"Oh, this is good," Marsha leaned forward.

"Don't you dare sell it to the tabloids," I warned her.

"Only if he treats you shabbily," Marsha promised.

I turned my attention back to Detective Rove. "Clyde and I knew each other in New York. We worked the Straw Hat circuit in the 30s: Ivoryton in Connecticut, Cape Playhouse in Dennis, Ogunquit Playhouse in Maine. He went to England, and we lost touch. Didn't know he was Cliff Guest until we came face to face, after the murder."

"Again, why not tell me?"

"Didn't think it mattered."

"Everything matters in a murder, Mrs. Race."

"I'm gonna use that line, detective." When it didn't get a smile from him, I sighed. "Is Cliff a suspect?"

"Everyone on that set is a suspect, especially with all these 'reinvented' identities." He watched me. "You don't seem upset that you're a suspect."

"I know I didn't kill the guy," I said. "You seem like a smart guy. I'm sure you'll figure it out."

"What do you know about Gil Reynolds?"

"Just what the publicity folks wrote up on his bio," I said. "First time I ever worked with the guy, although I've seen him in a few films." I watched the detective. "As I'm sure Ben told you, we only came onto the film earlier this week. Previous writer was fired."

"Because his writing was bad?"

"Well, yeah, it was bad, but he was fired because he drank rather than worked on the rewrites." I shook my head. "I'm glad for the job, I'm having a good time out here, but this film? I can't see any way to save it. We're just trying to survive it."

"Any reason you can think why your predecessor would have a beef with Nicky Johnson?"

"Unless Johnson got between him and a bottle of bourbon, can't see one," I said.

Detective Rove stood up and tipped his hat to me. "Thank you for your time, Mrs. Race."

He sauntered out. I'm sure he was aware of the appreciative female attention to his retreating figure.

* * *

"She's so mean." I overheard some of the gals from the publicity department talking in the commissary as I tucked into my bacon and eggs the next morning. I wanted to turn around, but I was more interested in what they said than letting them know I eavesdropped.

"She's upset because she doesn't want anyone to know she's from the Midwest," the young woman continued. "It's not like we don't have dozens of girls coming to Hollywood from all over the country." There was a large sigh. "My boss is furious that we have to reprint all those press pages. Blames me, of course, because he couldn't blame *her*."

"She could be an inspiration to girls just like her," one of the other young women added.

"She doesn't want the competition coming out here like she did," a third young woman snickered.

"Changing her name and all," the first young woman said.

"That's the game," said the third woman. "We always change their names."

"'Sandra' is a perfectly nice name. Plenty of good Sandras out there," the first woman said.

"Not flashy enough," the third woman said. "We save the 'Sandras' and 'Sandys' for more wholesome girls. That one's not wholesome. We'll have our hands full with her if she starts getting the kind of attention she wants."

181

I pulled my compact out of my purse and acted like I was touching up my face. Instead, I tilted the mirror to identify them. I'd make friends in that building.

* * *

"Hey, Gil, you look a little green around the gills this morning," I said, walking into the makeup room. "No pun intended. Have a little too much fun last night?" I nodded to the woman doing his make-up. "Hello, Louise."

"Hello, yourself. Did you get a look at that handsome detective yesterday? I'd get myself arrested just to spend more time with him."

I laughed, but Gil didn't.

"You don't think the murderer is some loony picking us off one by one, do ya, hon?" Louise's eyes widened.

"That's Agatha Christie. We can't afford her," I retorted. I turned my attention to the actor in the makeup chair. "What's going on, Gil?"

"I didn't realize it was Nicky who was dead." Gil dropped his script onto the floor. I picked it up and gave it back. "I got him the job here."

"You knew him?"

"Oh, hon, I'm sorry," said Louise.

Gil nodded. "We were in Navy boot camp together out in Illinois. He went to the Pacific, I went to Europe, but we spent our first few weeks helping each other survive. When he turned up in town a few weeks back, I was happy he was alive and then talked Wes into hiring him."

"Good of you," I said.

"No." Gil shook his head. "The experience changes you, y'know? Preparing for war? Then out there fighting? But neither of us was much good keeping in touch."

"You know the girl he was so crazy about?" I asked.

"Gosh, he did nothing but talk about her when we were in training. 'Sandy' this and 'Sandy' that."

"Ever see a photo of her?"

Gil shook his head. "She was supposed to give him one before he left, but she didn't. She promised to send him one, but never even wrote him a letter while we trained."

"Sounds like the relationship was a bit one-sided."

"He was determined to marry her if he made it home once the war was over."

"Then why was he here and not back wherever home was?"

"She'd dumped him and came out here to be in pictures," said Gil. "He was determined to track her down."

"Any idea where she is?"

Gil shook his head. "He was good with a camera, so I told him I'd try to keep him on pictures with me until he found her. Since I got the dark hair, they keep pairing me with the blondes, and if she really wanted to make it out here, she'd become a blonde. But he didn't buy it. He couldn't imagine her as anything other than the cute little brunette he knew."

"And we all know you like your blondes, especially when they're your co-stars." Louise gave me a wink.

My hair's auburn, so I had nothing to worry about from Gil. Not that I couldn't take care of myself, in any event. But it made me wonder if maybe Gil and Nicky had a falling out about a very specific non-natural blonde.

* * *

"I'm telling you, it's all taken care of." Cliff was on the phone when I joined Ben outside Cliff's office. "We don't have to worry about him anymore. No one has to worry about him anymore." He looked up and saw us in the doorway. There was a moment of consternation as he spotted us, but he mumbled, "Gotta get back to work," and put the receiver back into the cradle.

He motioned us in. "Good work on the rewrite. But we're gonna have to talk Sherry Anne into the scene. She doesn't think it makes her look good."

"She's the femme fatale of the piece," I said. "All she does is *look* good. Lights, costumes, writing."

"Talk to her, Gin," said Cliff.

"She's more likely to listen to Ben. She doesn't like other women much.

Doesn't even talk to the other actresses on set."

"She's staying in character."

"Oh," I said. "*That.*" I sighed. "I only met her that one time in her dressing room, the first day we were on the picture, and that was to say hello."

"I don't care how you work your magic, just do it. You were always good with the actors back east." Cliff looked at his watch. "We've got to get that scene shot tonight."

* * *

The publicity department was on the way to the dressing room bungalows, so I stopped there first. As usual, it was busy in the warren of offices, with actors, publicists, assistants, stylists, photographers, and all the others competing for attention.

I found the young woman who'd talked about the different Sandys. Her name was Veronica. "Call me Ronnie," she offered. "I saw you check me out in your compact."

"Purely professional," I assured her. "Good eye, catching that detail."

She shrugged. "Helps in my line of work. What can I do for you? Not sure we're doing much publicity for our writers."

"I'm curious about the former Sandy from the Midwest who's been giving you trouble."

"Figure she's giving you just as much trouble as the rest of us, seeing as she's on your picture."

* * *

"I'm here to talk about the new scene," I said when Sherry Anne admitted me to her dressing room. She wore a long, cream-colored silk robe that set off the highlights in her hair. "I hear you have a beef with it."

She shrugged, and sat at her dressing table, lighting a cigarette. Her hands shook. "It makes me look too much like the villain of the piece."

I looked at the photos taped to her mirror. There was one of her younger,

184

with a blonde wig, dressed as a mermaid. That's why Nicky's tattoo looked familiar. I'd seen the photo of her, probably the one that inspired the tattoo, right here in this room.

"Hon, you *are* the villain of the piece. On and off screen." I watched her.

She gave me a small smile. "I believe in creating my own reality, don't you?"

"My job is creating escape from reality for others," I said.

"Then you'll understand," said Sherry Anne.

"Why don't you explain to me why you killed Nicky Johnson?" I suggested. "Especially since he was in love with you."

"But I wasn't in love with him," said Sherry Anne. "He wouldn't take no for an answer. Not back in Kansas. Not out here." She glanced at me, then turned her attention to her reflection in the mirror. "I want to be good at this, really good, you know? Work my way out of these grind pictures and earn a role with meat, that makes people sit up and take notice that I can do some serious acting. Nicky wanted me to stay home and have babies. Even though, once he got the job here, he got bit by the moving pictures bug. We coulda been a team, but he only wanted a wife. I had no say in it."

"Stabbing him in the heart's a little melodramatic, don't you think?" I kept my voice gentle.

"Subtlety was always lost on him."

"You could have asked one of the boys to toss him off the film."

"He'd just hang around the gates, waiting for me. Or break into my house. Again."

"The police—"

"Do nothing in these situations." Sherry Anne held my gaze. "You know that. I know that. It's always our fault."

She had a point. "So you decided to take care of it yourself."

"He threatened to kill me, you know." Sherry Anne sounded almost bored. "If I didn't marry him. He had this big, romantic notion of a double suicide. Or a murder-suicide. Either way, I'd end up dead. I didn't want to die at his hands."

"You could have found a better way than stabbing him on set," I said.

"Pushed him off a cliff, given him a slow-acting poison. There are lots of ways to kill a guy that don't land you in the slammer."

"It was an impulse in the moment," said Sherry Anne. "I should have taken the time to think it through better, to plan. I could have gotten ideas from your books." At my look, she laughed. "Yes, I've read them. I can *read*, in spite of what they say about me. Your plots are clever, especially the way you do away with people. It was such a relief when you and Mr. Gold joined the film. I thought, now, my scenes will make sense. But Nicky kept bothering me between setups. I told him to wait, we'd talk away from set, but he wouldn't leave me alone. We argued, and he grabbed me. He frightened me and made me angry. So I reacted."

"The knife just happened to be nearby?"

She gave me a small smile. "He'd been cutting rope to tie up cable." She glanced at the door. "I suppose they're out there? The police?"

There was a soft knock on the door, and Detective Rove stepped in. I let out a breath I didn't realize I was holding, relieved that Ronnie fulfilled my request to put in the call. "Sherry Anne Sullivan, you're under arrest for the murder of Nicky Johnson."

"I'm sorry to put the film at risk," said Sherry Anne. "I'm not sorry Nicky's dead." She looked up at Detective Rove. "I'll make a compelling witness, testifying in my own defense."

"I'm sure you will, Miss Sullivan. Please get dressed. I'll wait outside."

Sherry Anne smirked at me. "What does the well-dressed woman wear to her police booking these days?"

I tried to laugh but failed. "I'm sorry."

"I thought I could tough it out, but I can't," she said. "Not because I loved him underneath it all. But because killing him sickened my soul." She looked at me. "Remember that, the next time you write a murderer."

I joined Detective Rove outside the bungalow and slumped against the wall. "I wish Matty was right, and it was someone from outside."

"It rarely is," said Detective Rove. "I'm sorry."

The gunshot startled me, but the detective didn't flinch. He opened the door, and we found Sherry Anne sprawled across her dressing table, a bullet through her temple, the gun on the floor beside her.

I rounded on Detective Rove. "You knew. You could have stopped her."

"I let her make her own choice, rather than being killed by the court." He glanced at her, then back at me. "You heard her. It was eating her up. Killing is different in life than in the pictures."

"How'd she get the gun?"

"It was probably Nicky Johnson's. Or belonged to whatever guy she was seeing while trying to get away from Johnson."

"I need a drink." My voice shook.

"Keep my card," said Jeremiah Rove, as more boys in blue showed up to clean up the mess. "I hope you use the number one day."

* * *

"I'm sorry things ended for Sherry Anne the way they did," Wes said. We were having dinner at the Musso & Frank Grill, supposedly the oldest eatery in Los Angeles, and with the best martinis. At least the martini part was true.

"So am I," I wondered if I should have a third martini. "I feel guilty she didn't think she could confide in me. Or in someone. He should have backed off a long time ago."

"But he didn't, and it got him killed," said Wes. "Gotta say, though, your friend Marsha's great in Sherry Anne's role."

"She is." I managed a smile. Ben and I rewrote it a bit, making room for her exuberance, along with the femme fatale sex appeal. I hoped this would be a break for her. If anyone ever saw it.

"The camera loves her, and she makes Gil Reynolds light up, too," said Wes. He watched me. "So what's next for you? Sticking around?"

"I'll work out my contract and then see," I said. Out of the corner of my eye, I spotted Jeremiah Rove at another table. He looked sharp in a dark suit, and the attractive woman with him was definitely not an actress. I wondered if I should have called the handwritten phone number on his business card. At least neither of us was alone. "Studio's got Ben and me writing a comedy."

"Nice change of pace." He took a drink of his Tom Collins, watching me over the rim of the glass. "Will you write about Sherry Anne someday?"

"Someday," I said. "But I won't keep on about it tonight."

"I'll listen if you like," Wes said. "I'll always listen."

"Attractive trait in a man," I said.

He smiled. "Glad you find me attractive."

"I hope it's mutual."

"One hundred percent." He leaned forward. "I have plans for us tonight."

I leaned in to meet him. "I like a man who knows how to plan."

"Moonlight plans."

"I like moonlight."

We smiled at each other, and I ordered that third martini.

Lola's Last Dance

By Kerry Hammond

She shot herself with a .45 and didn't even drop her cigarette. She may have pulled the trigger, but I refused to consider it a suicide. It was murder, pure and simple. I didn't know why she did it, but I knew who made her feel like it was the only option. I also knew what I was going to do about it.

Lola was her stage name, something she used for ten of the twenty-seven years she was on this earth. I had never known her by any other name, but I don't think anything else would suit her quite like Lola.

I met her back in '44 when she first arrived in the great state of California. She was chasing the dream of being a Hollywood actress, but ended up as a dancer at the Rooster Club. Back then, the clubs were classy and full of young girls who thought it was just a pitstop on the way to stardom. I was the piano player, and when I got the gig I thought I'd won the lottery. 'I get to play music and watch beautiful girls take their clothes off?' I thought. 'What could be better?' But then I got to know the girls, and I got to know the club owner.

Lola and I hit it off right away. The kid had spunk. This might sound like a line, but she was different from the other dancers. All the Rooster girls had survival instinct; they came with the territory. But Lola also had a heart of gold. That heart of gold, in the end, proved to be her downfall.

I had been there for about six months when she asked for my help. I thought she wanted me to help run her lines; she was always muttering to herself before she went for an audition. But it wasn't her lines she needed help with; it was a missing person. One of the dancers had gone missing, and Lola knew that my old man was a retired homicide detective. She thought I could help. The missing dancer's boyfriend was starting to get frantic, and the police had no leads. No one could afford a private investigator in those days, so I agreed to ask around. Lola ended up giving me critical information that helped me locate the girl. Unfortunately, I arrived too late on that day, too. The whole incident earned me a reputation with the girls for finding the truth, which led to my actually becoming a PI. But I'm getting ahead of myself.

The Rooster Club was run by one of the biggest thugs in Los Angeles. His given name was Jimmy O'Shea, but everyone called him Jimmy the Ax. No degree in rocket science was necessary to figure out the origin of Jimmy's nickname; it aptly represented the weapon he used to dispatch his enemies. The cops were never able to pin anything on him, and because of that, he felt invincible. No surprise there.

It didn't help that the people Jimmy chose to get rid of weren't the type to be missed by law enforcement. Well, most of them anyway. Last year, Jimmy's girlfriend of four years went missing. Since there was no body, the police investigation went cold. Lola took it hard; she was friendly with Kitty and she told me she suspected that Jimmy had made Kitty 'disappear.' Given my success with her previous request, Lola asked me to look for Kitty. I tried, but I ran into dead end after dead end. If Jimmy was responsible, he was good at covering his tracks. It was my biggest regret that I couldn't solve that case for Lola. Well, it was my biggest regret until now.

Jimmy and I had history. I grew up on the streets and worked for him as an errand boy before I started playing piano at the club. We weren't on completely friendly terms; to Jimmy, we're all just employees. Our past connection was one of the reasons that he tolerated my questioning his girls when Lola asked me to. The other reason was Lola herself.

Lola was his favorite girl, and although he didn't like the connection I had formed with her, he knew he had to accept it. From the moment I met her, she brought out the big brother in me. I called her 'Kid' and everyone thought that it was because she was fifteen years my junior. Only she knew it was because she reminded me of my kid sister. Neither of us felt the need to enlighten anyone. It was our private joke.

Jimmy found Lola living on the streets. Since she couldn't get work as an actress, she didn't have money for a place to live. She was only seventeen, and he gave her a job at the Rooster, telling her that she could just work there until she made it big. He even found her an apartment she could afford.

She took to dancing like she'd been born doing it, and she loved the attention from the men who frequented the club. Most of Jimmy's girls did other jobs on the side—if you get my meaning—but Lola wasn't into that. Jimmy made sure everyone knew she wasn't on the market, and that tells you how he felt about her. He had a soft spot for her. Well, as soft as a gangster could muster anyway. But before you get all warm and mushy about Jimmy, let me point out that Lola was the one who brought the most money into the club. They came to see her dance, even if that's all they could get. Jimmy knew on which side his bread was buttered.

When tragedy hits, some people break down in tears. Others get angry and yell and scream. As I stood looking down at Lola's lifeless body, I felt a cold sort of clarity. I knew I would grieve, but that had to wait. First, there were things that I needed to do.

I picked up the .45 and left through the back door of Lola's apartment building. I quickly found a payphone on the corner and called the police. My anonymous tip stated that the body of a young woman could be found in apartment 201 of the Westward Arms building. I hung up before they could ask questions.

I walked into the Rooster around noon. There was a three-piece band playing, one dancer on stage, and two guys sitting in the front row watching. I never understood what sort of guy spends his lunch hour drinking beer at a dance club, but to each his own. It meant that I had a job.

"Hey Eddie, where's Jimmy?" Eddie had been tending bar at the Rooster for as long as I could remember. He was Jimmy's cousin, and they were tight. I tread carefully whenever I spoke to him.

Eddie was a man of few words, so I wasn't surprised when he gave me a nod of acknowledgment followed by a twitch of his head toward the back office. I headed back in search of Jimmy.

I found the club owner sitting behind his desk on a plush red velvet wingback chair. He called it his 'throne' and no one dared sit in it when Jimmy was within a hundred miles of the club. As I expected, he was alone in his office. Up until last week, you would never find Jimmy alone. A man with as many enemies as Jimmy knew better than to leave himself open for attack, so for the last five years, he employed a bodyguard by the name of Bruno.

If you think Lola's name suited her, you should have seen Bruno. He was a hulk of a man, probably weighed in at three fifty, but the fact that he stood six feet four inches made it look like he wore it well. He was dumb as a box of rocks, but Jimmy didn't hire him for his intellect. His main function was to intimidate, and he was great at his job.

A week ago, Jimmy showed up at the club and found Bruno lying in a heap on the floor of his office. Jimmy's papers had been rifled, and Bruno had a bloody dent in the back of his head in the same shape as the large marble paperweight that lay next to his body.

It goes without saying that no cops were called to the scene. When you've got as much to hide as Jimmy, you don't invite the police into your place of business. They tend to get nosy, and Jimmy didn't like nosy. I heard a rumor that some important documents were missing, but no one actually knew what those documents were or who took them, and Jimmy never said.

In the end, Bruno's body wasn't found in Jimmy's office; it was found in an alley near Hollywood Savings and Loan. The paperweight that killed him wasn't found with the body; that might connect the death to Jimmy, and he wanted no part of that. Given that the body was moved, the murder weapon was missing, and the victim worked for one of the most crooked business owners in the city, it wasn't a surprise that the case went cold. As previously stated, cases seemed to frequently go cold where Jimmy was concerned.

Jimmy didn't mourn the death of his bodyguard, but he did lament the fact that he would need to find a replacement. Apparently, good help is hard to find, since he still hadn't filled the position. Maybe he was collecting resumes. I wasn't complaining, since it meant that I now had his undivided attention.

"If it isn't my good friend Sam Ford," said Jimmy as I entered the office. "If I'm correct, you're not working today, Sam. What brings you to the Rooster on your day off?"

"I'm looking for information, Jimmy," I said, sitting down in the chair opposite his desk to show him I didn't plan to leave anytime soon.

"As you well know, most of the girls aren't in just yet, so you'll have to come back later if you want to question them." He wanted to make it clear that he knew I'd questioned the girls before.

"I don't need to talk to the girls. I need to talk to you." Jimmy's left cheek twitched. It was his tell. He didn't get nervous often, but when he did, his cheek gave him away. He'd had the tick for years, and I picked up on it when I witnessed his interactions with his late father, Jimmy Senior. Jimmy was terrified of his father and hadn't been able to lose the twitch in the ten years since his dad's death. I wondered if he even knew he had it.

What followed can only be described as a fencing match. Whenever I advanced, he would retreat. Jimmy could parry like a champ, but in the end, I got the answer I came for. Jimmy was responsible for Lola's death. I felt it in my bones, and my bones were never wrong.

I now knew the *who*, but not the *why*. You may wonder why that was important to me, why knowing the *who* wasn't enough. I have an analytical brain; it's why I love music so much. The notes are all there on the page, and if you play them in the right order, you get a beautiful sound. People like me need everything to be tidy. I've always been a fan of puzzles for the same reason, there is an order to the clues, and if you put them in the proper order, you get the solution. You can't just solve part of a puzzle and walk away. You have to put all the pieces in place before you feel like it's complete. I needed this to be complete.

The police came to question me the next day. I knew they would get to me; I just didn't know how quickly it would happen. My connection to Lola wasn't a secret; it just wasn't something I shouted from the rooftops.

The guy they sent was short and skinny with yellow teeth and a comb-over. His name was Thompson, and he clearly had a chip on his shoulder, or he remembered my father when he was on the job, and they weren't happy memories. My old man sometimes rubbed people the wrong way. He questioned me about my relationship with Lola, implying a romantic connection that didn't exist. He knew it would rankle me. He wasn't wrong.

I bit my tongue and sat on my hands. If I went to jail, it wouldn't help me figure out the *why*. His twenty-minute visit felt like it lasted an hour, but it was clear that the police were looking into Lola's life at the Rooster, hoping to find a lead. I didn't know if their team was just going through the motions, but decided it was better than nothing. I wanted them to do a deep dive into Jimmy's affairs, even though I knew they'd come up empty. I still hoped they would look really hard.

When Thompson left, I needed a drink. I knew just where to go to get one, so I made my excuses and left early. Jimmy wouldn't be happy, but Ronny, the saxophone player, said he'd cover for me.

I drove to The Painted Horse, a local pub run by a guy called Hamish, a Brit who thought that L.A. could use a little bit of what he termed 'British class.' I wasn't sure a pub constituted class, but the place served great beer and didn't charge you for the atmosphere, so I let him have it.

I had helped Hamish out of a bind with Jimmy when he first arrived in the city, and I was still working as an errand boy, so he kept me in the loop when I needed it. For a small fee, of course.

I was prepared to pay handsomely for what I needed to know about Lola's death, but I also knew that Hamish wouldn't charge me a cent. He knew how much Lola meant to me and whether or not he wanted to admit it, he cared about the girl too.

Hamish was behind the bar, writing in a ledger when I walked in. I could tell by the way he looked at me that he had already heard the news.

"Sam, I heard what happened. How are you doing, mate?"

"About as you would expect, thanks for asking." I sat at the bar across from him, and he handed me a whiskey. I drank it in one swallow and waved off a refill. "I need to keep my wits about me," I said. "Listen, Hamish, you probably already guessed that I won't be able to let this lie. I'm going to get the bastard who did this, and I'm going to need your help."

"I don't understand. I heard she killed herself."

"That may be, but you know that's not the whole story. You knew Lola, and there's no way that she would do this to herself, not without a reason. I plan to find that reason." He looked at a point on the wall somewhere past my left ear and slowly nodded his head in understanding.

"What do you need?"

"I need any information you can give me about the last week of Lola's life. Where she went, who she saw, what she said." I knew Hamish had cultivated connections throughout the city, and he was the best person to give me what I needed, but I didn't know he would have the key to the whole affair. I don't think even he knew how valuable he would prove to be.

Hamish told me that Lola had been asking around about Jimmy's enemies. Specifically, the ones who had kicked the oxygen habit, so to speak. Hamish didn't know why she was taking a tally of Jimmy's victims, but he warned her to stop poking the bear. It didn't work; he saw that she was on a mission.

I knew it all stemmed from Kitty's disappearance; she still wouldn't let that go. Maybe if I'd spent more time looking into it, she wouldn't have felt the need to take risks. That was something that would haunt me for the rest of my days.

Hamish suggested I talk to Eddie. He knew everything that went on at the Rooster, and he and Jimmy had had a falling out over the club's liquor sales. This was news to me. Apparently, Jimmy thought Eddie was skimming, and Eddie thought Jimmy should trust him. Eddie might be inclined to talk if they were on the outs. I figured it couldn't hurt to try.

I knew I couldn't approach Eddie at the club, so I waited until he was off duty and met him on his walk home.

"Hey Eddie, how's it going?" I said as I moved into step with the big man. Men like Eddie don't startle easily, but I could tell that I surprised him. I could also tell that he didn't want to talk to me.

"Can I buy you a beer and ask you a few questions?" I said.

"Buy me a beer? It's three o'clock in the morning. Where are you going to buy me a beer?"

"It was more a figure of speech; don't you have beer at your apartment? I won't keep you long, I just have a couple of things I'm trying to figure out, and I think you might be able to help me," I said.

"I got nothing to say," he said. "I think you should go home, Sam."

"I can't do that, Eddie. You see, Lola was like a sister to me. I *will* find out what happened, whether you help me or not."

Eddie stopped walking and turned to face me. "Listen," he said. "I told you, I've got nothing to say." The street was completely deserted, and for a moment, I regretted my decision to approach Jimmy's cousin in the middle of the night.

I gave him my best 'pretty please' look and stood my ground. The man's shoulders slumped, and he stepped down off the curb to look both ways, searching up and down the street. When he saw that no one was in sight, he put his hands in his pockets and looked me in the eye.

"Look, Sam, I really don't know anything about what happened to Lola. The last time I saw her, she was in a huddle, whispering to one of the other girls. The only word I made out was 'photograph.' That's all I can tell you." As if to punctuate this last part, he abruptly turned north and walked away. I stood on the sidewalk and watched him go. I knew that was all I was going to get from him. I also knew that it was enough.

I found the postcard in my mailbox three days after her death. It allowed me to put that last puzzle piece in place. She wrote it the morning she shot herself. Putting it in the post box was probably one of the last things she did. The fact that it was a postcard made me smile. She knew it would bug me that she didn't write me a letter, and I had to squint to read her tiny script.

Sam, please don't be mad at me, but it was easier for me to say goodbye in writing. I know you're going to do your thing and investigate, and you're the best in town, so I know you're going to find out the truth. I just wanted you to know that I left all the paperwork you'll need in an envelope with the desk clerk at the Grand Hotel. Take it to the police, and it'll put Jimmy away for the rest of his life. I didn't mean for anyone to get hurt, I really didn't. Bruno wasn't supposed to be there. I can't get past it, Sam. I feel like it makes me like him. I just can't live with that. You're the best big brother a girl could have. Yours, Kid.

The clerk at the Grand Hotel handed me the envelope, and I handed her a dollar tip. I got a smile for my efforts before she went back to her business. Back in my car, I opened the envelope and found the information Lola left for me. I found pages from Jimmy's journal detailing each of his victims, their crimes against him, and their dates of death. There was also a Polaroid of each death scene. Jimmy always was an arrogant prick. This was worse than taking a souvenir. This was a record of everything the police would need to put him away on multiple counts of murder. Even Jimmy couldn't pay off enough cops to make this go away.

The last photo in the pack was the worst. It was Kitty. The unnatural angle of her limbs would have been enough to confirm that she was dead, but the ax sticking out of her head clinched it. It confirmed what I already knew: Jimmy was a monster. I closed my eyes and leaned back in my seat.

I visited Lola's grave that morning. I hated that it was raining; it was so cliché. The headstone that I bought her had a ballet dancer etched into one corner and a clapboard slate in the other. I wanted to represent her love of dancing *and* the movies. The headstone read simply: Lola, you will be missed.

"You didn't have to do this, you know, Kid," I said to no one in particular. If you had told me a week ago that I would talk out loud to a gravestone, I would have told you that you were off your rocker. Somehow, though, standing here in front of Lola's grave, it seemed completely natural.

"I would have figured out a way to help you; I wouldn't have let you go to prison. There are lawyers we could have called, deals we could have made. I hate that you didn't come to me first." I dropped a carnation on the dirt mound in front of her stone. She was crazy about carnations. "Later, Kid," I said as I walked away.

It was noon when I walked into the Rooster. The place was empty. There were no dancers, no customers, and Eddie was not behind the bar. It was as if everyone had made themselves scarce.

Jimmy was sitting on his throne, a glass of whiskey sat on the desk next to his left hand, his journal lay open near his right. He looked up as I entered,

and his cheek gave a single twitch.
    I shot him with Lola's 45.
    Jimmy didn't smoke.

Dead Men Don't Kiss

By Matt Cost

She was so incredibly beautiful. Her eyes were two oceans of blue. Skin that was flawlessly smooth and creamy. A smile that would melt an iceberg and a body to kill for. The extraordinary exquisiteness of this dish was probably why I didn't react when she pressed the pistol to my head and pulled the trigger.

* * *

My name is Elton Connor, of the lineage lover of hounds and not hero or champion. How'd I end up in Hollywood? For the dames, of course. I had a beatnik pal who moved out here from our hometown of Nowhere, Ohio. He was home visiting his parents for Christmas, and I met up with him for a few bottles of that blue ribbon beer.

The conversation, as most do between young men, revolved around women. Donald yapped on and on about the dames out in Hollywood. It was his theory that all the barbecue migrated to the West Coast with dreams of Tinsel Town and the silver screen. Hardly any of them succeeded, some returned to Dullsville, but most of them stayed and played the role of eye candy.

Two weeks later, a solitary suitcase in the trunk of my Ford sedan, I hit the road. It turns out that an average-looking joe with little money still didn't reel in the barbecue dames, and it was two years before I had a proper conversation with any woman at all, and she was a client.

It was a day like any other. The sun was fiery like the first shot of whiskey going down the hatch. The smog hadn't yet drifted over from L.A., but the air was thick as pea soup. My feet were up on my desk in my dingy office on Vine between Sunset and Hollywood Boulevards. The focus of my thoughts hadn't changed in months now. The bills weren't being paid, and the clients weren't coming through the door. I was seriously on the nut.

I'd been a cop, see, back in Ohio, but that didn't get me a job out here in California. So, I took the exam to become a PI and had hung out my shingle, but that wasn't the same as making payola. Sure, there'd been a few jobs, mostly taking pictures of men cheating on their wives with their secretaries, with a few people faking injuries for the insurance money thrown in on top.

And then the door opened, illuminating the shadows of my one-room office, desk with a chair and two across from it, all picked up at the second-hand store around the corner, one stop short of being chopped into kindling to start a fire or carted off to the dump. There was a large window staring out at Vine Street, people bustling here and there, caught up in the importance of themselves, intent on quickly getting nowhere.

Her hair was cut in that style made famous by that new actress, Marilyn Monroe, only in this case, the bob was black as the ink in my Platignum pen. Her lips were luscious, glistening red and plummy, curving their way into a perfect cupid's bow. Smoldering and sultry eyes pierced the gloom of my office, and her skin radiated forth like she was the sunshine itself.

"I'm looking for Elton Connor." Her voice, my name on her lips, caressed my soul.

I swung my feet to the floor and stood. As stated earlier, I was no prize, just an average joe a couple inches under six feet, with a nose and a mouth and two eyes that didn't catch anybody's attention. Not really conducive to attracting the ladies, but darn helpful in being a gumshoe and going unnoticed when snooping around.

"That's me. Elton Connor. What can I do for you?"

She closed the door behind her. Turned those blue ocean orbs back at me.

"I'm afraid that my husband is cheating on me."

"Have a seat, Miss…?"

"I'm Veronica Anderson." She took two bold steps forward and sat across the desk from me. "And you are Elton Connor."

I nodded.

"You have come highly recommended."

I nodded. Listening is the number one skill of the gumshoe.

"Would you consider finding proof that my husband is having an affair?"

"Who is your husband?"

"The movie producer Douglas Ray."

This made sense to me. I knew her name, of course. Veronica Anderson was an up-and-coming starlet, not yet getting the marquee roles dominated by Hayworth and Day, or the new fresh faces of Monroe, Kelly, and Hepburn, but ready to burst forth at any moment.

"You have different last names," I said, if somewhat lamely.

"Show biz thing."

"Why do you want proof of your husband's infidelities?"

"To divorce him, of course, and take half of everything."

That made sense. "Who do you think he's having an affair with?"

"I suppose that is why I need to hire you."

Fair enough. "I suppose I can wedge you into my schedule."

"When can you get started?"

"Right off, I suppose."

She gave me that thousand-watt smile that promised to have melted more than one heart and ignited more than one fire. "The thing is, do you mind if I call you Elton?"

I nodded. "The thing is what?"

"The thing is, Elton." She leaned forward and put her hand on top of mine. "Is that I believe my husband is planning on killing me."

* * *

After she departed, I took a moment to savor her previous presence. That turned to reflection. It seemed that she was concerned that her husband, the movie producer Douglas Ray, wanted her dead. She'd discovered an unsent letter on his desk to a man named Albert Loomis, insinuating that her demise was necessary and that her removal could prove to be financially lucrative to the person who was responsible for planting her in the ground.

Veronica, yes, I was now on a first-name basis with her, gave me a C-note to get started. That was enough cabbage to stave off my creditors, who'd begun to gather like coyotes around a hamstrung mule deer. In other words, I would've taken the job even if it wasn't offered to me by Helen of Troy.

The first order of business was to pay a visit to Douglas Ray under false pretenses to get the measure of the man. Veronica had told me he'd be on set at Warner Studios over in Burbank. I was moving up in the world, rubbing elbows with the likes of Veronica Anderson and Douglas Ray, even if one wanted a divorce and the other wanted her dead.

Luckily, I'd done some shamus work for a Jew from Brooklyn, Irving "Swifty" Lazar, thus nicknamed for putting together three deals for Humphrey Bogart in a single day. Swifty owed me big time and was only too happy to grease the skids for me to ride into the 110-acre Warner metropolis in Burbank. The guard at the gate eyeballed my old Ford like it was dog poop on his shoe, but waved me through. I was on the list.

The Warner Studios were a sight to see if you were in an airplane flying overhead, but not quite so grand once you entered the streets between the humongous barn-like structures that housed the movie sets. It had a similar feel to the basic training barracks I'd visited before going on that Korean vacation a couple years back with a few million other Americans.

This was my first time inside the studio gates, and the careful instructions given by the guard still left me trolling through the fifteen or twenty edifices, all with stoplights outside the doors. Red, meaning stay out, filming was in process, and green was come right in with the proper credentials.

Finally, I located the right building, waited for the light to go from red to green, and went through the door. My eyes first went to the lighted set where people now milled around, several police officers, most likely the director sitting in a tall chair, a few fellows with greased hair, and a stunning beauty. I recognized James Dean and Natalie Wood, but didn't know any of the other people. They were filming some misunderstood youth thing called *Rebel Without a Cause*.

Standing off to the side with a young woman was Douglas Ray, exactly as described by Veronica. About fifty with an alderman protruding from his waist, a puffy face, blond hair swept back on his head, and a jagged beezer—all packed into a few inches over five feet tall.

I'd stopped by the library on my way over to do a bit of research on the gink.

When World War II ended, Ray had been poised for success with a factory selling, of all things, garbage disposals. He then invested in a home construction company that used assembly line techniques to mass produce houses to accommodate the returning GIs, their new brides, and the influx of children that followed. Five years back, he'd cashed out, brought his money to Hollywood, and began bankrolling films.

The point rolling around in my head was that if you were lousy with cabbage, you could look like a flying monkey from *The Wizard of Oz* and still have a gorgeous wife, a stunning assistant, and be having an affair on the side. I mentally kicked myself. Enough self-pity. With a bold step, I walked past the movie set and approached Ray and his lovely companion.

"Douglas Ray?"

He turned his gaze upon me, judged, calculated, and discarded in a flash. "What?"

"I'm here for Swifty. Did you get a phone call from him?"

His eyes did a recalculation, and he smiled and held out his hand. "You are Elton Connor."

I took his hand. It was pudgy and sweaty. "Yes. Mind if we jaw alone?"

Ray patted the dame on her ass. "Why don't you run back to the office, doll, and make those phone calls." Once she'd gone on her way, he turned back from watching her leave to look at me. "She's a sweet young thing, isn't she?"

She was, but I didn't need to voice that.

"Swifty promised that you'd have something of great interest for me."

Taking the man's arm, I leaned down to whisper in his ear. "Spencer Tracy is interested in making the jump from MGM to Warner."

His eyes went cha-ching like a slot machine hitting on all sevens. "I heard he was thinking of parting ways with that antiquated company. Is he all done filming that western? *Bad Day at Black Rock?*"

Douglas Ray emitted a very sweet scent, and I stepped away. "He would like to explore his options."

"Why come to me? Why not go straight to Jack Warner?"

"Spence would like you to produce a film he has in mind and would like your wife to co-star with him."

Ray chortled. "Now, that's rich. You're joking, right?"

"Not at all."

"Does Spencer Tracy know my wife?"

I shrugged. "He knows that she is an up-and-coming star."

Ray guffawed louder. "Veronica is a pretty twist to look at, but she can't act a lick. The entire artwork is ruined when she opens her mouth, on or off the set."

"That was not Spence's take on Veronica, Mr. Ray. But I suppose, you being married to her, would know better. Is there something I can bring back to Spence regarding this?"

The beady eyes looked at me intently, again calculating. "You tell Tracy that if he signs with Warner and gets me to produce his next film, he can sleep with Veronica but not co-star with her."

"Is she some kind of chippie?"

"Would it interest you to know that my wife is having an affair?"

Not much surprised me in this line of business. "Yeah? With who?"

"Gink by the name of Paris Rainier. Supposed to be some up-and-coming hotshot director. Ask me, he's a bottom feeder passing himself off as a shark."

Upsetting enough to kill, I wondered? "Sort of thing that makes you pretty goofy, I would imagine."

"Not at all. Her time has come and gone."

"What exactly do you mean by that?"

Ray looked left and right. Stepped closer. That sweet smell again. Sickly sweet. "I'm about to jettison her for a younger model, Elton. Sayonara. See you later. Goodbye." He looked at his watch. "As a matter of fact, I gotta get going."

I couldn't keep the surprise from my face. "A younger model? How old is Veronica?"

"Veronica? She's twenty-five. Ancient for a woman with no ability."

"You ready to give up half of everything you own to get rid of her?"

He leered at me. "Won't cost me a cent. I had one of those marital contracts drawn up by my lawyer. If we get divorced, no matter the circumstances, she don't get one goddamn cent."

* * *

Marriage contracts weren't a part of the public domain, so I had no easy way to confirm if what he said was true or not. But why would Ray lie about that, and at the same time, brag about cheating, divorcing Veronica, and moving on, leaving her penniless if it wasn't true? Was it possible that Veronica didn't understand what she'd been signing? Ray had indicated that she was a bimbo, but that didn't fit the image of the shrewd woman who'd come into my office to hire me to investigate her husband.

The wait wasn't long. I'd only been parked on the side of the road outside the Warner gate for about five minutes when Ray came barreling out through it in a red Mercedes-Benz coupe with the top down. It wasn't an easy task to keep my old Ford up with him as he raced down the streets, but I managed to stay with him all the way to Malibu, where he pulled into the driveway of a cottage overlooking the Pacific.

The place was nothing special, minus the location. It was nestled into the side of the bluff leading down to the beach, the front of the lodge on stilts, the back built right into the hill. The gasping waves lapped the sand and rocks below, and it was impossible to tell where the sea ended and the sky began.

I got a good picture of a young blonde girl who might've been eighteen, but not many days older than that, opening the door and locking lips with the paunchy Ray.

This was the part of the job that I despised most, that of being a peeping Tom, but something had to pay the bills. With a sigh, I clambered my way through the brushwood and was able to get photographs of Ray and the girl having drinks and canoodling in the sunroom. She had her bathing suit top off and was sitting on his lap before they moved into another room. It took me five minutes to find a vantage point to view the bedroom, and they were almost done, his face red and sweaty, her eyes bored and relegated.

Feeling dirty, I called it a day and went back to my car, camera in hand. This would be the proof of infidelity requested by Veronica that her husband was having an affair. But did it matter? If she'd signed a marriage contract, as Douglas Ray said, it wouldn't do her a lick of good. These thoughts carried me almost back to my office off Sunset Boulevard.

It was trying to muddle through what was going on that allowed the man to walk right up to my window at a stoplight and slug me in the jaw. He pulled open the door, dragged me forth, and hit me again, this time with the barrel of a pistol across the temple. At that point, I got just a tad groggy, and the next few minutes were a bit stilted.

My senses returning were aided by blue flashers from a prowler car. My eyes came into focus on the black and white as a shadowy figure emerged from the driver's seat. It was Captain Ludolf Klein. A copper so dirty and corrupt that he'd been able to avoid being singled out during World War II as a kraut, and what's more, been promoted up through the police hierarchy. Not a good enemy to have. I'd made the mistake of embarrassing him during a recent case, and he'd had it in for me ever since.

"What's going on here?" he asked, looking down at me lying in the street.

I rolled over, came to my knees, and then struggled to my feet. Blood streamed down my face from a gash over my right eye. "I was just looking for a penny I dropped."

Captain Klein swung his head from side to side. "Don't get smart with me, Connor."

There would be no quarter given by Captain Klein, even if I did talk about the mug who slugged me. The palooka was gone, the only memory being a scar on his left cheekbone, and gray, gun-metal eyes.

"Sorry, captain. I believe I fell out of my car and hit my head."

"Fell out of your car?"

"Yep."

He stared at me for a long moment. "I'm going to have to give you a ticket for public disturbance."

* * *

I had to get a doctor to put seven stitches in my head and then change from my bloodied clothes, so it wasn't until past six in the evening when I found myself driving up into the Santa Monica Mountains, about twelve miles from my office, to the neighborhood of Bel Air. Douglas and Veronica's mansion was impressive, but not more so than most of the places my old Ford spluttered past.

A houseman opened the door and led me through a labyrinth of hallways to a sitting room where Veronica reclined on a Davenport. She had a cigarette in a long holder in a white-gloved hand. Apparently, she hadn't gotten the memo that they now had filters, but it was also quite possible it was about appearance, a thing that seemed quite important to Veronica Anderson.

She lounged sideways on the Davenport, wearing a pencil skirt and a top that barely covered anything and a smile that would wear everything. "Elton…" she trailed off, swinging her bare feet to the floor. "What has happened to your face?"

"It's nothing, just a scratch."

"Sit down, you poor goose." She pulled me onto the Davenport, lightly touching the area around the bandage, her body pressed against mine, her scent engulfing me. "Tell me what happened."

A part of me wanted to play it tough and shrug it off as bumping my head on a door or some such hogwash, but I wanted to see her reaction, so I recounted the day to her. Seeing her husband and being told about the marriage contract, following him and taking pictures of his infidelities, and then being coldcocked by a goon at a stoplight who took the camera containing those very same photos.

"That thing about the marriage contract simply isn't true." Veronica's eyes got even wider if that was possible, wider and softer. "He tells everybody that so that they won't suspect him when he kills me."

"There is no contract at all?"

"There is a contract in his safety deposit box that states that I get half of everything if we are to divorce. And it is also filed with the courts. I'm not some Dumb Dora."

She was not any sort of simpleton. And she smelled incredible. "That would explain why the man waylaid me. To get the pictures back that I'd taken. How did he know I had them?"

"Did you get a look at the fellow who attacked you?"

"Not so much."

"He didn't happen to have a scar on his cheek, did he?"

Something tightened in my chest. An image of a man swinging a pistol barrel at my head flashed through my mind. "He did. And he had gray eyes."

Veronica nodded. "That would be Albert Loomis."

"The gunsel your husband hired to murder you?"

* * *

Veronica had copied down the address from the letter to Loomis, and she'd retrieved that and shared it with me. The hatchetman had an apartment in Culver City, in the no-man's land between Hughes Aircraft and MGM studios. It was in a mostly desolate building where the streetlights had been broken and bums slept in the doorways and alleyways.

It was almost nine o'clock when I parked my Ford on the side of the street, relishing the rare occasion when it was the nicest vehicle on the block. There was a buzzer at the entranceway, but it was broken, and the door was propped open.

The apartment was a third-floor walkup, the stairs littered with garbage and debris. My roscoe, which I rarely carried, was stuffed in my jacket pocket. It was a Model 36 Smith & Wesson 5-shot double-action revolver with a short barrel. I'd bought it after my first paycheck as a private dick, and this was the first time I'd carried it.

Apartment 8 was at the end of the hallway. I considered kicking in the door, but wasn't sure I'd succeed, so I went to plan number two and knocked. A voice called out to come in. The door swung inward on loose hinges. There was a standing lamp casting dark shadows across a living room devoid of furniture except for three sawbuck chairs.

Sitting across from me was the hombre with the scar, Albert Loomis. He held a large pistol, possibly a Colt .45. Across from him, with his back to me, was another man. The Colt was aimed at somewhere between the two of us.

"Mr. Connor. Come in." Loomis waved the pistol. "Sit."

Glenn Ford, in that film, *The Big Heat*, would've known to have his gun out when entering a derelict apartment in a rundown section of town looking to find a man who'd just pistol-whipped him. I had not thought to do so. One would suppose that the more you do something, the better you get at it, and that any career had a few bumps and mistakes along the way, but most jobs didn't end in death for a lapse in judgment.

I stepped across the broken shards of a vase and what might've been a toaster and sat down. The third man was Douglas Ray. His beady eyes were sunken into the flesh of his face, and his carefully coiffed blond hair had been ruffled to match his rumpled suit.

"You," Ray said. "What do you have to do with this?"

A terrible idea started to percolate in my brain. "I was hired by your wife to find proof of your infidelity. But you weren't lying to me, were you? You did draw up a reverse marriage contract, one that protected you and your money in case of divorce."

"Yes, of course I did, but what does that have to do with…." His voice trailed off and he looked from me to the man in the gray flannel suit with a gun. "You're here to kill me?"

The man sneered. "You catch on fast, Ray. Only it's going to look like you and the PI shot each other."

The man was not Albert Loomis at all, if such a fellow even existed. He was Paris Rainier, the man having an affair with Veronica, and the whole thing had been a plot to kill Ray and hang the murder on me, and to leave me dead and unable to defend myself.

"Why me?" I asked. "Just bad luck."

The sneer was back on Rainier's face. Or maybe it never left. Maybe it was permanent. "You're the perfect patsy, Connor. You're a nobody. No family. No friends. And that copper, Captain Ludolf Wagner, hates you. He's outside now, ready to come in. Nobody's going to dig too deep into this one. That, my friend, is what is called an open and shut case."

"If I'm dead, Veronica gets all my money," Ray said.

It was good to see that somebody was a tad slower on the uptake than me. Rainier stood up, grinned wickedly, somehow still sneering, and took two steps toward Ray and shot him in the head.

My roscoe was in my hand, and as the big Colt swept in my direction, I pulled the trigger, once, twice, three times.

Rainier stared at me with a shocked expression, three neat circles of red blossoming on his shirt like a greenhouse on Valentine's Day. Ray, slowly toppled from his chair, one neat rose-hole drilled into his head. Rainer wavered, pulled the trigger twice, the bullets spitting into the floor, and then he followed them down with a heavy thunk.

I let the pistol dangle to my side, it suddenly feeling enormously heavy in my hand, and stared at the two dead men, wondering what I would say when Captain Wagner came through the door.

There was a creak of the floor, a slightly intoxicating perfume wafting in the air, and I turned my gaze on the gorgeous Veronica Anderson.

She was so incredibly beautiful. Her eyes were two oceans of blue. Skin that was flawlessly smooth and creamy. A smile that would melt an iceberg and a body to kill for. The extraordinary exquisiteness of this dish was probably why I didn't react when she pressed the pistol to my head and pulled the trigger.

Nothing happened. The gun had jammed. There was a pounding on the stairs. Veronica dropped the pistol. Leaned over and kissed me fiercely on the lips.

With a gasp, she broke the lip lock, pulled back, and gave me that killer smile. "Sorry about the coppers, but at least you're not dead and unable to defend yourself."

Captain Wagner burst into the room with two flatties hot on his heels. "What's going on here?" he demanded.

Veronica pointed a shaky finger at me, not unlike the pistol that she'd so recently aimed my way, and perhaps just as deadly. "This man just shot these fellows."

As I was being manhandled, punched around, and having the bracelets put on, I saw Veronica Anderson slip out the door. I had to disagree with her husband. She was quite the fabulous actress.

I doubted the coppers would be able to make the murder charge stick. Rainier had a gun in hand, and it was his lead that had killed Ray, plus two more shells in the floor. Being alive, I'd be able to connect the dots for them as to what had actually gone down.

I'd guess that Veronica Anderson would be skipping town. Maybe with the money. Maybe broke to try her game again. Truth be told, I was about as happy as a lark.

Why?

Dead men don't kiss.

Picture Palace Blues

By Colin Campbell

"Okay. Here's a question for you. How do you know if she's a femme fatale?"

McNulty threw Donk a sideways look. "What kind of question is that?"

Donk nodded at the plush red curtains that had just swished closed across the cinema screen. "In these old black and white films? When the woman's making eyes at Humphrey Bogart? How do you know if she's a damsel in distress or the femme fatale?"

McNulty stretched in his chair as the house lights came up and the intermission music began to play. An usherette in a vintage uniform slowly walked backwards down the aisle with a tray of ice lollies and Cornettos. She almost tripped going down the step beside McNulty's seat. McNulty instinctively reached to catch her, but she regained her balance. He wouldn't describe the smile she gave him as making eyes at him, but it was a smile. He bought a Cornetto so she wouldn't feel embarrassed, then turned to face Donk.

"She won't be selling ice cream. I'll tell you that."

* * *

Vince McNulty had been watching films at Hyde Park Picture House since he was a kid. The ancient cinema, with its Ionic columns supporting retro signage and a carved Dutch gable, had undergone its fair share of ups and downs since then, but it had been lovingly restored. The auditorium was bedecked with glittering chandeliers and alcove lights, set against velvet curtains and deep red wallpaper. It had gone through a phase of showing adult movies, cartoon clubs, and third-run feature films, but the main attraction for McNulty had always been the classic movie nights. Late night showings of such favourites as *The Dirty Dozen* and *Von Ryan's Express*.

Donkey Flowers had been more interested in the adult movies, but discovered classic cinema through his friendship with McNulty. Friendship wasn't how it had started. McNulty, a uniformed police officer at the time, had arrested Flowers so many times that Donk began giving himself up whenever McNulty passed Donk's house. Not long after that, McNulty persuaded Donk to forsake a life of crime—more or less—and McNulty joined the Vice Squad. Busting massage parlours had been his thing. Until he was suspended and fired for beating up Daniel Roach, a kiddy-fiddler who had been molesting his seven-year-old sister.

But that was all water under the bridge. McNulty had been redeemed after helping close down the Northern X child-sex gang, and Donkey Flowers had helped him. Now, they went to the pictures whenever McNulty was back in Leeds. Usually, when Hyde Park was showing classic war films, with one of his favourite closing lines.

"I once told you, Ryan. If only one gets out, it's a victory."

McNulty had been misquoting Trevor Howard for years, swearing that he had called Frank Sinatra, Von Ryan, but that had been one of the other prisoners. Tonight, it was a film noir double bill.

Standing outside before the show, a sulky Donk had said, "Should be showing *Casablanca*. Bogart's best."

McNulty had let out a sigh. "It's not film noir. Classic? Yes. Moody lighting? Yes. But noir? No. Noir is stylized Hollywood crime drama, with stark lighting and cynical heroes."

"*Casablanca* has stark lighting. And Bogart's never been more cynical."

"It's a war movie. Not crime."

"What about *The Maltese Falcon*? That's crime."

"That's next week. Tonight, it's Bogart times two."

Donk stood in a pool of light, looking at the posters for *The Big Sleep* and *Key Largo* outside the cinema. "Should have been *Casablanca*."

Grant tried one last time. "Other thing film noir has is a femme fatale. Ingrid Bergman was too sweet to be a femme fatale. So, stop complaining. Get your money out and buy the tickets."

* * *

McNulty watched the usherette back all the way to the front of the auditorium and stand under a spotlight serving ice cream and drinks. She looked strong and athletic, and completely ill-suited for the tight-fitting vintage dress and apron. At least they hadn't forced her to wear one of those silly hats that usherettes used to wear. She smiled at the customers. Laughed at their jokes. But every now and again, she would glance along the aisle and lock eyes with McNulty.

Maybe she *was* making eyes at him. He considered going to the front of the screen to buy another Cornetto, but decided that would be too cheesy. Especially since he hadn't finished eating the first one yet.

Donk followed McNulty's gaze and smiled. "Maybe I'll buy you a Kia-Ora on her way back."

McNulty snorted a laugh to hide his embarrassment. "Most watered-down orange juice in the world."

Donk laughed too. "With the smallest straw you've ever sucked."

McNulty took another bite of his Cornetto. "Bogart wouldn't be caught dead sucking a straw."

Donk patted his trouser pockets. "I'm all out of cash anyway. Unless I can pay by card."

McNulty shook his head. "Cash only. Same as the ticket booth. This is full-retro. Cinema the old-fashioned way."

The intermission music segued into the theme for *Key Largo*, and the ornate chandeliers began to dim. The usherette gathered up the heavy tray hanging around her neck and started walking up the aisle, more careful of the steps this time. She gave McNulty an extra Cornetto and smiled as she passed his seat. Making eyes? Maybe. But there was something else behind the smile. Fear. When she saw that McNulty recognised it, she nodded towards the foyer, then continued walking.

* * *

Legend has it that the plot for *The Big Sleep* was so complicated that the director, Howard Hawks, had called Raymond Chandler to check who killed the chauffeur, and even Chandler didn't know. The second film of the night was easier to follow. Edward G Robinson and his gang were bad. Humphrey Bogart was good. And they all met on a stormy night at *Key Largo*.

As McNulty sat through the opening titles, it felt like he was in for a stormy night himself. The look behind the usherette's smile. The nod towards the foyer. The fact that there were only two members of staff, the usherette and the ticket clerk. And the knowledge that Hyde Park Picture House had gone full retro, even at the ticket booth. McNulty scanned the auditorium. It was a full house. That was a lot of ticket sales. Not to mention ice lollies and Cornettos.

McNulty waited until the film got into its stride. He dropped the extra Cornetto into the cupholder at the end of the armrest, said a few words to Donk, then stepped into the aisle and headed towards the back of the cinema. The storm raged at *Key Largo* on the screen behind him. The storm up ahead hadn't begun yet.

* * *

The two men looked up from what they were doing when McNulty came through the door. From the stalls, not the balcony. Balcony tickets were more expensive, but more importantly, the seats were further away from the screen. McNulty preferred sitting halfway along the stalls, looking up. Looking down from the balcony, the silver screen felt more like a giant TV.

"You fellas know where the toilets are?"

One of the men was big and solid. The other one was small and weedy. The weedy one did the talking. "Second on the left, past *Casablanca*."

"They've still got that, huh? Thought they'd have changed it by now."

The foyer was the main focus of full-retro. The wallpaper was still deep red, but the walls were adorned with classic movie posters and lobby cards. A UK Quad of *The Italian Job* stood out against the wall opposite the ticket booth. *Butch Cassidy and the Sundance Kid* stood guard at the top of the stairs to the balcony seating. And *Casablanca* guided the way to the toilets.

Mr. Weedy looked at McNulty. "If you know about *Casablanca*, how come you don't know where the toilets are?"

McNulty made a twirling gesture with one hand. "They keep moving the posters. *Casablanca* used to be at the top of the stairs."

"They haven't moved the toilets."

McNulty shrugged. "It's been a while. Sometimes I get mixed up with Cottage Road Cinema."

"Cottage Road doesn't have a balcony."

"Doesn't have talking arseholes either. But when you need a leak, the mind kind of goes blank."

McNulty gestured towards the gloomy corridor. "And I need a leak. So, if you don't mind."

He didn't wait for permission. He walked past *Casablanca* and through the badly painted door, his eyes taking in everything about the situation at the ticket booth and the lack of popcorn at the concession stand.

The situation at the ticket booth was this. There was no sign of the round bald ticket clerk through the cashier's window. The little door at the side was partly open. The usherette was standing, wide-eyed behind the concessions counter. Mr. Big and Mr. Weedy were kneeling on the floor trying to close a leather holdall that looked too full to close. And the concertina grill had been pulled across the front doors.

The concertina grill was the tipping point. Fire regulations had been strictly enforced ever since a local business consortium had renovated the former laughing stock of Leeds. There was a printout of the regulations on the wall next to the front doors for all to see. One of the main rules was printed in red. Fire exits shall be clear and unobstructed at all times. The front door was a fire exit. Closing the security grill while customers were still inside meant it was definitely not unobstructed.

McNulty opened the toilet door a crack and peered through the gap. Muffled dialogue from *Key Largo* sounded from the auditorium. From this angle, he couldn't see the usherette, but he could see the two men stuffing banknotes into the bag. Mr. Big squashed the holdall while Mr. Weedy zipped it shut. Then Mr. Weedy paused, and McNulty thought the game was up. But no. Mr. Weedy checked his watch and held up a finger. He said something to his accomplice, then dashed up the stairs.

That left one robber and the usherette. The usherette was the damsel in distress. Leaving McNulty to be Humphrey Bogart. Bogart flushed the toilet and started the hand dryer, then opened the door.

* * *

It had been a long time since McNulty served in the West Yorkshire Police, but whenever he saw a crime scene on the news, he always felt like one of the police guarding the scene. Once a cop, always a cop. That had been his mantra for as long as he could remember. It was a mindset that had persuaded Larry Unger to hire him as technical adviser for Titanic Productions in America. It was the mindset that kicked in whenever he saw innocents being victimized. The round bald guy and the usherette were being victimized.

But the big fella was much bigger than Bogart, so McNulty would have to play it cool. Being cool was usually his friend, Jim Grant's modus operandi. McNulty normally lost his temper and charged in. He didn't lose his temper this time. Not yet. He played it cool.

"You need a hand with the bag?"

The big man stood up. "No."

McNulty moved into the foyer. "Looked like you were having trouble getting it closed, is why I ask."

"So?"

"So, I thought you might need a hand."

"No."

McNulty was beginning to understand why Mr. Weedy did all the talking. This fella didn't say any more than he had to. Standing over the bulging holdall like the Colossus of Rhodes, he didn't need to say anything at all. McNulty glanced at the usherette, whose eyes had calmed down slightly. Then he took a sideways step to give an angle on Colossus and the sweeping staircase where Mr. Weedy had gone. It also opened an angle on the ticket booth.

The door was slightly open, light spilling out through the narrow opening. The single bulb picked out the interior. To call the ticket booth spartan was doing a disservice to Gerard Butler. There was a swivel stool, a cash register, and a ticket machine that fed tickets through a slot in the sales counter. The ticket clerk wasn't sitting on the stool; he was curled up on the floor.

McNulty felt anger begin to dilute his attempt at playing it cool. The ticket clerk had seemed like a quiet, placid man who didn't deserve to be knocked to the ground. The bruise on the side of the head was leaking blood. His eyes had been bandaged from the First Aid kit on the wall, forming a makeshift blindfold. A pair of cushioned headphones covered his ears. That seemed like an odd choice for a smash-and-grab.

McNulty opened the ticket booth door, then glared at Mr. Big. "You didn't need to do that."

Mr. Big braced his shoulders. The usherette shrank back from the concessions stand. Mr. Weedy paused on the half-landing coming down the stairs. "He didn't do that. She did."

The usherette puffed out her cheeks and threw Mr. Weedy a disbelieving look. McNulty saw her with fresh eyes. Not Ingrid Bergman. Femme fatale.

* * *

The mechanics of plot construction and red herrings had never been McNulty's strong suit. He didn't understand who shot the chauffeur either.

The Dirty Dozen was much easier to understand. Not to mention, *Von Ryan's Express*. "If one gets out, it's a victory," was a much easier concept to get your head around. Double-crosses? False trails? Inside jobs? They never happened in real life. Rule of thumb, when McNulty had served in the West Yorkshire Police, was that if you caught a man with a bag of money at a crime, he was the one that stole it.

Misdirection? Now, that was something else entirely. Get the police looking one way, while the burglars ran off in the other direction. Steve McQueen had done that in *The Getaway*, and Boyd Crowder had copied him in *Justified*. This felt like misdirection.

McNulty looked at the little man coming down the stairs. "She must be stronger than she looks, then. Maybe it's hefting that tray around for three shows a day."

The usherette let out a sigh. "Thank you." Back to being Ingrid Bergman.

McNulty was busy piecing things together. "Besides. Since she works here, there'd be no need to blindfold him and cover his ears. He knows who she is."

He indicated Mr. Big with a wave of the hand. "Now Big Fella here, I'll bet he's got a helluva left hook. And he doesn't sell ice cream. So, once he floored the ticket guy, the only reason to make him deaf and blind was so he didn't hear the projectionist telling him what to do."

He gestured towards the top of the stairs. "You were up there changing the first reel, weren't you?"

The projectionist came down the stairs and stood next to the bag. Mr. Big took his cue and walked over to the concessions stand. Fear showed in the usherette's eyes again as she shrank away from him. McNulty felt the anger building again. Very un-Jim Grant-like. Very not cool.

Mr. Weedy kept his tone light. His attack dog gave him the upper hand. "And you should have been in there watching *Key Largo*."

He snapped his fingers, and Mr. Big lifted the flap in the concessions counter. The girl let out a little yelp. *Key Largo* rumbled through the speakers in the auditorium. The projectionist walked over to the ticket booth and closed the door. There was no need to risk the ticket clerk seeing anything through the bandages.

"So, you either step aside, or the girl gets it."

McNulty stifled a laugh. "Did you get that from the Film Noir Season? Threaten to shoot the girl if the hero doesn't give them *The Maltese Falcon?*"

"Doesn't matter where I got it."

McNulty disagreed. "Well, it kind of does. Since in America, there's an outside chance you might shoot the girl."

He lowered his voice. "But this is Yorkshire. What you going to do? Threaten her with a Cornetto?"

He nodded at the holdall. "For what?" He feigned doing the maths in his head. "Two hundred and seventy-five seats at eight pounds each? About two grand? Give or take? You want to go to prison for life over two thousand pounds?"

He held up a hand as he did a quick recalculation. "Split four ways?"

Nobody queried who the four ways was for. Nobody spoke. Leaving McNulty to continue playing house detective. "Unless two thousand pounds is an excuse to fake the robbery. And what you're really after is *The Maltese Falcon.*"

* * *

Legend has it, Part Two. Not so much a legend as a rumour. A serious rumour that was rooted in Hyde Park Picture House's history. Back in its heyday, but not all the way back to 1914, when the cinema had opened. The 1930s, after the advent of the talkies. At the height of the American gangster movie and beyond. In the unique shadow of film noir.

The serious rumour told how the original owner, Henry Child, had loved gangster movies so much that he had contacted Warner Bros Studios in Hollywood and bought the cigarette holder Sidney Greenstreet had used in *The Maltese Falcon* and *Casablanca*. He had tried for Humphrey Bogart's Zippo lighter but couldn't afford it. Even so, the cigarette holder was one-of-a-kind. Polished ivory with Greenstreet's initials carved into the bowl. It had cost a tidy sum in 1946. It would be worth a fortune now. Almost as much as the original Maltese Falcon itself. The rumour further told how Child had incorporated the holder into the ornate carvings somewhere in the cinema. And it had never been found.

McNulty took a deep breath. "You found it, didn't you?"

The projectionist played it close to his chest. "The Maltese Falcon? They found that years ago."

"The cigarette holder."

"They found that as well. Kept it behind bulletproof glass in the projection booth, so that spillage from the projector made it glow."

McNulty nodded. "Oh yes. I remember now. About the time the cinema was granted Grade Two listed building status in nineteen-ninety-six."

The projectionist nodded. "The gas lamp outside as well."

"Turned the Picture House into an expensive property."

"Especially with Sidney Greenstreet enshrined in the foundations."

McNulty made a throwaway gesture. "Glass case in the projection booth isn't exactly the foundations."

"Might as well have been. Projection booth is the heart of any cinema. Can't watch films without a projectionist."

McNulty nodded his understanding. "The least valued person in any cinema."

"Least valued person anywhere. Never seen. Ever-present."

"So, you decided to strike a blow for projectionists everywhere."

"I decided to strike a blow for me."

"But you couldn't just take it."

The projectionist smiled. "It would look a bit suspicious. Man in the booth would be prime suspect."

McNulty admired the audacity of it. "Unless somebody robbed the takings. And took Greenstreet too. A valued heirloom. Cushioned in a bag of money."

Mr. Weedy didn't seem so weedy anymore. He straightened and puffed his chest out. "Sounds like you've been watching too many movies."

McNulty ignored the interruption. "Knocking the ticket fella over the head was a bit excessive."

Mr. Not So Weedy shrugged. "Had to earn his share."

"The innocent victim? And authenticator? Prove you were really robbed."

"The Picture House was really robbed. We're just the staff."

McNulty jerked a thumb at the ticket booth. "Him taking a bump on the head." Then nodded at the usherette. "While she makes sure everyone's back in their seats after the intermission."

The projectionist turned a hard stare on the usherette. "Didn't do a very good job, did she?"

McNulty threw her a disappointed look. "Oh, don't be too hard on her. A man's got to go when a man's got to go."

The projectionist didn't look crestfallen. "Very good. If you were a detective gathering the suspects in the parlour. And not some just schmuck come to watch *The Big Sleep*."

The usherette spoke for the first time since she'd sought shelter behind the concessions stand, the fear in her eyes replaced by hard practicality. "He's not just some schmuck who came to watch the film. He's the copper who shut down Northern X and blew up the torture porn factory."

Recognition showed on the projectionist's face. "Ex-copper. Dishonourable discharge, wasn't it? Pension rights suspended."

McNulty kept his eyes on the little man. "They were reinstated."

"But you're still an ex. As in not current. No longer with a power of arrest."

McNulty could see the big man out of the corner of his eye. "Technically, there's always common law. Citizen's arrest. If that's what I wanted."

The projectionist nodded towards his attack dog. "That might be feasible if it wasn't four against one."

McNulty shook his head. "It's two against one. Ticket fella's out for the count." Then nodded towards the concessions stand. "And she's hiding behind the Cornettos."

The projectionist wasn't fazed. "I've got Colossus."

McNulty wasn't fazed either. "I've got Donk."

* * *

One thing the projectionist had got right was the fact that McNulty wasn't in the police anymore. He wasn't even in England, not as a resident anyway. He lived in America. This was just a flying visit to catch up with old friends and watch a few movies. Arresting people for robbery with violence wasn't how he wanted to spend his last night before flying back to Boston.

That being said, he didn't want Hyde Park Picture House going bust either. Not because some arsehole with a grudge had stolen the weekly takings. The local legend was different. It wasn't as if the customers ever got to see Sidney Greenstreet's cigarette holder. It had been cooped up in the projection booth since nineteen-whatever. McNulty's anger dialed down a touch now that he knew the ticket clerk wasn't the victim of assault and battery. McNulty could afford to play it cool. With the support of his own Colossus.

Donk came out of the shadows and stood in front of *The Italian Job*. McNulty moved towards *Casablanca*. Between the two of them, they had the unlikely robbers in a pincer movement. Colossus tried to look intimidating, but facing Donk was a different proposition from faking it with the ticket clerk.

McNulty took out his phone. "Now, the way I see it, you've got two choices. We have a knockdown, drag-out fight, and Donk kicks the living crap out of Colossus here."

He held the phone up for everyone to see. "Or I call nine-nine-nine, and the police kick the living crap out of both of you."

The projectionist glanced at Donk, then looked at McNulty. "The police don't kick the living crap out of people."

"Really? When was the last time you were arrested for armed robbery?"

"We're not armed."

"Not what I'll say when I tell them I'm in fear of my life. They'll kick first and ask questions later."

"That's not how it works."

"No? Ask Telfon Speed." McNulty held up a hand. "Oh, hang on. You can't. Because he got blown up along with Northern X, the last time the police kicked the living crap out of somebody."

"I heard it was a gas leak that blew him up."

McNulty was growing impatient. He put added grit in his voice. "You want a gas leak? We can arrange that."

The seriousness of the situation appeared to sink in. Colossus didn't look like he wanted to mix it with Donk. The projectionist didn't look like he wanted to be beaten for resisting arrest. The only person who seemed happy was the usherette. She let out a sigh and gave McNulty a little nod. A half-smile played across her lips. The look of fear in her eyes had gone. Leaving McNulty to wonder just how complicit she was in the theft of *The Maltese Falcon*.

She looked calm and relaxed now that the robbery had been foiled. Maybe the threat of Colossus had forced her to act as a lookout, which was effectively all she had been. Making sure the audience were back in their seats after the intermission. It was the only explanation for her warning McNulty, the ex-cop who had made national headlines for closing down Northern X. She had recognised him when he'd tried to save her from falling. The dashing hero helping the damsel in distress. And she had given the only signal she was able to give. A free Cornetto and a nervous glance towards the foyer.

McNulty looked into her eyes and gave a little nod of his own. Job done. The girl had saved the day. But it wouldn't stop her from getting arrested as an accessory, despite there being mitigating circumstances. McNulty knew how that worked. Shit sticks. She might well be found not guilty, but her reputation would be forever tarnished. He couldn't do that to Ingrid Bergman.

McNulty surveyed the room. The bulging holdall on the floor. The ticket booth with its guilty secret. The little man with his bodyguard, and the damsel in distress. He looked at the projectionist. "Or you could go with option number three."

* * *

The thing about being an ex-cop and not a current cop was that you didn't have to play by the rules. Some cops didn't play by the rules anyway, but there were no rules at all if you were Joe Public, just out for a night at the pictures. McNulty was just out for a night at the pictures.

"You all like the movies, or you wouldn't be working here. Let's see if we can work out a final reel that sends the audience home happy."

Talk of a final reel sparked panic in the projectionist's eyes. He checked his watch and looked at McNulty. Rumbling noises of the storm that was engulfing *Key Largo* came from the auditorium. McNulty glanced at the antique clock that had been reclaimed from the Gaumont cinema, and nodded his understanding. The final reel change.

"Come straight back."

The projectionist dashed up the stairs and disappeared. The projection booth was half a floor up from the balcony seating. The projectionist's dedication supported McNulty's decision. It wasn't strictly a legal one. He doubted the West Yorkshire Police would agree with it. While the final reel was being changed, McNulty indicated the ticket booth with a wave of the hand.

"Wake him up. Make sure he's okay."

Colossus didn't need asking twice. He opened the narrow door and nudged the prone figure with the toe of his boot. The ticket clerk raised his head and spoke to the room. "Is it finished?"

He hadn't been unconscious at all; he had been listening to *Key Largo* through his Bluetooth headphones.

McNulty reached in and took the headphones off. "No, but you are."

The round bald man tugged the blindfold off. "Oh shit."

McNulty stood over him. "Yes, shit. But not as deep as you deserve."

He pointed at the blood on the side of the man's face. "What is that?"

The ticket clerk wiped the blood and licked his fingers. "Ketchup. From the hot dog stand."

"You sell hot dogs?"

The ticket clerk struggled to his feet. "Replaced the popcorn maker. Hot dogs are a bigger seller. Place needs all the profits it can get."

McNulty stepped away from the booth. "All the profits in the bag, you mean?"

The clerk recognised the man who had shut down Northern X. "Oh shit."

Full circle. But the clerk's reaction mirrored the projectionist's dedication.

Like all small businesses, Hyde Park Picture House survived on the goodwill of staff and volunteers. Whatever they had planned to do with the takings, it was the cigarette holder that had been the prize. That had been their final reel. McNulty thought he knew what they'd intended to do with it. That, and the fact that nobody had been hurt, made his decision easier.

The projectionist came back down the stairs. The ticket clerk wiped ketchup off his face. Colossus just stood with the holdall between his feet. Donk stood with his back to the concertina security gate in case anybody made a break for it. Nobody was going to make a break for it. This wasn't the crime of the century; it was *The Lavender Hill Mob*.

McNulty gathered the suspects and played house detective.

"Okay, here's what we're going to do."

* * *

McNulty's plan for a fair and impartial solution worked fine, right until it didn't. Everybody agreed to abide by the ruling of the court; the court in this instance being the court of Vince McNulty and his bailiff, Donkey Flowers. To be fair, Donk thought McNulty had lost his marbles, but was prepared to go along with him if it meant avoiding the police. Despite having gone straight and joined the Navy, the law was still a touchy subject for the man McNulty had arrested more times than he'd had hot dinners.

Before McNulty outlined his plan, he tapped his watch and looked at the projectionist. "Don't you have to do stuff when the film finishes?"

"Rewind the spool and turn the projector off. The rest is automated. House lights and curtains." He nodded towards the auditorium. "I'll know it's time to reset when they start coming out."

McNulty checked the clock. Just gone midnight. The late-night double-bill was due to end at quarter past. "We'd better get a move on then." He gave everyone a hard stare. "Here's how you keep from going to prison."

This was the part where Donk thought McNulty had lost his marbles.

McNulty focused on the three men, since they were the ones who had faked the robbery. He ignored the usherette. "Firstly. The definition of theft is: the dishonest appropriation of property belonging to another with the intention to permanently deprive the other of it. So far, nothing has been stolen. If you put the money back right now."

He paused before continuing. "Secondly. Nobody got assaulted. Ketchup doesn't count. And Hyde Park Picture House need be none the wiser."

Max Steiner's film score rumbled through the doors, building up to the finale of *Key Largo*. Bogart saved the day. Lauren Bacall was probably smiling. McNulty glanced at the clock again, then waved the projectionist towards the stairs. "Go up and end the show."

He pointed at Colossus and the ticket clerk. "You two had better put the money back in the cash drawer."

He nodded at the main doors. "Donk. Open the security gates."

The projectionist nodded his thanks and dashed up the stairs. The ticket clerk went into the booth and opened the cash drawer. Colossus unzipped the bag. Donk pulled the concertina grill until it clicked into place outside. The music reached its crescendo as the movie ended. There was a collective rush as people came out to catch the last bus. Another retro vibe from the bygone days of cinema. There were probably a lot more motorists than in the good old days.

The ticket clerk stashed coins and banknotes into the register. Colossus sifted through the bag. The crowd surged through the foyer, voices muttering and laughing and generally having a good time. That would normally have been Donk and McNulty going to The King's Arms to discuss *Von Ryan's Express*. Tonight, Donk was guarding the front door, and McNulty was supervising the return of the money.

No crime. No police. All good. But something was wrong. Colossus rummaged around in the holdall. All the money had been taken out apart from a few fivers and a smattering of loose coins. He put the bag on the ticket counter. The clerk searched the bag too, then looked at McNulty.

"It's not here."

McNulty was confused. "What?"

Colossus said more than he'd said all night. "*The Maltese Falcon*."

McNulty pushed through the crowd to the ticket booth. "The cigarette holder? It's only small. You sure it's not wedged in the seam?"

The crowd was beginning to thin. Donk came over to see what the fuss was about. "Something wrong?"

"The valued heirloom cushioned in a bag of money? It's gone."

Donk wasn't looking at the bag; he was looking over McNulty's shoulder. "So is she."

McNulty spun around. The concession stand was empty. He turned back to the ticket clerk. "Describe it."

The clerk rubbed his chin while he thought for a moment. "Stained ivory. Initials carved on the bowl. Thick at one end. Long and thin at the other."

McNulty wasn't interested in the colour. "How long?"

The clerk held his thumb and forefinger about five inches apart.

McNulty looked at Donk.

Donk understood. "Cornetto."

They both pushed against the thinning crowd and walked down the aisle to their seats. The cup holder in the armrest was empty. The Cornetto had gone. McNulty let out a sigh and looked at the fire exit door next to the velvet curtain.

Donk gave McNulty a sideways look. "You know, when you said the femme fatale wouldn't be selling ice cream?"

McNulty ignored the jibe. What he was thinking was, *I preferred it when she'd been Ingrid Bergman.*

A Note from the Editor

Historically, I have not been a lover of short stories. My major complaint is that so many of them I have read are not really, to my mind, stories—beginning, middle, end—being my requirements. I would call many "stories" out there vignettes, or sketches, or character studies. But I grew up on great short stories. More specifically, my Dad introduced me to the great Frederic Brown, who has many writing credentials in both the mystery and science fiction genres. And this spoiled me for any other stories I have read since.

This anthology was created from a call for stories by Level Best Books. In reading all the submissions, it was wonderful to see the many ways that "noir" had been invoked and interpreted. There were many really good stories—in the end, there were seventeen stories that I felt rose to the level of great stories. I look for a strong voice, a complete story, and a satisfying ending, and these all delivered that in spades.

I grouped the stories by era—the first batch was from the thirties to post WWII, the second was set in the changing landscape of the 50s and 60s, and the last stories were closer to contemporary. Since we had an almost even number of male and female narrators in the anthology, I alternated the stories between the two voices.

I hope readers enjoy these stories and that they go out and discover more works written by this cadre of incredibly talented authors.

About the Authors

Colin Campbell—Ex Army, retired cop and former Scenes of Crime Officer. Colin Campbell is the author of British crime novels, *Blue Knight White Cross,* and *Northern Ex,* and US thrillers *Jamaica Plain, Montecito Heights, Beacon Hill* and *Final Cut.* His Jim Grant thrillers bring a rogue Yorkshire cop to America where culture clash and violence ensue. He has also written YA books, *Silent Flight Holy Night,* and *The Early Grave of Sophie Laville.*

Away from writing, Campbell has played tennis for Yorkshire, and represented Great Britain in the World Police/Fire Games, winning gold medals in Adelaide and Rotterdam. For more info visit www.campbellficti on.com.

Matt Cost—Over the years, Cost has owned a video store, a mystery bookstore, and a gym. He has also taught history and coached just about every sport imaginable. Cost has just published his seventeenth book, "The Not So Merry Adventures of Max Creed". Cost now spends his days at the computer, writing mainly mysteries.

P.A. De Voe, an anthropologist and Asian specialist, is a Silver Falchion award winner, and a twice Silver Falchion, Next Generation Indie Book, and Agatha award finalist. Her short story, *The Immortality Mushroom,* was in the Anthony Award winning anthology **Murder Under the Oaks** edited by Art Taylor. Find her at padevoe.com.

Devon Ellington is a full-time writer, publishing under multiple names in fiction and nonfiction, and an internationally produced playwright and radio writer. She spent decades working professionally in theatre and film/television production, including as a dresser on Broadway. She is the author of 10 novels, dozens of short stories, and is a member of the Boiler House Poets Collective. www.devonellingtonwork.com.

C.C. Guthrie's short stories have appeared in mystery and crime anthologies and Black Cat Weekly. C. C. is a member of Sisters In Crime, the SinC Guppy Chapter, and the Short Mystery Fiction Society and has been a Derringer finalist and a finalist for the Bill Crider Prize for Short Fiction.

Kerry Hammond is a fully recovered attorney living in Denver, Colorado. Several of her short stories have been published in mystery anthologies and her latest, "Sins of the Father," was nominated for an Agatha Award. One of her stories was featured in *The Mysterious Bookshop Presents the Best Mystery Stories of 2023*. She also enjoys creating downloadable Murder Mystery party games for BlameTheButler.com.

Wendy Harrison is a retired prosecutor who turned to short mystery fiction during the pandemic. Her stories have been published in numerous anthologies and online magazines. When Hurricane Ian destroyed her home in Florida, she moved to the Pacific Northwest. When she isn't writing, she is weaving or reading or walking the steep hills around her new home.

Peter W. J. Hayes is the author of the six-book Vic Lenoski mystery series. His almost thirty published short stories have appeared in multiple mystery magazines and crime-writing anthologies, including the Best Mystery Stories of the Year (2024) and The Best New England Crime Stories. He is also a past finalist for the Silver Falchion, Derringer, and Al Blanchard awards.

Greg Herren is the award winning author of over forty novels, fifty short stories, and has edited over twenty anthologies. He lives in New Orleans with his partner of thirty years. His next novel, *Hurricane Party Hustle,* will be released in fall of 2025.

Deborah Lacy grew up near Los Angeles listening to the *Dr. Demento* radio show where she first heard the song, *Pico & Sepulveda*. She is the editor of THE MOST DANGEROUS GAMES short story anthology, and her short mystery fiction has appeared in many magazines and anthologies. Her website is deborahlacy.com.

Robert Lopresti is a retired librarian whose stories have been published in most mystery magazines and reprinted in *Best American Mystery Stories*. He recently edited *Crimes Against Nature: New Stories of Environmental Villainy*. His previous adventures of Madame Matilda appeared in the anthologies *Monkey Business* and *Party Crashers*. He blogs at SleuthSayers and Little Big Crimes.

Nicky Nielsen, PhD, is a Danish-born Egyptologist living in the United Kingdom. He is the author of the Victorian crime thriller *Death on Stanley Dock* (Level Best Press, 2025) and has also written extensively for nonfiction magazines. He currently writes a column on ancient burial customs and funerary beliefs for*Atlas Obscura.*"

M.E. Proctor (www.shawmystery.com) is the author of *Love You Till Tuesday* and *Catch Me on a Blue Day* (Declan Shaw PI series), as well as *Family and Other Ailments*, a short story collection. She co-authored a retro-noir novella, *Bop City Swing*. A Derringer nominee, her short fiction has appeared in various magazines and anthologies. She lives in Texas.

Jeff Tanner lives on Virginia's beautiful Eastern Shore, where the internet and cell coverage sucks but it's a great place to write. Currently, I'm pitching my debut mystery novel and have published fifteen nonfiction books. Thank you, MUSEketeers, my writing group, and Level Best author Marlie Wasserman for critiquing early versions.

Gabriel Valjan is the author of *The Company Files*, and the *Shane Cleary Mysteries* with Level Best Books. He has been nominated for the Agatha,

Anthony, Derringer, and Silver Falchion awards. He received the 2021 Macavity Award for Best Short Story and the Shamus Award for Best PI in 2023. Gabriel is a member of the Historical Novel Society, ITW, MWA, and Sisters in Crime. He lives in Boston and answers to a tuxedo cat named Munchkin. He can be found at: Bluesky: @gvaljan.bsky.social; IG: @gabrielvaljan; Web: gabrielvaljan.com; Amazon Author page: https://rb.gy/tsntz

Nina Wachsman writes historical mystery novels set in 17th Century Venice. Her novels, "The Gallery of Beauties" and "The Courtesan's Secret", were both finalists for Agatha and Silver Falchion awards, and "The Courtesan's Pirate" was published by Level Best Books in September 2024. She lives in New York City, but frequently visits Venice.

J. J. White has had articles and stories published in several anthologies and magazines including, *Pithead Chapel, Sherlock Holmes Mystery Magazine* and *Mystery Weekly Magazine*. His novels, *Deviant Acts*, and *Nisei* were published by Open Road Media. He was nominated for the Pushcart Prize for his short piece, "Tour Bus." He lives in Merritt Island, Florida.

Website: www.jjwhitebooks.com

About the Editor

Deborah Well is an editor, marketing consultant, and digital strategist. After working for several decades in the finance realm, she has been happy to see her English degree get put to good use in her "retirement career" in the publishing world. Deb lives in Boston's South End with her partner, author Gabriel Valjan, and their much-memed tuxedo cat, Munchkin.